LOVING AN EARL

Widows of Mayfair, Book 1

Christine Donovan

ARE YOU SIGNED UP FOR DRAGONBLADE'S BLOG?

You'll get the latest news and information on exclusive giveaways, exclusive excerpts, coming releases, sales, free books, cover reveals and more.

Check out our complete list of authors, too!

No spam, no junk. That's a promise!

Sign Up Here

www.dragonbladepublishing.com

Dearest Reader;

Thank you for your support of a small press. At Dragonblade Publishing, we strive to bring you the highest quality Historical Romance from some of the best authors in the business. Without your support, there is no 'us', so we sincerely hope you adore these stories and find some new favorite authors along the way.

Happy Reading!

CEO, Dragonblade Publishing

CHAPTER ONE

Langford Manor
Kent 1814

LILLY ST. CLAIRE'S body had trembled as she'd released heart-wrenching sobs from deep inside her soul as she'd stood over her papa's grave so soon after she'd wed the Earl of Langford—mere hours, really. As she sat in Langford's carriage now, tears ran unabashedly down her cheeks, and she was surprised she had any left to shed after her episode earlier in the day. Her new husband sat opposite her, looking almost as heartbroken as she. This was unsurprising since her papa and Langford had known each other for nearly thirty years. And that friendship had led to her marrying the earl this day.

The earl was something of a recluse and rarely traveled to London except when Parliament was in session. The crowds, noises, and smells of London made him nervous, he said, and he preferred the peace and quiet of his country estate in Kent. Lilly was very grateful Langford preferred the country. Not that she knew much about London, as she'd never been, though she'd always dreamed of visiting. Nevertheless, now that she was married to Langford, she could only imagine the scandal when London Society learned the earl had married a vicar's daughter who was only seventeen. Her fear of becoming the talk of London had her trembling again.

"Are you cold, my child?" Langford possessed a gentle, soft-spoken voice. He always referred to her as a child, which had never bothered her before, but it sounded inappropriate now that they were married.

"Just a little. Please call me Lilly." She had lied about being cold, and her fingers gripped her cloak, pulling it tighter around her body. But there was no sense in admitting her panic about her new life and what it would entail.

"We are almost to the estate. And you must call me Henry."

With half-lidded eyes, she studied her husband. At his advanced age, he still clung to the handsome younger self she'd seen in a portrait hanging in the gallery at Langford Manor. Although his hair was white and his frame lean, he still appeared strong, and his mind was sharp. Suddenly, her insides churned. Would he try to get an heir with her? Would that not be the reason he had accepted her father's request? She'd not been instructed in the goings on of the marriage bed, since her mama died many years ago, and she'd been too young then. What would Henry expect of her? Would he want to consummate the marriage tonight even though they both mourned her papa?

"You may relax, my child," Henry said in his soothing voice. "When we arrive at Langford Manor, I have instructed my housekeeper to whisk you away to your chambers and prepare a bath and light repast for you before bed." He paused, leaned forward, and gently covered her hands with his thin, slightly bent ones. "There's no need to fret about tonight. The loss of your dear papa saddens us both, and I imagine you would prefer to mourn in private, as would I."

Before she could ask what he meant by fret, the carriage stopped before the large stone manor. The household were lined up outside, ready to welcome her even though she'd been here many times. This time, however, she was introduced as their new countess. Her insides quivered at the look of pity she witnessed in many of their eyes, making her wonder if the pity was for her papa's death, or for marrying the old earl, or both.

She paid the closest attention to Mrs. Pemberton, the housekeeper, and Miss Daisy Campbell, who'd been introduced as her maid, as they would work closely with her.

When formal introductions were complete, Mrs. Pemberton led her up a grand marble staircase. The beautiful staircase gently curved and split off to the right and left. They stayed to the right, going up another flight to the private family rooms.

"Please accept my condolences on losing your father, your ladyship. There will never be another vicar with a heart as kind and gentle as his." Mrs. Pemberton cleared her throat and smiled sadly. "Campbell and I unpacked your belongings." She opened the door, and Lilly gasped at the beauty surrounding her. The room was decorated in soft shades of cream and mauve with little touches of light blue. The furniture consisted of a large sleigh bed with matching nightstands, and a lovely ornate carved secretary, which doubled as a dressing table. Opposite the bed was an impressive fireplace and a beautiful mauve chaise longue. She could imagine spending afternoons reading on it with the flames from the hearth warming her. A more welcoming and soothing bedchamber she'd never seen. Not that she'd seen many.

"The dressing room is just over there." Mrs. Pemberton pointed to a door next to the secretary. "And this way." She led Lilly to another doorway to the left of the fireplace which opened to a modest sitting area. "This is your shared sitting room, and his lordship's chamber is right through that door."

Lily didn't know how she felt about being in such close proximity to the earl, even though they were wed. By law, since speaking their marriage vows, he could do with her as he wished. She was essentially his property. Though the thought of that didn't unnerve her as she initially believed it would. He was kind and gentle on the surface, and she believed his heart was as well. She would not panic now and believe he hid any odd tendencies, though the thought did bring her mind back to consummating the marriage. Lily clasped her hands together to hide the trembling as the housekeeper led her back through her room and into the dressing room, where a tub filled with steaming water awaited her. The scent of roses filled the air and tickled her senses.

"I will leave you in Campbell's capable hands." Mrs. Pemberton bobbed. "Good evening, my lady, and welcome to your new home."

Lilly found herself being undressed and helped into the soothing bathwater. "I will see to the rest myself, Miss Campbell."

She dipped. "Yes, my lady."

How odd to have a maid of her own. Perhaps Miss Campbell would allow Lilly to call her Daisy. Perhaps that would make this all feel a bit less strange and formal. She'd have to ask her tomorrow, Lilly thought, as the young maid left.

Alone at last, Lilly sank into the tub up to her shoulders and relished the scented and soothing water. Her hand touched the small emerald pendant that had belonged to her mother. It was a necklace she rarely took off. Even though her memories of her mother had faded, she felt close to her when she wore her necklace.

Lilly closed her eyes and concentrated on the warm water cradling her body, hoping it would help to tame her runaway mind and heart about how unprepared she was for her new role as a married woman. Managing a household, even as large as the earl's, did not frighten her. She had managed her papa's affairs, which had included the whole village, for many years. Surely, along with the housekeeper and the butler, she could manage Langford Manor. What she didn't know was how to be a wife. Everything she'd learned about married couples had been observed in public places. She hadn't a clue about the intimate details of a marriage.

She didn't bother with washing her hair, as she'd done so that morning. After scrubbing her skin and realizing she couldn't hide in the cooling water forever, she exited the tub, dried off, and donned the night rail and matching robe laid out by her new maid. When she entered her bedchamber, she froze when she came face to face with Henry dressed in a thick blue banyan and looking flushed.

"I hope your accommodations are to your liking, my chi . . . Lilly."

Swallowing the lump in her throat, she replied, "Yes. Very much so."

"The cook prepared a delicious feast for us. Come into the adjoining room so we may partake." As soon as he finished speaking, he turned and walked through the doorway into the sitting room. He stood by a chair at a table filled with covered dishes and a platter full of cheese, fruits, and slices of bread, waiting to seat her.

As she sat and murmured, "Thank you," she hoped she'd managed to hide her nervousness from her new husband.

"My pleasure," he said as he sat and placed a napkin on his lap. "This looks wonderful."

Draping her napkin across her lap, Lilly removed the cover from her plate and found roasted pheasant, crispy small potatoes, and candied carrots. "It all smells divine." She hadn't realized until this moment that she was hungry. With all that had happened today, she'd not eaten since breakfast. Her heart pained, and tears stung her eyes as reality set in.

Her papa was gone. Forever.

Her life as she knew it was gone. Forever.

How had she gotten here? To this pivotal point in her life?

She wiped her tears from her face. "I'm sorry to cry. Please forgive me."

Henry reached across the small table and wiped more of her tears with his bare hand. "There is nothing to forgive. You have lost your papa, and I have lost my dear friend. We both are entitled to mourn for as long as we need."

How had she been so fortunate as to marry such a kind man? "It hurts."

"It does. From my experience, the pain will lessen as time goes on, but you will never forget. He will always be with you."

Henry ate nearly his entire plate while Lilly only nibbled. Yes, she was hungry, but nothing seemed to settle well. She thought it best to eat light.

When they were both finished, Henry helped her up and escorted her to her chamber. All the while, Lilly's insides vibrated, her mind raced with unseen scenarios, and she thought she might cast up her accounts.

They stopped near her bed.

"You have had a heartbreaking day, so I will bid you good-night." He bent and lightly brushed his lips on her cheek. "We will talk tomorrow about what our marriage will entail."

Lilly's feet refused to move as she watched her new husband exit her room and close the adjoining sitting room door. Her feet remained stuck to the floor, and her eyes never wavered from the closed door Henry had gone through, leaving her both relieved and anxious. She was relieved that her wedding night was postponed, but she was anxious because surely it was better to get it over with and not have it looming over her, wasn't it? How could she relax and sleep when worry swirled around inside her mind and body?

When his closest friend and local vicar, George St. Claire, asked Henry to marry his daughter, Lilly, the answer came quickly and easily. It was the least he could do to repay his friend for all but saving his soul many years ago during a dark and tragic time.

Henry had never married by choice, although he had come close once. He never worried about an heir because he had a nephew, Edmund, who knew from an early age that he would inherit the earldom since his father, Henry's younger brother, had died when Edmund was young. It was public knowledge that Henry never planned on marrying and producing an heir.

Never say never.

He had finally married, after all.

Could produce an heir if he wanted to.

Which made him think about the lovely young woman close by. His wife. She was like a daughter to him—he'd known her since her birth. Could he bed her and consummate the marriage?

Even though Henry had people reporting to him on his nephew's actions and whereabouts over the years, deep down, he didn't know what sort of man he was. Edmund hadn't visited since leaving university, which bothered Henry. He appeared well-liked in social circles, an affable fellow if somewhat of a rakehell. He owned a shipping import and export company with two other gentlemen, and by all accounts, it had become very prosperous. The business took him out of England for many months, if not years at a time.

However, what if the marriage wasn't consummated and Edmund found out? Henry never wanted Lilly's status as his countess to come into question once he passed on. Would Edmund cast Lilly out, penniless with nowhere to go? Was Henry willing to risk her future? No, he wasn't. It was the whole purpose of George asking him to marry her and keep her safe. A meeting with his solicitor was needed to set up a trust in Lilly's name. He would not leave her future to the whim of his nephew.

His thoughts returned to consummating his marriage. He would have to impress upon Lilly to keep this knowledge to herself after he was gone. That way no one could ever question the legality of their marriage.

Lately, he'd had trouble sleeping, so he spent most nights in the library. A warm blaze glowing in the hearth as he sat in a comfortable chair, his feet on an ottoman, reading from any book on the shelf, it didn't matter which, and a nice glass of brandy in hand. This night was no different, although he'd never had a wife waiting upstairs for him before. He snorted. Waiting might be a stretch. The poor child was probably frightened to death that he would visit her bed and demand his husbandly rights.

What had George been thinking? Marrying his daughter to an old man? Of course, Henry knew why. If the roles had been reversed, Henry would have done the same. He may never have had a child, but he understood parents, especially fathers with their daughters. They would do anything for them, anything to keep them safe and to secure their future.

A cold chill crept up his spine at the thought of what would have happened to Lilly if George had died suddenly and not been able to secure her future. If she had been fortunate, she would have procured a position in a household as a governess or a maid or married a member of the local gentry. But none of those guaranteed her safety. Henry refused to think what may have happened to the innocent, sweet girl who'd become his countess if they had not wed. And would he have had the whither all to intercede on her behalf?

Swirling the amber liquid in his glass, he shrugged his shoulders. It was a good thing he'd married her. George could join his beloved wife in heaven and rest easy knowing their daughter was safe and cared for.

THE CREAKING OF the door woke Lilly up as her maid came in. "I'm sorry about the squeak. I'll have someone oil the hinges today," Campbell said as she opened the curtains, letting in the cloudy daylight. She went back out into the hallway and returned with a breakfast tray, settling it on the bed next to her.

"His lordship thought you may want your breakfast brought to you. I'll return soon to help you dress."

Alone again, Lilly's reality of her new life weighed heavily on her heart and mind. It was difficult enough dealing with her papa's death, which made breathing difficult this morning, but finding herself suddenly married to the earl baffled her brain. Two shocks she needed to deal with. If she could only bury herself beneath her covers and never leave these beautiful rooms to face her future life. She'd only recently turned seventeen and wasn't prepared for what lay ahead. She hoped Henry was a patient man.

Sighing heavily, Lilly fluffed her pillows against the headboard and sat up, realizing she was famished. After she'd finished her tea, toast, and eggs, Campbell returned and helped her prepare for her day. And what, pray tell, would her day hold?

"His lordship wishes to see you in his study right away. I'll show you the way," Campbell said as she put the last few pins in her hair. "Also, Mrs. Pemberton wanted me to say that a seamstress will be coming to fit you with a new wardrobe this afternoon."

Lilly wasn't surprised about the new wardrobe. She hardly had clothing fit for a countess. When they traveled to London, she certainly didn't want to embarrass Henry with her country attire. Thinking of London had her chest constricting again. The earl could dress her to look like a countess, but underneath, she'd still be the vicar's daughter. Oh dear, would she ever be ready for a foray into London Society? She wondered how long she had before Parliament was in session.

Once Lilly stood outside Henry's open study door, she smoothed down her plain blue skirt. It was more to settle her nerves than because it was wrinkled. It also gave her trembling hands something to do.

"Enter, my dear."

Lilly's nerves eased somewhat when she heard Henry's soothing voice and also because he hadn't referred to her as a child. She needed to be treated as an adult now, whether she wanted to or not. Since finding out her papa was dying, she felt she had aged ten years anyway. Gone was her idealistic younger self.

"Good morning, Henry," she said, trying to make her voice sound, if not happy, at least not sad.

"Good morning to you, Lilly." He stood and came around his desk, gesturing to one of the two chairs opposite his large mahogany desk. "Please sit."

She sat down, arranged her skirts, and then entwined her

hands on her lap. Henry sat in the chair next to hers.

"I hope you slept well and found your room comfortable."

Was that nerves she heard in his voice? Could he be as uncomfortable with their sudden circumstances as she? After all, he was elderly and had never been married before. "Yes. I slept quite well, all things considered." He looked at her, raised his brows, his soft brown eyes questioning. Her stomach sank to her toes. Oh dear, she hoped she hadn't insulted him. "I didn't mean . . ."

"I know what you meant. Yesterday was a shock to both of us. No need to explain." Once again, he proved how kind and understanding a man he was. "I requested your presence so we may discuss what is expected of you within our marriage."

Her body tensed against her will, and she fervently hoped he didn't notice.

Gently, he placed one of his warm hands on top of hers briefly. "If I say anything you object to, please interrupt me as I tend to prattle on at my age. I want to tell you a story about myself in the hope that you will understand me better. And then perhaps you will share some things about yourself, your hopes and dreams."

"I will." She held her breath, waiting and anxious to hear what he had to say.

"Many years ago, when I first inherited the earldom, I spent much of my time in London enjoying myself. I was young and rich, relishing my time as a new earl. I had a small group of friends I'd known since Eton, and we belonged to all the same clubs." He paused, took a deep breath. "Some things I say may shock you, so I will apologize now. But know that everything I say relates to my life and the decisions I've made and will continue to make. So where was I? Oh yes, my friends and I were known as rakes. We drank, gambled, and socialized to excess. We spent many hours in brothels and snubbed our noses at our Parliament obligations. This went on for several years, I'm afraid."

Rising, he went to the sideboard, poured amber liquid into a tumbler, and sat back down. "During this time, I met a duke's daughter during her first season. She was beautiful and shy and had sapphire eyes that I drowned in. I was smitten immediately. I sent flowers, called upon her, and tried my hardest to prove to her father that I wasn't a wastrel. For weeks I called upon her during the proper visiting hours, but her father refused to allow me to court her. Evelyn was as devastated by her father's refusal as I was. I will never really know why she fell in love with me, but by the grace of God, she did. I even stayed away from my friends and my clubs. All to prove to the duke I was worthy of his only daughter."

Lilly sat motionless, hanging onto his every word. She couldn't take her eyes off his face. A face that, even now, all these years later, was saddened by the retelling of his story. And if she weren't mistaken, tears glistened in his eyes.

"After being relentless for many weeks, I was finally allowed by the duke to court his daughter, which led to my marriage proposal. But Evelyn fell ill as we waited for the banns to be posted and the wedding to be planned." Henry cleared his throat, removed his handkerchief from his coat pocket, and dried his eyes. "Forgive me. I still get emotional even though it's been forty years."

"I'm so sorry."

"We decided to have a private ceremony, but she passed the night before it took place. Their family physician could never tell us why she had taken ill. All I know is that over the course of a month, I sat at her bedside and watched as the lovely young lady I'd fallen in love with wasted away to nothing."

This time, Lilly placed her hand on his and squeezed, hoping to give him what little comfort she could. "How terribly sad for both of you."

"Within another month, I'd moved here. I hated London after that because I saw her beautiful face everywhere I went, which drove me to the brink of madness. Or perhaps not true madness, but I was mad for a time. The country air soothed me, as did busying myself with the estate. Eventually, my heart healed, but not enough to give it away to anyone else. Even though Evelyn and I never married, she was the wife of my heart."

Lilly touched his hand again. "I don't know what to say. Except thank you for marrying me. I know it couldn't have been an easy decision to make. I nearly died of embarrassment when Papa told me he'd asked you."

He turned his hand over and squeezed hers. "It was easy. Your father asked—the man who saved me from myself all those years ago. You see, I skipped an important part. The part where I met your father."

Tears welled in her eyes, and her lungs constricted, making it hard to speak. "Will you tell me?" she whispered.

"For almost a year after Evelyn's death, I buried myself in drink. I was careless with myself. I went riding across the countryside at breakneck speeds, inebriated and not caring if I lived or died. One afternoon as I led my horse by the reins, too drunk to ride, even by my standard, I came across your father and he kindly invited me into his home. He introduced me to his young bride, your mother, and served me soup and bread. Both of them treated me with such kindness, never judging me for my drunken behavior in the middle of the day. That was the first day of a long friendship with both your parents. But an even longer one with your father. Months later, after your father had helped me truly begin to deal with my grief and anger, I thanked my horse, my household, and your father for keeping me alive."

Lilly sniffled most unladylike. "Thank you for telling me."

"Thank you for listening to an old man babble about his lost love. Which brings me to our marriage."

Tension coiled inside her body, causing her stomach to ache.

"Ours will be a marriage in name alone. I'm an old man and do not wish to produce heirs or take a child bride to my bed. If this is shocking to you or you object, please say so now."

What did she think? Truly think? The tension drained from

her body, and she inhaled and exhaled in relief. If Henry had said he wanted heirs, she would have performed her wifely duty in the marriage bed, even if she didn't know exactly what that entailed. But she could only think about how relieved she was because he didn't. And sad for Henry. About how lonely a life he'd led never having loved again.

"If that is what you want, I will agree. But if you change your . . ."

"I won't. Someday, when I'm gone, you will find a good gentleman to love and one who will love you in return, give you babies, and you will thank me. Do not waste your innocence and love on me."

Her mouth opened to speak, but words escaped her. There were so many things to thank Henry for, but she didn't know where to begin. For however long he had left, she would take over her papa's role in the earl's life and be his closest friend and confidant.

CHAPTER TWO

THE FOLLOWING YEAR flew by with daily rides with Henry, picnics, and stimulating conversations. He treated her as an equal, sharing everything with her. She also accompanied him on his visits to his tenants. The time they spent in London for him to sit at his place in the House of Lords was not as fearful as Lilly had believed. They attended the opera and the theater but refused all invitations to private balls and small dinner parties. Henry had no yearning to relive his early years in London. Lilly was thankful he felt that way because she had no desire to mingle with strangers or to be gossiped about.

She spent much of her time with Henry's young cousin Emmeline, and Lilly was thrilled to have a friend. Henry's maternal uncle, Baron Connolly, had married a younger woman after his first wife's death, and his new, young wife had given him a daughter named Emmeline. At eighteen, Emmeline had married Mr. Aiden Fitzpatrick. At twenty-two she became a widow. The young widow Fitzpatrick was a Godsend to Lilly, teaching her everything she needed to know about London's social scene and more gossip and stories than she had room for in her memory.

Lilly couldn't have been happier or more content with her life. Thinking back to the day she'd married Henry, she would never have believed what a wonderful life they would have together.

Until it was no more.

The sun shone bright that early spring day, making it feel warmer than it was. Henry and Lilly had the cook pack them a picnic lunch, and they headed out for their usual ride. During the past year, she'd become quite a horsewoman and loved to race Henry. And the true gentleman that he was, he always let her win. Today was no exception. Only when Lilly pulled the reins on her mare and glanced over her shoulder, her heart stopped, and she cried out, "No, no, no!"

Turning her horse around, she bolted back toward Henry, lying on the ground at an awkward angle, his loyal bay beside him. Jumping off Rose Petal, her heart in her throat, Lilly dropped to the ground. Henry's eyes stared up at her sightless. Even though she recognized death, she clumsily felt around his neck for a pulse. Nothing. She threw her head back and screamed and screamed until no sound emerged. Tears and anguish clogged her throat, and she covered Henry with her body and sobbed.

"My lady." A gentle hand touched her shoulder, and she ignored it.

"Go away." Her voice was broken and hoarse.

"I can't. His lordship is gone. I must escort you home so he may be retrieved."

"I can't leave him alone."

"He won't be. My eldest son will stay with him."

With these kind words, Lilly finally mounted her horse, and the local farmer, Mr. Mahoney, held Rose Petal's reins and walked them back to Langford Manor. Many members of the household met them, no doubt seeing them approaching and wondering where their lord was.

Wilson, the butler, helped Lilly down from Rose Petal, a panic-stricken look on his face. "Where's his lordship?"

Eyes wide and mouth open, Lilly couldn't speak. No words could get past the lump in her throat.

Mr. Mahoney, standing beside her, eyes cast down, removed his hat, clutched it to his chest, and said in a voice laced with sadness, "He is dead. Appears to have fallen off his horse."

Every fiber in Lilly's body wanted to yell out that he wasn't dead and that Henry would never fall off his mount, but she stood, tears silently rolling down her face as Mrs. Pemberton and Campbell each had an arm around her waist.

After that, everything was a blur. Henry's body was returned, prepared, and laid out in the public drawing room. Messages were sent to his cousin and his solicitor, who would inform his nephew of his inheritance. Emmeline sent word that she was ill and couldn't travel, but she insisted Lilly come to London and stay with her. They could mourn Henry together. Nothing arrived from the new earl, and Lilly shivered with dread. How could someone be so cold as not to attend his uncle's showing? In her mind, she already disliked the young man she'd never met.

Standing in the family cemetery, a cold, windy rain blasting her body, her heavy cloak doing little to keep her dry as the wind blew off her hood. Lilly watched with burning eyes and a heavy heart as Henry's casket went into the ground. A sadness she'd only felt once before when her papa died settled inside her soul. She'd been too young when her mama died to remember. Her heart was broken and her throat sore from all her crying as her mind screamed, *why Henry?* He'd become her everything. How would she survive without his love, friendship, and guidance?

As she rested that evening on the chaise longue before the blazing hearth in her bedchamber, Lilly closed her eyes and tried to sleep. Her bed didn't interest her. Even though she and Henry hadn't shared it, he'd visited her nightly, hugged her, and kissed her cheek. Sleeping without their nightly ritual didn't feel right.

The next day, Lilly had her belongings moved to another room as far down the hall as she could get from her and Henry's old chambers. It was a smaller room but no less lovely. And she may as well prepare for the arrival of the new earl. Of course, he might not come here at all and instead move directly into Henry's London residence in Mayfair, corresponding about the estate and earldom through the family solicitor and Henry's estate manager.

Having never received word from his nephew during the year of their marriage, Lilly also didn't know whether he was married or single. Did she now possess the title of Dowager Countess of Langford? Only time would tell.

MR. EDMUND WESTON, Mr. James Caldwell, and Andrew Hampton, the Earl of Quincy—the three owners of Mayfair Imports and Exports—each traveled from the West Indies on different ships with cargo holds full of goods to sell in London and beyond. As Edmund's ship traveled up the Thames on a bright clear day toward the docks and their warehouse, the tension of the long trip eased from his shoulders. *London.* He had been traveling for business for nearly eight years, ever since the inception of their company—the last three of those years with only quick stops in London.

The years had been full of adventure, hard work, foreign politics, women, gambling, and much more. But recently, he'd missed his life in England and decided to come home with plans to travel less. It was time to put down roots and prepare for the earldom which would one day be his. Uncle Henry was in good health, as far as he knew, but he was getting up in age. Edmund figured it couldn't hurt to be prepared.

After settling business affairs in London, he was going to Langford Manor to see his uncle and spend time learning his day-to-day routine. He would visit the tenants and ease any concerns they had about him taking over at some point. He wanted to make his uncle proud and know he was leaving everything in good hands. Give him no regrets about never marrying and producing an heir.

Finally standing on solid ground, Edmund's body swayed as though he were still on the open seas. He was used to the feeling, so he went about his business. By the end of the day, Quincy and

Caldwell, his business partners, also arrived safely to port and Edmund sighed with relief. They'd had a relatively calm voyage, but calm waters didn't always mean safe travels. Pirates could come upon them at any time.

"Another safe journey," Quincy said as he entered the warehouse office along with Caldwell. Both men looked tired but in good spirits, as they should be with the fortune in cargo their ships had hauled into port.

Edmund sat at one of three desks in the large room and eyed the large piles of correspondence. "Caldwell, would you pour three glasses of brandy? We should celebrate another successful adventure."

The three friends sat drinking and discussing their shipments, which were being unloaded into their warehouse at that very moment, when a gentleman knocked on the open office door and said, "Excuse me, gentlemen. I'm looking for Mr. Edmund Weston."

"I am he. And you are?"

"I am Randal Beauregard, solicitor to Henry Weston, the late Earl of Langford. I have a letter for you, my lord. Your uncle Henry passed on two months ago. You have inherited the earldom." He handed Edmund a sealed missive. "I am very sorry for your loss. Please come to my office tomorrow. We have things to discuss and paperwork to sign." He bowed and left as quickly as he'd arrived.

"I'm sorry for your loss," Quincy said as he looked thoughtfully into his drink. "And congratulations on your title and inheritance. I find it very awkward when titles transfer. Strange circumstances."

"Most definitely," Caldwell said as he refilled everyone's glasses.

Edmund stared at the letter in his unsteady hand. Once he opened it, everything in his life as he knew it would change. He broke the seal on the letter from Beauregard, unfolded it and read:

Dear Edmund Weston, The Earl of Langford,

It is with terrible regret that I inform you of the death of Henry Weston, the 5th Earl of Langford, on 21 April 1815, in a riding accident. He leaves his widow, Lilliana Weston, the Countess of Langford . . .

He didn't bother reading the rest. "Uncle Henry had a wife." Surprise did not begin to express how he felt about learning that Uncle Henry had finally married. He was glad he'd had someone to share his last years with, but his heart ached for his widow that she would spend her elderly years alone. One of the first things Edmund needed to find out was whether there was a dower house at Langford Manor. Surely, she would not want to live in that enormous manor alone when he was not in residence.

Both of his friends' heads turned his way.

"I'm shocked," Quincy said, pulling Edmund out of his musings. "We certainly haven't been very well informed during our years abroad. I think something as interesting as the Earl of Langford taking a bride at his age would've made the newspapers we received."

"One would think." Edmund studied the empty glass in his hand. "I imagine she is upset with me for not coming right away. Not that I could have. I hope someone explained that I was out of the country and wouldn't receive word until now. I would hate our relationship to be stained before we've met." He should write to her himself, try to undo any awkwardness that might exist between them on account of his absence.

Quincy stood and placed his glass on the sideboard. "I'm going home. I have no idea if my parents received my message informing them of my arrival. Hopefully, I won't cause my mother to have a fainting spell when I appear."

Caldwell snorted and stood to follow his friend out. "Since I live in single gentlemen's quarters, I'm free to do as I please."

Alone at last with his thoughts, Edmund made a list of important things he needed to do starting tomorrow. Before he traveled to Langford Manor, he needed to visit Baron Winslow and inquire about his daughter, Annabelle. The thought of Annabelle stabbed his heart. He'd once cared for her deeply. It was almost ten years since he'd seen her, and he hoped she was happy, healthy, and alive, wherever she was. Neither the baron nor he had been able to locate her since she'd left all those years ago. The last time Edmund had been in London, he had spent many days and nights wandering the poorer sections of town in the hope of finding her. The baron was getting on in age, and he wanted to see his beloved daughter once last time before he met his maker.

TWO MONTHS HAD passed since Henry's death, and the household had prepared to welcome their new lordship each day to no avail.

Until a letter arrived stamped with the Earl of Langford's seal.

Her hands trembling, Lilly sat alone in the family drawing room, awaiting afternoon tea while she broke the seal. Opening the short correspondence, she began to read:

My Dearest Aunt Lilliana,

Please forgive me for writing to you months after my uncle's passing. I returned to the country only days ago, having been abroad for many years, and I just learned of his death. I also only just found out he married, and I am very sorry for your loss.

It is with a saddened heart that I write to you now. I remember my uncle from when I was a boy, and I regret that I didn't spend more time with him as an adult.

I will arrive at Langford Manor on 15 June 1815 to meet with the estate manager and visit the tenants. I sincerely hope that you will make time to spend a meal or two with me so we can discuss your plans for the future.

Your Humble Nephew,

Edmund

Lilly folded the missive and slumped down into the settee in a most unladylike way. Who cared? No one would see her except for the maid bringing her tea. So he'd been abroad and hadn't known Henry had passed or that he had wed? How interesting. It also sounded as though he was single, which was in her favor. He would probably spend all his time in London.

Before knowing whether he was wed or not, Lilly had it in her mind to spend some time with Emmeline in London. London didn't frighten her as it once did. However, she thought now she would wait until her year of mourning was over before leaving. By then, perhaps she would be ready for public gatherings.

But until she met with the new earl, her future plans really were up in the air.

EDMUND, HATING THE confinement of a carriage, rode his gelding, Bear, in front of the matching four hauling his trunks. Accompanying him were his driver and two outriders. He spent so much time in close quarters on his fleet of ships that he craved the vast open space whenever the chance arose. At six feet tall, no carriage or ship's cabin catered to his height. Even his captain's quarters on his ships had low ceilings, causing him to crouch. Such was life at sea.

They were almost to Langford Manor, and Edmund had no idea what sort of welcome was waiting for him. As a grown man, he shouldn't have an anxious knot in his belly, but he did. Would his aunt resent him? She'd lost her husband, and her life was changed forever. But he had no plans to live in the country and wouldn't interrupt her daily life. His ships sailed in and out of London. His warehouse was there, so that was where he needed to be. He would juggle his business and the responsibilities of the earldom from there. And if he couldn't, his partner, Mr. James

Caldwell, who was unmarried and untitled, could take on more responsibility in the business.

Several servants hurried out the door and down the manor's steps to greet him. They took the reins to Bear as he dismounted. Ignoring the need to stretch his limbs, he turned toward the people who he supposed were his household now.

"My lord, welcome to Langford Manor." The small, middle-aged man Edmund recognized as the butler bowed. "I am Mr. Wilson, your butler. Please accept all the household's condolences on the loss of your uncle."

"Thank you," Edmund said.

Wilson proceeded to introduce the remaining servants to him. As well as remembering the butler, he remembered the valet and housekeeper from when he was a child.

His uncle's valet, Mullens—now his, he supposed—came forward and bowed. "I will have your things brought to the earl's chambers and unpacked immediately."

Upon entering the manor, Edmund relaxed and looked around the sizeable, marbled entry. If this were any indication, the house wouldn't need any repairs or redecorating. He'd forgotten his uncle had impeccable taste. Most likely, nothing would need to be changed, as with the London townhome. Until one day in the future, of course, when he took a bride and she wanted to make modifications.

"I would like to freshen up and then meet my uncle's widow. Could you ask her to meet me in the drawing room in half an hour? And please bring a tea tray."

Edmund hurried up the stairs to the master chambers. He remembered where they were and found the large bedchamber clean and tastefully decorated in dark blue and beige. He opened the door to the dressing room and found nothing of his uncle's left inside. A quick peek into the adjoining sitting room found it clean and smelling faintly of roses. He wrinkled his nose and shut the door.

Mullens brought a basin of warm water for him to freshen up

with. While splashing the soothing water on his face, several servants brought in his trunks, and Mullens oversaw the unpacking of his things. "Leave the small brown trunk. I will take care of that myself," Edmund said. Inside the smaller trunk held Edmunds's personal papers and things he preferred nobody to handle but him.

Half an hour later, Edmund went down the hall to the family's private drawing room to find a small woman standing, gazing out the sunny window with her back to him. He studied the woman in a plain, black mourning dress, her light hair done up in a neat chignon. One delicate hand leaned against the molding around the window. He frowned as his heart thumped hard inside his chest. Something appeared off. Suddenly, he didn't know whether to address her as aunt, countess, or Lady Langford. He chose the latter.

"Lady Langford."

When she turned to face him with a gentle smile and spoke the words, "Please call me Lilly," with a sweet melody of a voice, he stumbled forward as though he'd been punched in the gut. Was his mind playing tricks on him? Because standing before him was but a girl. If she were a day over twenty, he'd eat his gloves. This was his uncle's widow? This beautiful young woman? He'd expected someone closer to his uncle's age. His suspicious nature had chills climbing up his spine. He ignored the feeling for now.

"Lilly, let me express my deepest condolences on the loss of Lord Langford. I admired my uncle greatly and will miss him."

"Thank you. I miss him very much."

"I must admit I was shocked to find out my uncle finally married. And to marry someone such as yourself . . ."

She looked at him with confusion. "Such as myself? What does that mean?"

What does that mean? Had she never thought it would seem odd that a man of his uncle's advanced years would be married to someone her age? Surely, this girl and her family had somehow taken advantage of his uncle in his old, lonely years, hoping to swindle him out of his fortune. Why else would someone so young tie herself to an aging gentleman?

His words came out sharp as his suspicions grew. "Where did you come from, and how on earth did you convince my Uncle Henry to marry you? Has your family stolen all the Langford jewels? Was he supporting all your relatives? Because if he was, the money is no more. I will not be taken advantage of as he was. You and yours will not see a farthing from me."

As he ranted on, Lilly rose to her full height. Her arms crossed in front of her chest, and her facial expression, once warm and welcome, had turned frigid. Her bright-blue eyes were now dark and stormy.

For one brief moment, he felt contrite for his angry and harsh words. Perhaps he had spoken too quickly. Perhaps he should have given her a chance to tell the story of their marriage and how it came about. But his confusion and shock at the situation had made him forget his manners completely, and the hurtful diatribe had poured from his mouth without thinking.

Putting a wedge between himself and Uncle Henry's widow would no doubt be something he regretted later.

CHAPTER THREE

LILLY COULD NOT believe her ears. What right did he have to speak to her in such a way? When she'd first turned around and faced Henry's tall and handsome nephew, she'd smiled in welcome. And for a moment, he'd appeared genuinely happy to make her acquaintance. That was until his dark eyes narrowed, and he'd rudely looked her up and down from head to toe. Right before her eyes, his features changed from friend to foe, making her wonder what she'd done to cause such a drastic change in him. And then he'd said such horrible things to her.

Well, two could play at this. She shut down her feelings and faced the man, *Edmund*, with ice flowing in her veins. He'd insulted her and poor, deceased Henry. He'd insulted her, because he thought she'd married him only for his fortune, and Henry, because he thought he was so old and feeble that such a person could swindle him. He hadn't known his uncle at all. And it was too bad this man would take over Henry's titles and lands that he appreciated, honored, and loved so very much.

With her chin up, she mustered her haughtiest voice—she didn't know if she even had one, but she would try. "How dare you come in here and speak to me so? I *am* the Countess of Langford and deserve your respect. Henry and I loved each other and had a wonderful marriage. I never took anything from him but the basic necessities. When you are ready to atone for your behavior, ask Mrs. Pemberton where you may find me."

Quitting the room and out of that man's view, she gathered up her skirts and ran down the hall. Behind her closed door, she slithered to the floor against the door and sobbed into her hands. If it were possible, her heart cracked right down the middle all over again, causing pain to radiate throughout her entire being.

"That . . . that . . . bloody arse," she cursed, her voice vibrating with both heartache and seething anger, "cannot be the Earl of Langford!"

A knock on the door startled her. She stood, wiping tears from her eyes and cheeks, and opened the door to see Mrs. Pemberton looking concerned.

Lilly opened the door wider to let her enter and found herself engulfed in the housekeeper's comforting arms.

"There, there, my lady, I'm sure the earl didn't mean what he said."

"How did you know?" Lilly gasped into Mrs. Pemberton's ample bosom, which made a soft pillow.

"I was right outside the door with the tea tray ready to enter when I heard his lordship accuse you of those dreadful things." She huffed. "Someone needs to teach him some manners or box his ears or both. Come, let me tuck you into bed. A nice nap will make you feel better."

Exhausted all of a sudden, she believed a nap would be nice. Mrs. Pemberton helped her undress to her chemise, tucked her in, and closed the window curtains, leaving Lilly in darkness. Snuggling beneath the counterpane, Lilly sighed and put the events from earlier out of her head as she succumbed to a restless sleep.

Where was she? She was shivering in the cold, clutching a thread-bare cloak to her chest, and her feet were numb in her tattered kid boots. Her toes nearly peeked through the top of the worn leather. Why was she not at Langford Manor? Confused, she stood outside the cottage where she had lived with her papa and found it empty. There was no sign that anyone resided there. She rested for a spell, then headed out into the elements.

Where was Henry? Walking the two miles to Langford Manor took everything she had inside her. She knew if she stopped and curled up to sleep, which she wanted so desperately to do, she would die. The cold would freeze her body, and wolves would eat her. How terribly sad Henry would be.

She shuffled up the steps on legs she could no longer feel and banged on the large wooden door. She almost fell to the ground in gratitude when Wilson opened the door. Her happiness didn't last long when he glared at her. "What are you doing here? Your husband, the earl, is dead, and you are no longer welcome. His heir cast you out for your sins. Be gone and never come back." Tears silently trickled down her cheeks as the door slammed in her face. Henry was dead. Why did she not remember him dying? And why had his nephew thrown her out? She was a countess. Making her way to the stables, she snuck inside so the stable boy wouldn't see her and cast her out. Finding the stall with Rose Petal, her mare who welcomed her, Lilly lay down on what clean hay she could gather and fell into an exhausted and troubled sleep.

"No!" Lilly screamed as she sat up, shaking and sweating, her heart pounding against her ribcage. Hurrying from the bed, she threw open the curtains and ran around the room, checking to see if all her belongings were accounted for. Sinking into the chair at the dressing table, she sighed with relief. Her dream had seemed so real. Was it a premonition of what would come? Surely the earl, no matter what he desired, wouldn't throw her out, leaving her destitute and homeless? Wasn't that why Henry set up a trust in her name alone? To secure a comfortable future for her?

Mrs. Pemberton knocked on Lilly's door and entered. "Forgive me, my lady, but the earl has requested you join him for dinner." Her voice was soft, and her features apologetic. "Campbell will be right in."

Lilly's shoulders slumped forward, and she fought the tears pooling in her eyes. She wanted to refuse, to put off coming face to face with that despicable man. But she knew deep down that it was only putting off the inevitable. She would have to see him eventually, and it may as well be at dinner.

Just then her maid entered the room, her face as solemn as Mrs. Pemberton's. Clearly, the whole household heard what transpired between the earl and her that afternoon.

"Daisy, please bring my plainest black dress. I'll not have the earl think I'm trying to make an impression dressing up for him. Also, I'll wear the small hat with the half veil." That way, she could eat, but he couldn't see her eyes. He would get no respect from her after the way he treated her.

"Yes, my lady."

Lilly studied herself in the looking glass and cringed as tears stung her eyes. Where had she gone? Where was the young lady who had just begun to enjoy her life being married to Henry? More importantly, what was to become of her? She needed to keep her chin up and fight the melancholy and the uncertainty of her future.

She swept into the dining room to find Langford seated at the head of the table, sipping a glass of wine and following her movements over the goblet's rim. A quick glance at the table sent Lilly's stomach tumbling. The only other place setting lay directly to his right. With the help of a footman, Lilly took her seat and welcomed the wine that was being poured into her glass. Without acknowledging the earl, she picked up her wine glass and took a nice sip before dabbing her lips dry with her napkin— anything to postpone having to look at or speak to him.

"I must apologize for my rash actions this afternoon," Langford said with a deep voice that Lilly didn't believe sounded contrite at all. In fact he sounded like an arrogant, entitled arse. "I was shocked when I found out Uncle Henry married so late in life. And, well . . ." he paused and cleared his throat, "to find he married someone so young."

She couldn't bear to listen to him babble anymore. "Yes. I'm sure you were shocked. Many people were."

"Why did he marry you?"

His question sounded more like a demand for information.

Lilly took her time answering. She sipped her wine. Signaled the serving footman for a refill. Sipped again. And she refused to look his way. Wearing the half veil was her best idea ever. "Your uncle decided he wanted children. Unfortunately, we were not blessed in the short time we were wed."

His snort had her fighting back a smile.

When the dessert ended, Lilly excused herself and left Langford staring after her with his mouth open. Hurrying down the hall, she entered the library, collapsed into a chair before the hearth, tossed her veiled hat to the side and sighed. "Well, that was trying," she whispered into the empty room full of floor-to-ceiling bookshelves. Her body froze when footfalls traveled down the hall and paused inside the library.

"Forgive me. I'm not following you. I seek something to read."

Lilly's breath suspended inside her lungs as her eyes followed his every movement. He may be her enemy, but he cut a fine figure in his tan-and-brown print waistcoat, his white linen shirt, and nicely tied cravat. His brown trousers were tucked into even darker brown Hessians. Between the dining room and here, he'd discarded his jacket. His hair was short and dark as night. His eyes were the darkest brown. They almost appeared as dark as the devil's.

Heat curled in her stomach. A strange sensation. One she'd never felt before, but she recognized it as desire, and she didn't like it being associated with Langford at all. Her traitorous body had better behave. She attributed her reaction to being in close proximity to a gentleman close to her age for the first time ever.

"Can you recommend something?"

"No." She could, but she had no interest in doing so.

"Well then, I hope you don't mind sharing the room because I may be a while."

"Take your time. I was just leaving. Good night."

EDMUND SPUN AROUND, his eyes riveted on Lilly as she exited the room with the grace and ease of someone much older. What game was she playing? It had started during dinner and continued in the library, and he didn't yet understand it.

He may have apologized for his accusations and hurtful words he'd spoken that afternoon, but he hadn't meant them. Every single person in this house was hiding something from him. He'd spent the afternoon drilling the servants, trying to get a view on his uncle and Lilly's marriage. The only thing anyone said was that it was a love match. "Bloody hell," he mumbled. They lied to his face. His household lied to him so easily. It was so obvious they were keeping secrets. And damn it if they weren't completely devoted and loyal to Lilly, as he supposed it should be.

But he was the new earl, and he also deserved their loyalty. Only a few members of the household knew him, but the others would learn soon enough he was loyal, too, hardworking, and devoted to the earldom. As for Lilly, she had his insides tied up in knots. There was no denying she was beautiful and alluring, even dressed in dreary black. If he'd met her under different circum-stances . . . he moaned and raked his hands through his newly cut hair. *Do not think about her in that way.* She was his uncle's widow and off-limits to him. The best thing for him to do to keep the peace between the two of them was to complete all his estate business as quickly as possible and go back to London. They would barely have to see each other. His hand rubbed his chest to ease the sudden tightness.

When he'd arrived today, he'd expected to be greeted by an elderly, kind widow who would be happy to retire to the dower house. And if Langford Manor didn't have one, he'd build one for her and she'd live out her remaining years there. For some reason, he no longer saw that happening anytime soon. Nor should it. Lilly was too young to retire from life. He picked a tome off the shelf without even reading the title and strolled up to his rooms, wondering what tomorrow would bring.

On the pillow on his bed was a sealed letter that hadn't been there before dinner. It was addressed to him and was sealed with the Langford seal. The hairs on the back of his neck rose as he knew, without a doubt, that this was a letter from Uncle Henry written to him before his death. He tore it open, his eyes widening as he read the letter in his uncle's handwriting.

My Dearest Nephew,

When this letter reaches your hand, I will be dead and you will have taken my place as the Earl of Langford. I have faith in you that you will be a fair and honest landowner to your tenants and will do the names Weston and Langford great honor. I'm so very proud of what you have made of yourself and your business enterprise.

I have a great favor to ask, though. I married the lovely and young Lilliana. I ask you to look out for her, as we kept mostly to ourselves when in London, and I'm afraid London Society will eat her alive. She is kind, honest, and smart. But she is inexperienced with members of the ton. Please help her navigate Society. As she is so young, my greatest wish for her is to make another love match for herself, one that can produce children. Please take my request to help her and see her happily married to an honorable gentleman very seriously. I am relying on you, Edmund.

From the other side,
Henry

After reading the letter three times, he folded it and placed it on the bedside table. *From the other side.* Edmund shivered. Did Henry have to make it sound as though he were watching him from the grave, making him feel guilty for how he'd treated her today when they first met? Putting that thought aside, he had to come to terms with his uncle's two requests. He had the feeling that after today, Lilly would not welcome his assistance in entering London Society or help with finding herself a suitable husband. He shuddered. A love match. Did they even exist? Yes, of course he knew they did. But they were rare.

⋙✦⋘

HAVING TOSSED AND turned around in her bed, the sheets tangling up with her limbs, and unable to sleep, Lilly was up and dressed before Daisy came to wake her. "I don't need your assistance with anything this morning, Daisy. I'm going to take my breakfast in the morning room."

Daisy bobbed her head. "Yes, my lady."

The thought of having a tray brought up to her room and hiding from Langford tempted her, but if they were to coexist in the same house, she'd better get used to him. Although, he never said he would be staying at Langford Manor. He would seek a bride now that he was an earl and would, no doubt, return to London in the hope of finding one. Also, he may insist she move to the dower house. Lilly wrinkled her nose. The dower house was a lovely large cottage not far from the main manor house, but she had no intention of living there. The dower house was for older widows. Not someone of her young age. Besides, she hadn't really lived a life outside of the country in Kent. As much as the idea of London's polite Society still frightened her, a part of her was excited to experience it firsthand. What little she'd taken part in when Henry lived was nothing that she imagined a widow would experience.

When her year of mourning concluded, she wanted to experience new things and perhaps find a husband not three times her age. Henry's cousin, Emmeline Fitzpatrick, had already invited her to stay with her and her mother. As soon as she felt ready, she would write her and take her up on her offer.

Lilly entered the morning room, found it empty, and sighed

with relief. She relaxed her face, which hurt from the forced smile she had adopted to greet Langford with if necessary. After fixing a plate at the sideboard, a footman helped her sit and poured her a cup of hot chocolate. "Thank you, Stevens."

Just as her first forkful of egg made its way into her mouth, Langford swept into the room with dark circles under his eyes. So, it appeared she wasn't the only one who hadn't slept.

"Good morning, Langford."

"Good morning," he mumbled as he fixed a plate.

Even though she'd lost her appetite with Langford's arrival, she forced herself to eat, knowing she would be hungry later if she didn't. It was the method she adopted for supper as well, and every meal she found herself sharing with the new earl.

Mrs. Pemberton reported to her, every day for a fortnight, that his lordship was still drilling the servants for any tidbits surrounding her marriage. He tore apart Henry's study several times, seeking papers. Lilly's heart dropped with the knowledge. It was a good thing Mr. Beauregard possessed the banking and legal documents for the trust Henry had set up for her. And as far as she knew, Henry didn't have a copy in the house.

Langford continued to treat her with disdain and indifference. He didn't come out and accuse her again of stealing, but he still implied it. They sat together each night for supper per his request. A request she chose not to ignore as it would only make things worse between them. Tension swelled thick in the air as they ate in silence, making her question why he would torture both of them. Eating separately would ease both their constitutions. She didn't know about him, but she felt sick each night when she climbed in bed. What food she consumed felt like a rock in her stomach.

Each morning, she woke up exhausted, knowing it would be an exact repeat of the day before.

Edmund was an insufferable bore. And after two weeks she decided she'd had enough of living this way. Sitting at her small writing desk, she grabbed paper and dipped the quill into the inkwell and penned a letter to Henry's cousin.

> *Dearest Emmeline,*
>
> *I hope this missive finds you well. I would like to take you up on your offer to visit you in London. I will arrive in a few weeks, if it is agreeable to you.*
>
> *Your Humble Cousin,*
> *Lilly*

Now that that was resolved, she rang the bell for Daisy to begin preparing for their eventual departure immediately. Lilly would not so much as leave a stocking behind as she never planned to step foot in this house again. "I'm sorry, Henry," she whispered as she rubbed her chest while tears slid down her cheeks. "I can't stay here. I have to make a new life for myself. I know it's what you wanted for me, but it hurts to say goodbye."

When she arrived in London, she would have about nine months left of mourning to prepare herself to enter Society. During these months, she knew she would need to learn to dance. One could hardly expect to attend social functions without knowing how to dance properly. She also needed to visit a modiste and add several ballgowns to her wardrobe.

After Daisy helped her dress for afternoon tea, she made her way to the family drawing room, hoping Langford wasn't there. If he were, she would take tea in the public drawing room. She had reached her breaking point with his antics. One moment he seemed able to manage civility and respect for her station as Henry's widow, but then the next minute he would be rude again. Fortunately for her, this time the room was empty, and she enjoyed the privacy and quiet of taking tea and biscuits in solitude without Edmund taking up space in the room. She supposed she should start thinking of him solely as Langford, but it stung. Henry was Langford, but not anymore.

Lilly wasn't fool enough to think she could leave Langford Manor without the earl taking notice, but she wanted to put the confrontation off as long as possible. Once she had received a welcoming reply from Emmeline, Wilson quietly arranged for the earl's carriage to take her to London a few days later. Days that couldn't go by fast enough, her patience was so strained. Sometimes, dealing with the new earl had her feeling like a child. At other times, she felt ancient.

Sipping her tea, a pain sparked inside her chest at the thought of never returning to the only village she had lived in. Henry's household had been most kind to her, and she would miss them. Suddenly an idea occurred to her, and she rang for Wilson. "Please have my horse saddled and a groomsman ready to accompany me. I shall visit Papa's and Henry's graves."

The two miles to the cemetery where her papa was buried didn't take long on this glorious day, weather-wise at least. With the groomsman's help, she dismounted and made her way to the small headstone marking both of her parents' graves.

"Mama, Papa," she said as she knelt before the marker, "I've come to say goodbye." Tears pooled in her eyes, and breathing proved difficult with the heaviness inside her chest. "I'm moving to London and don't know if I will return. Henry died, and the new earl is a dreadful man. I cannot live under the same roof as him. I know when I am not wanted. Henry's cousin, Emmeline, a lovely childless widow, invited me to stay with her. I don't find London as frightening as I once did, and I look forward to immersing myself in its lifestyle." She clasped her hands and bowed her head in silent prayer.

"Please forgive me for leaving, but I must do what is best. Henry's biggest hope for me, when he no longer lived, was for me to marry a kind man for love. I also pray for this. And it will not come to fruition here." She gasped for air, fighting back her sobs. "I will always love and miss you both." As she stumbled away, her hand clutching her chest, she knew a large section of her heart stayed behind with her parents.

Her next stop was the Langford family burial ground. Kneeling at Henry's grave, she kissed her finger and touched his headstone. "Hello, Henry. I miss you so. Life with you was simple and easy. You made me feel welcome and wanted, even though deep down you didn't want to marry me." She smiled sadly. "You honored a dying man's request. Your breed of aristocracy is dying if your nephew's behavior is any indication. I'm going to London to live with Emmeline as she has offered, and I think it is for the best. The new earl doesn't need me underfoot as he acclimates to his new duties. And I won't lie, I look forward to living in London. If I never return, know I loved you in my own way and I will always be grateful." She wiped the tears from her eyes so she could see as she mounted her horse with the groom's help.

"Time to go, Peters."

"Yes, my lady."

CHAPTER FOUR

Nine Months Later
London 1816

"HOW DOES IT feel, cousin, to be out of mourning?" Emmeline asked Lilly as they entered Madam Serena's, the most sought-after modiste in all of London. Today, both of them had final fittings for several new ballgowns, day dresses, and cloaks to add to their wardrobe.

How did she feel? Lilly felt nervous, excited, and terrified to begin this next chapter of her life. Now, nothing kept her from attending balls, soirees, Almack's, the theater, and the opera; indeed, her head spun. There was nothing at all to keep her from accepting the many invitations that came to Emmeline's house daily.

"I'm nervous. I suddenly find myself out of mourning as the Widow Countess of Langford. It appears as if everyone who is anyone in London's elite Society wants to meet me. I'm afraid they all have ulterior motives in making my acquaintance. As if they want something from me." She paused, trying to ignore all the sweeping emotions coursing through her veins. "You know Henry and I kept to ourselves when we came to London. He was afraid Society would overwhelm me and kept me sheltered. Thinking back on it now, I'm not convinced he did me any favor. Nothing is stopping anyone from treating me cruelly now."

Emmeline placed a comforting, gloved hand on her arm. "I

am your family, as is my mother, and we will protect you. You have a cousin and aunt looking out for you."

Before Lilly could respond, Madam Serena swept out of the back room, closed off by a dark-blue velvet curtain. "Lady Langford, Mrs. Fitzpatrick, you are right on time for your final fitting." She curtsied. "Please come with me."

It was quite some time later when Lilly and Emmeline left the dressmaker's shop. Lilly had added a day dress at the last minute—an emerald green which matched her pendant perfectly—and couldn't wait for it to be delivered. "I've never owned such fine pieces of clothing, and Henry was quite generous with my allowance. But I never needed more than two ballgowns before. Now I have six." Lilly said, linking arms with Emmeline. "I spoiled myself. Mr. Beauregard's jaw will drop when he receives the extravagant bill."

Quiet laughter came from Emmeline, who was beautiful at twenty-eight. "As my solicitor will be when he receives mine," Emmeline said with a smile.

Emmeline had thick raven hair, light-blue eyes, and a lush figure dressed today in a royal-blue day dress and matching spencer with seed pearls as accents. She looked closer to Lilly's age, which made Lilly wonder if two widows of such young age should be traveling Bond Street and the rest of London on their own.

"Is it proper for us to be about without a chaperone?"

Emmeline laughed. "We are both widows and are allowed certain freedoms because of it. Nonetheless, I have already decided to have my mother accompany us to nightly social gatherings. She is not so old that she doesn't appreciate socializing." Emmeline looked around to confirm no one could overhear. "During our special outings set up by the Duchess of Greenville, we always have a driver looking after our safety. Please remember we have a meeting tomorrow."

"I haven't forgotten." How could Lilly ever forget the Ladies' Society of Mayfair to which they belonged? It had kept her sane during her time of mourning. She had never been one to embroider, sew, or play an instrument, which had given her very little to do the past year. Instead, she immersed herself in the workings of the Society, guided by the Duchess of Greenville, a very kind woman in her early forties who had no children and dedicated her time to helping those less fortunate.

Lilly had visited St. Giles with some regularity in the name of the Society to deliver necessary food, clothing, and medicine to the less fortunate which gave her purpose. The few times she'd ventured out beneath the darkness of night had her heart pumping so she knew she was still alive. Fortunately, those dangerous trips at night were due only to emergencies. They were few and far between, but Lilly always volunteered, as did Emmeline. It could be dangerous for the ladies in the Society to do the deliveries, but many of the women living in the slums were leery of men for good reason and would only take donations from other women.

They stopped at Gunter's for lemon ices, and Lilly tried to ignore the stares directed at her. Everyone appeared interested. Several ladies approached their table and Emmeline made introductions: The Duchess of Fairway, Lady Brennan, and Mrs. Smythe. Lilly was surprised at what appeared to be genuine kindness and sympathy for her loss of Henry. It gave her high hopes that everyone she met would treat her in such a way.

It wasn't long before she realized that was not to be true.

"Oh my," Emmeline whispered, "don't look now, but Lady Wilmington is coming this way with her two daughters. She has been unfriendly to me since my first ball as a debutante when I met my late husband. Apparently, her eldest daughter, who has since died, had set her sights on Aiden."

"Mrs. Fitzpatrick, how nice to see you," Lady Wilmington said with a nasally voice and an insincere smile. "And who is this lovely creature with you?"

Lilly cringed at the lady's false words.

"Lady Wilmington, this is my cousin, Lilliana Weston, Countess of Langford."

Lady Wilmington made a big show. She grabbed both of Lilly's hands with her own and squeezed. "How terribly dreadful to be widowed at such a young age. How *old* are you, my dear?"

Emeline and Lilly eyed one another, knowing she only wanted to know her age to surmise if she was a threat to her two daughters and their chances of snagging husbands this season. "I'm nineteen."

"Oh, my. So young, but looking . . ." She frowned, then whispered, "Perhaps you should use cucumber slices on your eyes to ease the puffiness."

Before Lilly could gasp in outrage, Lady Wilmington bid them farewell and left with her daughters in tow.

Her fingers flew to her eyes. "Do I have puffy eyes?"

"No," Emmeline said reassuring her. "It was Lady Wilmington's way to hurt you. She sees you as competition for her daughters, whom she didn't bother introducing. Lady Grace is the taller one, although I'm afraid there's nothing graceful about her. She's twenty-two. Her sister is your age and not very bright I fear. Her name is Lady Faith. Both of them are pretty, sweet, and kind, nothing like their mother. I feel bad for them; they can never get a word in with the way their mother prattles on. No eligible bachelor wants Lady Wilmington as a mother-in-law, so the girls have become wallflowers."

"How unfortunate. What happened to the older sister?"

"Sad, really. She died in a carriage accident shortly after I married Aiden."

"How tragic," Lilly said as they gathered up their things and left Gunter's to find Simon, their coachman, outside waiting for them.

Fortunately for Emmeline, because her husband didn't possess a title, nothing he owned belonged to the crown. He named her the beneficiary of his will and everything was put in a trust for her, so it would all stay hers when and if she married again, including her townhome in London. Not unlike her trust, Lilly thought. When she married again, she would retain the funds.

THAT EVENING, WITH the help of Daisy, Lilly prepared for her first ball of the Season, held at the Duke and Duchess of Westport's London residence. As promised, Madam Serena delivered Lilly's and Emmeline's gowns late that afternoon. Lilly sighed with relief as she surveyed herself in front of the mirror. The lovely silk gown in sage green emphasized the green of her eyes, and the high waist and scooped neckline did wonders for her figure. The white satin ribbon woven through her hair matched the ribbon trimming beneath her breasts and at the hemline. All she needed was her matching cloak, reticule, and fan, as she already had the slippers on her feet, and she'd be ready to go. Her pulse soared with excitement and nerves.

Just then, Emmeline swept into the room dressed in a sapphire-blue gown, looking gorgeous. Lilly was envious of her cousin's dark hair and light-blue eyes.

"You will have every gentleman vying for your attention tonight," Emmeline said with a twinkle in her eye.

"As will you," Lilly said, touching her stomach. "I'm so nervous. My very first ball. I'm afraid I'll embarrass myself and cast up my accounts."

"NONSENSE." EMMELINE WRAPPED Lilly's arm around hers and led them out to the hallway and down the stairs where her mother, Vivian, the Dowager Baroness Connolly, awaited.

"Ah, my girls, you both look stunning. I'll be beating the gentlemen off with my fan tonight." She smiled as they approached.

Immediately, they went out the door and into the coach. The

ride was not a long one, but Emmeline knew the queue for exiting the coach would be. Everyone who was anyone would be in attendance tonight, which had her insides humming with excitement. She'd had her sights on one particular gentleman for a long time. The only problem was she didn't think he noticed her at all anymore, even though they had been close friends at one time. Why would he look her way at her old age of twenty-eight? Not with the young debutantes and the ladies in their second or third Season available. He would need an heir. Even if they married, could she give him one?

Nonsense, she scolded herself. Many women had children well into their thirties. But would he think her worth the risk?

"You have become quiet suddenly," Lilly said from her seat opposite her and her mother.

"Forgive me. I was thinking about whether a certain gentleman would be in attendance tonight. He is in partnership with Langford and Caldwell, and since they are both in London, perhaps he is as well."

Her mother humphed. "You know he will be."

"He may be in attendance, but he may not want to see me."

"Do you think I don't remember two young gentlemen vying for your affections ten years ago? I will never forget you crying in my arms, trying to decide between the two. As I understand, he never wed. And you are a widow, beautiful, and kindhearted. He will be there tonight. Approach him."

"But he's a duke now. *A duke.* He needs a young bride to give him heirs." She had known him as the Earl of Quincy, but right before he'd returned to London, his father had passed making him the new Duke of Blackstone.

"Heirs," Vivian flicked her wrist, "which you can give him. Nothing says he cannot marry a young widow."

"Thank you, Mother, but I think you are biased. He is good friends with the Earl of Langford. I highly doubt the new earl speaks kindly of me anymore."

"Why ever not?"

Inhaling deeply, Emmeline held her breath for five counts, then exhaled. She did this three times. "Because Lilly has been staying with me. Not to mention the fact that Langford hasn't been in London for several years, and when he was last, he wasn't very friendly to me. I'd married one of his closest friends. And I think he blames me for Aiden's death. As though I caused the horse to throw him off to his death." Emmeline gasped for breath, removed her delicate handkerchief from her reticule, and dabbed at her teary eyes. "Perhaps the duke thinks the same about me."

Lilly leaned forward and grasped her hands. "Nonsense. Nobody blames you. How can they? From what you told me, they were with him during the tragic accident, not you. They were the ones who got inebriated during a hunting party and decided to race willy-nilly on horseback without regard to any of their lives. You were back at the estate having tea with the other guests."

"Dry your eyes, daughter. We are next in the queue. Do not stay away from Langford or Blackstone because you think they blame you. Did you ever stop to think that perhaps they feel guilty because they were with him? That you are reading the signs wrong? That they stay away from you because of their guilt?"

⊱⊱⊰⊰

"YOUR MOTHER IS a wise woman," Lilly said. "Although I don't relish coming face to face with Langford." She shivered. "What a bear of a man."

Emmeline's soft laughter rang out in the carriage. "Did you know it's the name of his horse?"

Lilly frowned. "Horse?"

"Bear. It's his horse's name."

"It figures." Lilly fought the urge to fidget as they made their way up the wide marble staircase, awaiting the receiving line. She didn't have to look around to see people staring at her, wondering who she was, or already knowing and curious to see the young lady who had married the reclusive, elderly Earl of Langford.

Well, let them wonder and stare. Lilly already had it in her mind to join the Wilmington sisters along the wall. A widow and the wallflowers, how exciting. She knew she was an imposter and didn't belong there. Her only saving grace was that Henry and Emmeline had trained her well on how to act in public. She didn't resemble an imposter on the outside, but inside, she was still the vicar's country daughter, through and through.

"Stop touching your hair," Aunt Vivian whispered. "People are already curious enough about you. Let's not have them think you have a nervous disposition."

Oh dear, she hadn't realized she was doing it. "Sorry," she whispered, gripping her reticule with both hands in front of her tightly, hoping she wasn't crushing the delicate silk fan inside. She would need that to hide behind in the ballroom.

Finally, they were at the top of the stairs with only a few people ahead. Lilly's knees were knocking together. Then Vivian made the introductions to the Duke and Duchess of Westport. Lilly curtsied deeply. "Your Graces, it is an honor to meet you both and to be welcomed into your home."

The duchess smiled warmly, putting Lilly somewhat at ease. "My dear, your departed husband was our longtime friend. Meeting you, I see now why he married you." She winked at Lilly, and her eyes twinkled. Lilly curtsied again, wondering what the look was about. "Thank you, Your Grace."

Emmeline wrapped her arm around Lilly's as they entered the crowded ballroom once they were announced. The room glowed from the chandeliers hanging from the ceiling and in sconces along the walls. The ballroom, decorated in gold and cream, resembled a fairytale. Never had Lilly seen anything so breathtaking in all her life. What in the world was she doing here? She should be living in a small village in the country with a landed-gentry husband. Not at a massive London estate at a ball attended by all of the aristocracy. There was even a rumor that the Regent might make an appearance.

"Pinch me," she murmured to Emmeline.

"Why?"

"Because this must be a dream."

"No dream. Hold tight because once our names were announced, all eyes turned to you."

"Oh." She had been so engrossed in the beauty of the elegant ballroom that she hadn't noticed. "Why?"

"Because people are curious. The Earl of Langford married you after sixty-six years of bachelorhood. Members of the *ton* are fickle and love to gossip. Tonight, it's you. Tomorrow, someone else."

"Where did your mother go?"

"To sit with the older ladies and watch us young folks dance and socialize. Let us take a turn around the room."

Lilly scanned the ballroom as they promenaded behind a line of people doing the same around the outer circumference of the ballroom.

"I should mention that even though you are a widow and allowed certain transgressions, I advise you not to cause a scandal. Pretend you are a debutante and abide by those rules. I don't want your reputation destroyed on the Season's opening night. And trust me, there will be people hoping for it—people such as Lady Wilmington. I wouldn't put it past her to send some rogues your way."

"What rules and what rogues?" Lilly asked with a sudden knot in her stomach.

"Oh dear, Henry never told you?"

"Why would he? We were married."

"Do not dance with the same gentleman more than twice. Do not go off alone with a man, no matter how much you want to. Unless you go out to the veranda in plain sight. Say no if he asks you to stroll in the gardens. Nothing good comes from strolling dimly lit gardens at night." She sighed wistfully. "Well, mostly nothing."

"Is that all?" Lilly's heart thrummed inside her chest. She could count the beats. "What about the rogues?"

"If I see any rogues heading your way, I'll warn you." Emmeline patted her hand. "You'll be fine." Her steps faltered, forcing Lilly to stop. Emmeline recovered quickly, and they continued.

"What is it?"

"Quincy . . . Blackstone. Dressed in navy. Staring daggers at me."

Lilly looked around and saw two handsome gentlemen looking their way. One looked vaguely familiar and very nearly took her breath away. "Who is the man with him with the dark wavy hair and dressed in charcoal and black?"

Emmeline led them off to the side of the room, looking puzzled. "Do you need spectacles?"

Lilly giggled. "No. I see perfectly. Why?"

"That, my dear Lilly, is Langford."

If she hadn't been standing still, she would have tripped over her own feet. All the color drained from her face. She didn't need to see it—she physically felt it slide down her neck. And she swallowed to keep from casting up her accounts. "Henry's nephew? The new earl? That's impossible. I met him. Surely I would remember what he looked like." She refused to believe that was him. That the handsome-as-sin gentleman regarding her intently was her nemesis. Oh, how cruel fate could be sometimes.

"Don't panic, but here they come." Emmeline squeezed her hand, causing Lilly to wince.

"Please let go of me." Lilly squeaked out.

"Oh, sorry, I didn't realize."

"They're almost to us. Is it too late to hitch up our skirts and run for the exit?" Lilly's eyes darted around, looking for the quickest escape route.

"Surely you jest?"

"Not at all." It was too late. They were upon them, and Lilly willed her body to stop trembling.

"Mrs. Fitzpatrick," the duke's intense, unwelcome gaze never left Emmeline's face. She didn't offer her hand, but he reached out and took it nonetheless and bowed most gallantly. At least Lilly thought so.

When he dropped her hand, Emmeline curtsied, her eyes downcast. "Your Grace."

"Will you please introduce me to this lovely lady?"

"Your Grace, may I present Lilliana Weston, the Countess of Langford."

Blackstone grinned, and Langford's eyes widened. Langford hadn't recognized her, either. Just then, she realized how odd it was that she was the Countess of Langford and he was the Earl of Langford. She curtsied. "Your Grace. It is a pleasure to make your acquaintance."

She rose and Blackstone took Lilly's offered hand and bowed, staring inquisitively into her eyes. "Countess, the pleasure is all mine." Blackstone glanced at Langford, his eyes mischievous. "You remember your uncle's widow?"

"Yes. How could I forget?" Langford bowed, his face grave as he briefly made eye contact. "Countess."

Somehow, Lilly managed to move and curtsy. "Langford." She couldn't get over the shock that this was the beast she'd met a couple months after Henry's death. Where had the ogre gone? No doubt lurking just below the surface. His hair had been closely cropped then. Now he sported it on the long side and it had curls.

Surely that must be what had thrown her off as to his identity.

EDMUND WAS GOING to kill Blackstone—he was still getting used to calling him that instead of Quincy. His friend had received news of his father's passing the same day Edmund had learned about his uncle. It had been quite a homecoming for all of them.

Edmund hadn't heard the ladies' names being called when they'd entered the ballroom. All he knew was that he looked at the mysterious woman with Emmeline and his heart stopped. She had appeared familiar, yet not. He'd asked Blackstone if he knew the lady's name, and he'd looked at him like Edmund belonged in Bedlam, shook his head, and grinned. Now he knew why. Edmund had known his uncle's widow lived with Emmeline now, but not in a thousand years had he thought that was her.

As the four of them stood in their intimate circle, Blackstone entertained the ladies while Edmund studied the countess with new eyes. Young, petite, thin, but not so thin that she didn't have ample curves where it mattered. Her features were delicate, which complemented her light hair and green eyes. Her white teeth had the tiniest gap between her front teeth. How had he never noticed it before?

When he'd met her at Langford Manor all those months ago, he'd been so shocked at her young age that he'd hardly taken in her looks. No, that was a lie. He had noticed, just not noticed enough. His insides cringed at the memory when he thought back to his accusations. What a bloody arse he'd been. No wonder she'd run off mere weeks later without a word to him. The following months spent at Langford Manor had been tainted. The servants, while treating him with respect due to his station, didn't befriend him. They kept their distance. Obviously, they favored Lilly and saw him as the enemy—the new nasty earl who'd run off their beloved widow of the previous earl.

A fortnight ago, he arrived in London, taking up residence in Langford House in Mayfair. He had visited his clubs and spent much time at his warehouse office, dealing with the affairs of his business. Thankfully, James Caldwell, his and Blackstone's other partner in their enterprise, had everything under control.

"Langford." Blackstone nudged him with his elbow. "The countess asked you a question."

He snapped his mind back to the present. "Forgive me, Lady Langford."

"I was inquiring about the household at Langford Manor. I hope everyone is healthy and happy with their new lord?"

Edmund tried to school his features but thought he had given away his frustration. "Everyone is well. They asked me, if I saw you, to extend their good wishes and say that they miss you."

Were those tears pooling in her eyes?

"Thank you. Please give them my best." Her voice came out a little stifled. It appeared she loved them as much as they did her.

CHAPTER FIVE

WHILE THEY WERE chatting, the dancing began with a quadrille, which Lilly was thrilled to miss out on. Even though she'd danced it with her dancing master, she knew the dance made her nervous that she would make a mistake. Lilly listened to the three others reminisce about the days when Emmeline's husband was alive and how they all missed him. Blackstone also mentioned a Mr. James Caldwell, and they all wondered why he had not arrived yet. Lilly felt bad for Emmeline—though Blackstone was polite, he treated her indifferently.

But as they conversed, Lilly learned several things about Langford. He had arrived in London two weeks ago after spending all those months she'd been away at Langford Manor. Along with Mr. James Caldwell, he had started a lucrative shipping business some years ago. Blackstone had also bought into their business sometime later, adding him as a third partner. And the three men had spent the three years before his uncle's death traveling to the West Indies and back. They owned four ships and a warehouse on the Thames. Emmeline teased both men, asking them now that they inherited titles, lands, and everything that went with them, would they do their duty and seek brides this Season?

When both men coughed into their gloved hands, Lilly

smiled.

Blackstone spoke up first. "My dear, Emmeline," he paused, uncertainty flashing in his eyes. "May I still call you Emmeline?" There was that cool tone again, even though his words were friendly.

Emmeline blushed, and her eyes softened. Poor Emmeline, she really did have deep feelings for Blackstone. "Emmeline is fine." Her cheeks took on a darker shade of red. "We have been friends for ten years. You don't need to stand on formality. Pray tell, what shall I call you now?"

He chuckled, letting his guard down and Lilly swore he blushed. So perhaps he wasn't that indifferent to Emmeline. "His Grace, Duke, or Blackstone will suffice in public. In private, you can call me Andrew as you used to."

Lost in listening to Blackstone and Emmeline's conversation, Lilly didn't notice the orchestra beginning the first strings of a waltz until Langford turned, bowed, and held out his hand. "May I have this dance if it's not promised to another?"

No need to look at her dance card tied to her wrist by a ribbon, for Lilly to know it hadn't a name written on it. "Y-yes," she stammered with shock. Langford wanted to waltz with her? She put her hand in his and he transferred it to his forearm and led them out into the middle of the dance floor, which was quickly becoming a crush of couples. As they began to dance, she noticed the looks and whispers following them around the floor. She fought hard not to let her nerves get the best of her. If she didn't relax somewhat, she was liable to trip up.

"Look at me and breathe," Langford said. "In, out. Again. In, out. Let them stare and wonder. We will be fodder for their gossip whether we dance or not."

So she studied his handsome face with his warm brown eyes, strong jaw, and straight nose, and she breathed.

"Better?"

"Yes. Thank you." And it was better. Concentrating on his face and nothing else made the people and the room around them disappear. The tension eased from her back and shoulders until her mind became a traitor again. "Why are you being kind to me?"

He stepped on her toe; she winced at the pain but ignored it. So he wasn't as relaxed and comfortable around her as she believed.

She knew a waltz was still a bit scandalous and had always pictured it as a slow dance where the partners could get close and have an intimate conversation. And then her dancing master taught her how to waltz, and she was disappointed to find that, though there was an uncommon measure of touching and closeness, the dancers moved quickly around the room. Though a couple could converse, it wasn't intimate. One had to speak rather loud and fast.

His brows lowered, and he frowned. "Why wouldn't I?"

"Because last we met, you were not nice. You accused me of terrible things."

His frown deepened. "Forgive me. I was not myself that day."

She widened her eyes in silent question.

His brows drew together. "Fine. For several weeks. You gave me quite a shock when you turned around from looking out the window that first moment we met. I didn't expect a lady as young as yourself." He paused and his lips curved up into a tight smile. "I was shocked and have regretted my actions ever since that day. By the way, the household barely speak to me. You must have cast a spell on them. They love and miss you."

A lightness entered her body and she smiled, remembering happier times when she resided at Langford Manor and Henry lived. "I love them as well. I have known most of them my entire life. My father was the vicar and Henry's closest friend. I spent many a day at Langford Manor while growing up."

His eyes widened and then relaxed as if he hadn't known this information. How strange. Had no servant or villager told him? He seemed to shake himself and changed the subject.

"Forgive me for speaking of finances, but I hope Mr. Beauregard sent word that an account was set up for you with a monthly allowance, and you are to send your bills to him for payment."

"Yes he did. Thank you."

"May I ask a personal question? And forgive me if I overstep, but how did it come about that my uncle married you?"

Now it was Lilly's turn to step on Langford's foot. She quickly recovered, and his only concession to acknowledging it was one raised brow. Was this why he'd asked her to dance? To fish for the information he'd never been able to get out of the Langford household?

"I'm sorry. There is nothing to tell. I can't say why he decided to marry at that time in his life. Only Henry knows. However, he hinted at wanting an heir. Perhaps he wasn't pleased with you." She ignored his gasp at her lies. "Why did he choose me? That is also a mystery." She hoped her words made him think again about asking such intimate questions that were none of his business. What had transpired between Henry and her was their business and no one else's.

She was saved from future questions when the waltz ended, and he escorted her back to Emmeline and Blackstone, who had not danced. He bowed, his expression serious with a touch of anger. "Please excuse me." Lilly watched him make his way across the room, nodding to several gentlemen trying to get his attention. He exited the double leaf doors, which she assumed led to a veranda.

"Why did he run off?" Blackstone asked with a knowing smirk.

Lilly wanted to know what Blackstone knew. And why he hinted at things. Had Langford confided in him what transpired between them the day they met? She would have loved to have overheard that conversation. "We had a lovely dance. The man is dark and brooding. Perhaps he needs fresh air to lighten his mood."

Blackstone threw back his head and laughed, drawing eyes to them. It was the first time Lilly had seen the duke relaxed and unguarded. "You know Langford so well already." He bowed. "If you'll excuse me, ladies, I should seek out my friend."

Emmeline's eyes followed Blackstone as he swaggered toward the doors to the veranda. Unlike Langford, he didn't acknowledge those vying for his attention. Perhaps Lilly would think of him as the Haughty Duke of Blackstone.

"Tell me what happened," Emmeline said, her eyes still following Blackstone.

Lilly humphed. "I now see why you are taken with Blackstone. He is beyond handsome, mysterious, and witty. Although not to you, which I don't understand unless your mother is correct and he suffers from guilt surrounding Aiden's death."

"Many years ago, he was friendly and lighthearted with me," Emmeline said with a sigh, her eyes still trailing Blackstone as he disappeared outside. "And then Aiden died. He began treating me coldly and kept his distance. He had a hard time the following year. He drank and gambled to excess. From what I heard, his father stepped in, refusing to cover his markers and cut off his allowance."

"What happened?"

"He went to work with Langford and Caldwell and spent three years on their ships. I heard he amassed enough money to pay his debts and buy into Langford and Caldwell's shipping empire. From the rumors I hear, the three are now richer than the Crown." She paused. "Why did Langford stomp off?"

Lilly smiled. "He did, didn't he? I have no idea why. Well, except that he asked me why Henry married me, and I told him it was because he wanted an heir, perhaps because he was displeased with the one he had."

Emmeline laughed, then covered her mouth with her gloved hand, the same sapphire shade as her dress. "What a little devil. I didn't realize you could lie so easily."

"It wasn't a total lie. Henry never said he wanted an heir, but it wasn't beyond possibility." Perhaps she was a good liar after all.

"Come, I'm hungry. Let's see what they are serving," Emmeline said as they strolled arm and arm out of the ballroom, making their way to the drawing room. "As a debutante, I would eat before I came. My mother wouldn't let me eat at any of the balls or soirees. She was afraid I would spill on my gown or a gentleman would think me a cow for eating too much. I was only allowed to eat at small, intimate gatherings where sit-down dinners were served. Most of the debutantes attending tonight will have stuffed their faces before coming here for the same reason I did."

"That's a little harsh."

"Yes, well, as widows, we can eat to our heart's content." Emmeline glanced around. "Unless my mother sees us. We must eat in here so she doesn't. She might still want to enforce that rule."

Lilly laughed as she took a small plate from a server. "Then we must eat quickly not to be found out."

"Exactly."

"Exactly what?" asked a deep voice belonging to Blackstone.

Emmeline was startled and nearly dropped her plate. "Your Grace, didn't your mother teach you manners? You should never sneak up on a lady."

"Forgive me." He smirked, then looked at Lilly and winked. What a devil he was—one moment glaring at Emmeline, then the next teasing her. If Emmeline managed to snare the duke, her life would never be boring. So far this evening, Lilly hadn't seen him dance with anyone, even though she had caught several debutantes eyeing him hopefully, and their mamas looking longingly with greed and some with lust, which shocked Lilly.

On the other hand, Langford had danced nearly every dance since they waltzed, or she should say, since he reentered the ballroom after he stomped off in a huff. He plowed through the debutantes like a farmer plowing his fields—not that she was particularly noticing or anything. No, another lie. Enemies they were, but he had magnetism, and she wasn't immune.

Why couldn't she be attracted to the duke instead of Langford? Although on reflection, that would be so much worse. Emmeline was in love with him.

As Blackstone escorted both Emmeline and her back into the ballroom, their host, the Duke of Westport approached. "I've requested a waltz. I would like to dance with my dear friend Henry's widow." He bowed slightly, holding out his arm, clearly expecting Lilly to take it.

Panicking, Lilly's eyes swung from Emmeline to Blackstone, then to the duke, a man Henry's age. And as with Henry, he was handsome and fit. They both had aged well, but the similarities ended there. Her entire being shivered. She believed the duke hid some depraved part of himself from the outside world. She could not explain how she knew. She just did. However, believing she had no choice in refusing, she accepted and ignored the chills tingling up her spine.

"It is an honor to dance with you, Your Grace." Another lie. She was indeed becoming proficient in lying. Not something she was proud of. Ten seconds into the waltz, Lilly regretted her decision. The duke held her too close at every opportunity the dance allowed. Mostly when they twirled around fast and he thought she might stumble. His dark, beady eyes stared down her bodice, and he licked his lips repeatedly as though he wanted to devour her. Or perhaps it was to stop himself from drooling. She had to breathe through her mouth because the heavy, perfumed scent of musk mingled with body odor had her stomach revolting. During the receiving line, she had paid little attention to the duke since the duchess had drawn her in with her smile and chatter. She regretted that now. He was positively repulsive.

Finally, he lifted his eyes from her bosom. The depravity she saw inside them had the chills creeping up her spine, intensifying and confirming what she believed earlier. Her eyes darted around the ballroom, hoping to find a savior. No one noticed his leering or her panic.

He licked his lips again, and when he spoke, spittle hit her in the face. Her entire being screamed for help as she fought not to gag.

"My dear Countess, may I call you Lilliana?"

There was no need to respond as he went right on leering, spitting, and talking in what he seemed to believe was a deep, seductive voice. When in reality, it was the voice of nightmares.

"Since you are a widow and are used to certain activities of the flesh, I was hoping you would consent to become my mistress. I want to lick you from head to toe and the sweetness between your thighs." His lips curled up into the most frightening thing she'd ever seen, and her entire body trembled. She wanted to run away and hide.

"Good," he moaned, licking his lips again. "You are excited. Once the waltz is over, meet me in the library, and we will make plans. Perhaps you will allow me a sample of your sweet flesh." If the waltz didn't end soon, Lilly was afraid she would be sick all over the duke. It would serve him right if she were.

As the final chord of the waltz ended, Lilly didn't wait for the duke to escort her back to Emmeline and Blackstone. She turned her back on him and hurried not to her friends but to the lady's retiring room, where she came face to face with the duchess.

"My dear, whatever is the matter?" she asked with a knowing smile. "Did my husband make advances? Ask you to become his mistress?" For a brief moment, she cringed. "Please forgive me if I planted the idea into my dear husband's mind. You see, I've done my duty and given him not one son but two, and three daughters. His touch is vile and makes me ill. Shall I say his taste runs sadistic? We haven't shared a bed in years. Unfortunately, his needs must be met, and most of the brothels won't allow him inside—bruised merchandise doesn't sell. But I thought since he and Henry used to be friends, perhaps they shared similar tastes in the bedroom and you wouldn't mind."

Was she daft? Lilly opened her mouth to speak twice before she could choose the right words. "How c-c-could you?" she stammered. Tears ran down her cheeks, tears of anguish and mortification, and she hated herself for showing the duchess any weakness. No doubt she would take even more advantage.

Instead, her face softened. "I'm sorry. I was desperate. Forgive me. Please keep this little incident between us."

Without another word, she left, and Lilly sank into a small chair and hugged herself, hoping to stop the trembles plaguing her body. How on earth would she continue the evening when all she wanted to do was go home, bury herself beneath the covers, and forget this night had ever happened? Instead, she went to the mirror, wiped the tears from her face, pinched her terribly pale cheeks, put a smile on her face, and exited the room. Before taking barely five steps, she bumped into Langford. He reached out with his hands to steady her.

"Easy there, Lilly . . . Countess." When his eyes narrowed on her face, he took her hand and pulled her down an empty hallway to a deserted sitting room, shutting the door behind them. He released her hand and studied her face, making her shiver. "What happened?"

"Nothing." She couldn't tell him.

"I saw you dancing with the duke. Never has a more immoral man ever existed." His features softened. "What did he say to you? You may not believe this, but you are the previous earl's widow and I, the current earl, am responsible for your well-being unless you marry. If you do not marry, then you will hold the title of Countess of Langford forever. And when I marry, you will become the Dowager Countess of Langford—still my responsibility. Please tell me what happened. I can't protect you if I don't know what we are up against."

We? There was no *we* as far as Lilly was concerned. "He asked me to become his mistress."

He growled. He actually growled like an animal, reminding her that she had called him a bear of a man once.

"He didn't?"

"He did, at the suggestion of his wife."

This time he managed to control his growl to a mere groan. "The bloody blackguard and the bitch."

His reaction puzzled Lilly. It seemed he really did think he was responsible for her. Something inside her broke when he took her hands again into his. The anger spiking in his dark eyes turned to distress as tears leaked down her cheeks and her body trembled.

"Please don't cry," he murmured as his fingers wiped away her tears. "He will never get near you again. I promise."

CHAPTER SIX

Pulling Lilly into his arms and rubbing her back as she sobbed into his chest had Edmund rethinking his knight-in-shining-armor behavior. Part of the reason he'd been cruel to her when they first met at Langford Manor—a reason he was only beginning to admit to himself—was that when she'd turned around and faced him for the first time, he had instantly wanted her. And he'd taken out his anger on her for his own inappropriate feelings.

He'd stayed in the country for so many months not just because there was work to do there, but because he'd been afraid to see her, knowing she was living in London with Emmeline. But he'd known he couldn't stay away from London forever, even though he also knew he would run into her at most society functions throughout the Season. He'd vowed to himself he would do everything in his power to stay away from her, knowing all the while it would be impossible. And holding her warm, soft body in his arms now broke down his resolve to keep his distance. Her hands gripped the front of his jacket as though she never wanted him to let her go.

He fought the urge to hold her even closer when all he wanted to do was pull her tight against his body and kiss her until neither of them had breath left in their lungs. The last thing she needed was to feel his desire for her after what the duke said, and he had an inkling the duke had said more to her than she'd admitted. The blackguard had a reputation as being a brutal, sadistic fuck. Rumor had it he'd seriously injured more than one courtesan while playing his sexual games. But being a duke had its advantages. Since these incidents happened in brothels, people looked the other way. What was one less working courtesan?

Well, he would never get close to Lilly again. And if he did, Langford would call the duke out. It didn't matter if duels were illegal; they still took place. And it would be worth risking the Regent's wrath to keep her safe.

It took him a moment to realize Lilly wasn't sobbing anymore. She stepped back from him, wiping her eyes with her gloved hands. "I'm sorry I cried all over you. I'm not usually a watering pot."

He smiled into her lovely green eyes sparkling with unshed tears. He touched her cheek with a hand he was shocked to see trembling when he wiped away the tears she'd missed. "Don't apologize."

Losing himself in her eyes, feeling a pull he did not fight, he lowered his lips to hers and found nothing but air. She had stepped aside and was glaring up at him with a fury he had not yet seen in her expressions.

"If you meant to kiss me, then you are no better than the duke," she cried out, her face red with anger, her eyes glaring like daggers. "I thought you said you were my protector!" She picked up her skirts, and exited the room, leaving him staring after her.

What the bloody hell? He smoothed down his jacket, tugged on his cuffs and straightened his cravat. She was absolutely right to throw his words back at him. He'd tried to take advantage of her at a vulnerable moment—it was beastly and completely inappropriate. Perhaps he should spend time finding her a husband instead of lusting after his uncle's widow.

When he entered the ballroom and found Blackstone standing alone, he inquired, "Where did the ladies go?"

Blackstone cocked a single brow. "You tell me. They took

their leave quite suddenly. Care to elaborate on what caused the lovely countess, flustered and blushing, to insist they leave posthaste?"

Edmund huffed and hated himself even more when he felt the heat from his neck rise up his face. "Nothing."

"You are a terrible liar." He smacked him on the back. "Let's go to White's. I'm angry at you. I was enjoying my time being standoffish with Emmeline."

AT A DIM room in the back of White's, Edmund and Blackstone sat on comfortable chairs in front of a blazing hearth drinking brandy. Edmund stared into the swirling amber liquid in his glass. Nerves refused to let his hand be still, so around and around the glass and liquid went.

"Never has a man found the answers inside a glass of spirits," Blackstone said as he stared at him.

"Don't be so sure about that." He stopped swirling the glass and took a healthy swallow. "Before you interrupted me, I believe I saw my future . . . bleak and lonely."

"You are in a mood tonight, my friend. What's bothering you?"

Edmund glanced around the room, making sure they were still alone. He shrugged his shoulders and sighed. "Besides the fact that I lust after my uncle's widow?"

Blackstone chuckled and Edmund glared at him. "I'm sorry. I don't mean to find humor in the situation. But there's no reason you can't pursue the lady."

"She hates me."

His friend swung his head to him, his eyes alight with curiosity. "Do tell."

"First, there's how abominably I behaved toward her when we met last year. Then tonight—let us just say I pressed my advantage. Wrongly."

"So that's why she marched up to Emmeline and me in the ballroom, flushed and her eyes intent on murder, demanding to leave at once." Blackstone downed his drink in one gulp. "A fine pair we make. I lust after the beautiful widow of one of my dearly departed friends, and you lust after your uncle's widow. What did we do to bring the wrath of the Fates down upon us?"

"Here you two are," Caldwell said as he dropped into an empty chair that one of White's attendants pulled forth in a hurry. "Whisky, please." A drink in his hand, he held it up. "Here's to the London Season." He took a deep pull and relaxed back in his chair. "Why the long faces?"

"We are a wicked lot. We are." Edmund signaled the server. "Just leave the bottle."

Caldwell lifted his brows, eyeing them both. "Speak for yourselves. I've never been wicked a day in my life."

"Oh, come now." Blackstone held up his empty glass and signaled Edmund to hand over the bottle. "You are the worst of us. At least Edmund and I lust after widows. You lust after . . . hell if I know. We have been away from London for so long that we've lost our touch."

"Widows?" Caldwell asked, his brows raised. "What widows do I know?" He smirked. "Yes. I remember now. You, my friend Blackstone, have always desired Emmeline for yourself. There's nothing standing in your way now. Aiden would be glad to know she found an honorable man—one who loves her."

"I can't entertain the thought. Besides, I have no honor," Blackstone said with a frown. "If she ever found out the truth, she would hate me. I need to keep her at a distance."

"As for Edmund." Caldwell shrugged his shoulders. "What widow? Your uncle's?"

"How did you . . ." Edmund choked out the words.

"I didn't, just a guess." Caldwell eyed his drink. "I'm feeling left out. Is there not another lovely widow to be had for me?"

The three gentlemen chuckled, none with lightness in their heart.

AUNT VIVIAN SLEPT on the ride home. Emmeline sat across from her, lost in her own thoughts, which suited Lilly just fine. She didn't want to talk about what had happened. But, she realized, she also wanted to confide in her. What was wrong with her?

Later, lying in bed, unable to sleep, she welcomed the knock on the door and the voice whispering. "Lilly. Are you awake?"

"Yes."

"I'm glad," Emmeline said as she entered and shut the door behind her. Without being invited, she crawled onto the other side of the bed, sitting up against the pillows. "I can't sleep. Tell me what happened. Both with the Duke of Westport and Langford. Because I knew something had happened when you stomped into the ballroom demanding we leave. Not to mention the blush on your neck and face."

Rearranging herself, Lilly sat up, leaning against the head-board, and sighed deeply. "I did not stomp. I was hurrying. Anyway." She ran her fingers down her plaited hair, checking the ribbon keeping it secure. "The duke is a terrible man. He said lewd things to me and asked me to be his mistress."

Emmeline inhaled deeply and said, "Sorry, I should've warned you. He did the same thing to me once."

Lilly glared at her. "Why didn't you say?"

"By the time I thought of it, he was asking for the dance." She made a noise in the back of her throat that resembled a growl. "He is a wicked man. I feel bad for the duchess."

"Don't." Lilly huffed. "She put the idea in his head."

Emmeline stared at her, her mouth open in a wide *O*. "She didn't."

"I assure you she did. She told me so herself. I could almost feel sorry for her, except that she sent her depraved husband after me."

"I'm shocked." Emmeline paused, fluffing the pillows behind

her back. "But at least that explains Westport. What about Langford?"

Langford. "He took me into an empty room to comfort me after dancing with the duke, which I might add, seems unlike Langford, but apparently he saw that I was upset. I cried all over his clothing while he vowed to protect me. Then he spoiled everything by trying to kiss me. What a hypocrite."

Emmeline sighed. "The fool. I'm sorry your first ball didn't go perfectly. And as for Langford, he *is* behaving unlike himself, now and last year—not at all like the Langford I used to know. I will hope he may yet come to his senses and improve." Emmeline hugged her. "I'll leave you to get some sleep. The good news is, we get to do all this again tomorrow. It's sure to be better."

Lilly closed her eyes, trying to sleep, but every time she did, the Duke of Westport's face and Langford's face flashed back and forth; she had to pop her eyes open to make the visions disappear. Struggling to keep her eyes wide open, she wondered if one could sleep that way.

As Lilly made her way to the morning room for breakfast, the sun shone in through the windows, putting a smile on her face. They'd had nothing but cold and rainy weather since the year began. If the weather held, perhaps they could take a ride in Hyde Park later in the day.

She fixed a plate with coddled eggs, sausages, and toast. With the help of a footman, she sat down at the empty table. Immediately, a hot cup of chocolate was placed in front of her. No sooner did she wonder what was taking Aunt Vivian and Emmeline so long to rise than they both entered the room. Aunt Vivian was chatting about last night's ball, and Emmeline was smiling, making Lilly wonder what had made her cousin so happy this morning.

"Did you stop in the hall and see the flowers on the entry table?" Emmeline queried as she fixed a plate.

"I went through, but I never looked around. My stomach was growling something fierce, and all I could think about was eating. Why?"

"There are several bouquets of flowers and cards on the table. Blackstone sent me beautiful white roses with a card. He's coming during afternoon tea." She looked at Lilly and smiled. "There are also yellow roses and a beautiful bouquet of wildflowers, both cards addressed to you." Emmeline produced the cards. "This is the roses card. Open it first." Her eyes were wide with excitement.

Taking the card from Emmeline with trembling hands, she was afraid to find out who the roses were from—probably from the debauched duke. She broke the seal but didn't recognize it, not that she would recognize any seal but the Langford one. Reading the card, her brows drew together as she tried to put a face to the name. "It's from the Marquess of Hollingsworth." She'd been introduced to several gentlemen last evening, but none were memorable other than the Dukes of Westport and Blackstone. "He will be calling on me today. Did I meet him?"

Emmeline and her mother exchanged looks. "He was in attendance last evening. You weren't introduced to him, but obviously, you caught his eye," Emmeline said. "He is thirty-five, most handsome, wealthy, and well-liked. His father recently passed, and he has inherited the title. I remember him well from my very first Season. All the debutantes vied for his affections. He stayed far away from them. I can only surmise he is hunting for a bride and an heir now that he's inherited his father's title and estates." She paused and frowned. "I would be remiss if I didn't mention there were rumors about him several years back. But the details are unknown to me and nothing came of it. At least, I don't think so."

"But why should he call on me?"

"Besides the fact you are beautiful?" Aunt Vivian added to the conversation.

"I suppose." She broke the seal on the second card. A seal she knew well this time. Her insides shivered.

My Dearest Lilly,

Please forgive me for last night. There are no excuses for my behavior. I will call upon you today to discuss a list of suitable gentlemen seeking brides. I think it's for the best.

Your Humble Servant,
Langford

"The pompous man," she said out loud with a huff. "It's from Langford. He's calling on me today to discuss possible husbands for me. Does he think he can just marry me off?"

"No, my dear, of course you are entitled to your own choice," Aunt Vivian's soft, placating voice resonated in the modest room. "I'm quite convinced he means well. As his uncle's widow, he feels responsible for you. You are still so very young. I'm sure he means to advise you so you aren't taken advantage of by a fortune hunter or a man unworthy of you. He's doing his duty to his uncle."

"There's no need. I can take care of myself. Make choices for myself."

"This is your real first time in Society. I'm appalled to say there are members of the *ton*—gentlemen and ladies both—who would have no scruples in ruining you or taking advantage of your naïve, young self."

"I have both of you," Lilly contradicted.

"Yes. You have us. But even ladies with protective families have fallen."

"Enough, Mama," Emmeline said. "She is a widow, and you know the rules are relaxed for her. Besides, I will be with her at all times. And Lilly is smart. Her father and Henry taught her well, as have we."

CHAPTER SEVEN

DAISY HELPED LILLY prepare for her afternoon visitors. Lilly chose a pretty, soft-blue muslin day dress with matching slippers and wrap, should she get chilled. Daisy prepared her hair in a simple coil with several wisps dangling on either side of her face to soften the look. Knowing she wouldn't get any more presentable, she went down the stairs to the drawing room to find Emmeline and Aunt Vivian sitting and awaiting the day's callers. Lilly sat beside Emmeline on the dark-blue settee, which perfectly complemented her dress. Emmeline wore a lovely shade of pink, and Aunt Vivian wore deep green and a fashionable turban in the same shade.

"I'm nervous," Lilly said to them as she adjusted her skirts and then clasped her hands together on her lap. "I've never received visitors, unless you count when I received friends and villagers to my father's house or Henry's. This is different." So very different. She had never been so nervous in all her life. Well, excluding her wedding night. Or perhaps when she met Edmund for the first time . . .

The butler, Harrison, entered the room and announced, "His Grace, the Duke of Blackstone. The Earl of Langford." After the formalities and greetings were concluded, the gentlemen sat in two of three chairs facing the settee. Aunt Vivian sat in a chair next to the settee.

Lilly didn't know how she felt seeing Langford today after crying all over him and his near kiss at the Westport ball. She would admit, though, he looked handsome in his dark-brown riding clothes. Her fingers fluttered to her lips and her cheeks warmed as she thought about their almost kiss. Her eyes glanced at him and she found him staring at her intently. His expression was unreadable. Immediately she lowered her gaze and her traitorous heart beat a fast staccato.

"Did you like the flowers I sent?" Langford asked her as he tugged on his cravat.

Was he nervous? "Yes. I love wildflowers. I used to pick them all the time in the fields near Langford Manor."

"Indeed. They are plentiful there. Do you miss Kent?"

Her heart pained at thinking about growing up there. "Yes. I spent my entire life there until Henry died. I can't help but miss it."

"I'm sorry. You can stay at Langford Manor, you know. I will be living in London for the most part, now that I have the estate business in hand. You can have the manor all to yourself if you'd like."

Tears pooled in her eyes, and she blinked them away. Why was he being nice to her? "Thank you. It is good to know I can visit at any time."

The tea tray arrived, and thankfully, Aunt Vivian offered to serve. Lilly didn't think her fingers would work. She could hardly take the cup and saucer handed to her without them clattering. Instead of risking drinking her tea, she placed it on the low table in front of her with more clattering. Lilly sat perched on the edge of the settee, mindful of her posture, and nibbled on a sweet biscuit, hoping someone would speak so she wouldn't have to continue conversing with Langford. She wasn't used to him being kind or thoughtful and it was unsettling to her.

"How lovely you look today, Mrs. Fitzpatrick," said Blackstone as he sipped his tea. The cup was swallowed by his large hands.

"Thank you, Your Grace. The weather is warm today. We are going to take a ride in Hyde Park later."

"Langford and I were just discussing that on our way here. Our horses could use the exercise." He nodded his head and smiled. "Perhaps we will see you."

His gaze shifted and lingered a moment on Emmeline. How Blackstone looked at Emmeline with his haunting green eyes almost had Lilly swooning. Except they were haunting in a sad and vulnerable way. What must Emmeline be thinking and feeling? She glanced at her to find Emmeline studying the duke.

The butler returned and announced, "The Marquess of Hollingsworth."

As greetings and, in her case, introductions were made, she studied the newly arrived gentleman. Emmeline had spoken truthfully when she said he was handsome. He stood tall, filling out his brown and tan riding clothes quite well. He had chestnut, wavy hair and kind, chocolate-brown eyes. When he took Lilly's hand and bowed, his smile was devastating. She had the feeling many ladies had swooned when they'd found themselves the recipient of that smile. She could see at a glance he was the very definition of a rakehell, and she had best lock up her heart.

Hollingsworth sat, his hat dangling from one hand. "It's nice to see you, Blackstone, Langford. Congratulations to you both on your inheritance. But also condolences on your losses. It's been a long time since you both graced London with your presence. Do I understand you are back to stay?"

"Yes." Blackstone also held his hat. "I won't be sailing off to the West Indies or anywhere else."

"Neither will I," Langford added. "Caldwell will handle most of the traveling. Although Blackstone and I will spend plenty of time at our warehouse, no doubt."

"You three have a gold mine in that company of yours. Too bad I didn't have the foresight to have invested with you."

Did the Marquess's words mean he was short on coin? Was that why he was calling on her? Did he need to marry a wealthy woman, such as herself, or a debutante with a large dowry because his coffers were empty? Lilly hoped not because, honestly, he intrigued her, rakehell or not.

Although he had no knowledge of her trust from Henry. Nobody did but her and Mr. Beauregard. Not even Langford knew. So technically, as far as anyone knew, the only money she had came from the earldom. She was not a rich woman in her own right. He could not need to marry for funds if he was calling on her.

After the proper visiting time was over, Lilly found herself sad when all three gentlemen bid farewell. Langford never broached the subject of a husband for her, thankfully. After their conversation when he'd first arrived, he became quiet and serious for the remainer of his visit. But she knew it was only putting off the inevitable.

"My, the marquess certainly is a handsome devil," Aunt Vivian said with a blush. "If only I were twenty years younger."

"Mama!" Emmeline gasped. "What a thing to say."

"I speak the truth. What did you think of Hollingsworth, Lilly?"

Before she could respond, she smiled and felt her cheeks warm. "He is definitely the most handsome man I've ever encountered. But I wonder if he has a serious bone in his body, as his eyes shone with amusement the entire time he was here. And I got the feeling it wasn't just for our benefit. He enjoyed getting under Langford's and Blackstone's skin with his jesting."

Emmeline's eyes studied her, and Lilly squirmed under the scrutiny. "I have heard there's more to the man than just another pretty face and affable personality. I think he would be perfect for you."

Lilly didn't know about that. She could see herself spending time with him, getting to know the real Hollingsworth. "I hope he calls upon me again."

"He will," Aunt Vivian said confidently.

"WHO DO YOU think Hollingsworth is interested in?" Blackstone queried as he and Langford entered the crowd in Hyde Park on horseback.

Edmund frowned. The answer to that question was very much on his mind. "We should have asked."

"And look jealous?" Blackstone laughed. "Are you out of your bloody mind?"

"Perhaps he called upon Lilly, and with any luck, he will propose, and I will no longer feel responsible for her. Or anything else for her. I could wipe my hands clean of her, knowing he would be kind to her. I can get on with my life without her haunting my dreams at night."

"I don't think that's what you want. Think very carefully before you encourage this match. Remember the rumors from years past?"

Damn Blackstone for his intuition and his memory. Of course it wasn't what he wanted, but helping her find a match was the right and honorable thing to do. He would bury his lust and desires for Lilly. Perhaps he would take a mistress to help slake his need. And bloody hell, he'd forgotten about Hollingsworth and the rumors surrounding his sexual preferences. Perhaps he wasn't the gentleman for Lilly after all. Hollingsworth had never refuted the rumors, but they were never proven true, either. He could still be a good match for Lilly. Only time would tell.

"Rotten Row is a crush today. If we go at this slow pace, we'll never make it around the park until midnight." Blackstone complained. He led his horse to the right of the path, his eyes and his horse's nose trained ahead.

"Tell me you are not looking for Emmeline?" Edmund eyed his friend who looked agitated sitting stiff and tall in his saddle.

"What if I am? Not that it matters. She deserves someone better than me."

"You could just bed her and get her out of your system," Langford suggested.

Blackstone's head whipped around, and he glared daggers at him. "If I weren't on horseback, I'd punch you for disrespecting her."

Langford had never heard his friend so cross. "Apologies."

"How would you like it if I spoke about Lady Langford that way?"

How would he? "Point taken—you're right. Do you see them?"

"No." He glanced over his shoulder and watched as Blackstone grimaced and mumbled something under his breath. "The blackguard! Here comes Hollingsworth sitting like a peacock on his mount. So help me, God, if he's after my Emmeline . . ."

Edmund was shocked at Blackstone. He looked positively ready to murder someone—that someone being most likely the marquess. Edmund told himself that he hoped Hollingsworth was interested in Lilly for his friend's sake, but it was a lie and the pain in this chest proved it. It would be even worse, though, if Hollingsworth's affections were for Emmeline. He'd hate to see his friend lose Emmeline to another man again, regardless of what Blackstone said about being wrong for her. If it hadn't been for their friend, Fitzpatrick, Blackstone and Emmeline would have been married ten years now.

When they'd been wet behind the ears and all of nineteen, both Fitzpatrick and Blackstone had fallen hard for Emmeline, who was eighteen at the time. There were times Edmund had worried for their friendship. As the Season had progressed toward summer that year, Blackstone had eased off when he witnessed how much Fitzpatrick loved her. They'd married that autumn and had four wonderful years together before the tragic riding accident took Fitzpatrick's life. Another six years had gone by now, and Edmund thought it was high time Blackstone made his move and married the woman he'd never stopped loving.

Hollingsworth caught up to them. "Gentlemen." He tipped his hat. "May I join you?"

"Only if you tell us which lady you are interested in," Edmund said, causing Blackstone to snort. Edmund looked at Blackstone and shrugged one shoulder. He had to ask. He hated seeing his friend twisted up in knots.

The marquess chuckled. "Perhaps I was merely paying a social call with no ulterior motive." He looked at both men with a grin Edmund wanted to wipe off his face with a slap from his gloved hand.

"If we weren't in public . . ." Blackstone threatened.

Hollingsworth chuckled, not the least bit bothered. "If you must know, I called upon the countess. And please tell me you both are not vying for Mrs. Fitzpatrick's favors. We don't need history repeating itself." He had the nerve to look concerned as though he really cared one way or another.

"No," Blackstone said, his posture now relaxed and a grin on his face.

Good for him. But Edmund's insides jumbled up like someone was scrambling eggs. Deep inside his mind, he knew this could be a favorable thing. Hollingsworth would make Lilly an advantageous match, sans the rumors—rumors he should set aside some time to look into, just to be sure.

"You have my permission to court her." Bloody hell, had he just blurted that out before he'd genuinely convinced his heart, mind, and body it was the proper thing to do?

Hollingsworth laughed. "I don't think I need it. She is a widow, after all."

Edmund glared at Hollingsworth, daring him to question him again. "She is my uncle's widow, therefore my responsibility. Forget her status as a widow and treat her as a debutante. She is, after all, only nineteen, and I will not have you ruining her reputation."

"For the love of God," Hollingsworth snapped. "She's been married. She's not innocent. Don't you think that allows her certain freedoms?"

"Normally."

The marquess didn't look happy, but he huffed. "Fine." His features softened and he looked at Blackstone. "I wouldn't wait long before making your intentions known to Mrs. Fitzpatrick. I heard several gentlemen discussing her last evening, and nothing they said involved marriage. Since you both have been out of the country, I'll let you in on a secret—there's been a wager on the books at White's for several years now on how long it will take to get her into someone's bed."

Blackstone growled.

"Relax, Duke, I don't believe she has looked at any man since Fitzpatrick died. I think she's been waiting for you to come to your senses and return to England. Now, if you'll excuse me." He lifted his hat, turned his horse around and rode off carefully picking his way through the crowd.

"That was enlightening," Edmund said as Hollingsworth rode off.

"Where the hell are the ladies?" Blackstone looked livid. "And when I get my hands on that blasted book at White's, I'm tearing those pages out and tossing them into the fire. Nobody will ever win that bet because the point will be moot. No bet will exist. I'm a bloody duke now, and nobody will dare question me."

"DO YOU SEE them?" Emmeline asked Lilly as they rode in an open-air carriage. Their driver went along slowly behind other carriages and riders on horseback.

"No, but I caught a glimpse of Hollingsworth."

"Hmmm."

Lilly felt herself blush. "Don't *hmmm* me. It was an observation, nothing else."

"I'm positive Blackstone said he was riding this afternoon. Perhaps we missed them," Emmeline said as she moved her head from side to side, scanning the park.

"I have never seen or heard you pout before. You sound like a five-year-old."

Emmeline leaned back and sighed. "If you were nearing thirty and considered to be back on the shelf you would be desperate to hurry Blackstone along, too."

Lilly took Emmeline's hand in hers, hoping to help soothe her worry. "I'm sorry. Perhaps you could take the reins, so to speak, and give him subtle hints. Although, by the way you looked at him today, he'd have to be blind not to notice your affection for him."

"Was I that obvious?"

"Yes and no." What did Lilly know about anything related to matters of the heart, courting and letting one's feelings for another show? What right did she have to think she was knowledgeable to advise Emmeline? She giggled. "I'm the last person who should be telling you anything. I know nothing. Listen to your heart and observe him. If I'm wrong about him and his feelings for you, I'll eat the feathers on my hat."

They both giggled.

CHAPTER EIGHT

THAT NIGHT, THEY attended the opera as last-minute guests of Hollingsworth. Aunt Vivian insisted on chaperoning. Hollingsworth escorted them to the Opera House in his carriage, complete with his family crest. Lilly's heart accelerated more the closer they came to their destination. She'd attended the opera twice with Henry and had loved every moment of it. They'd sat in the Langford private box, just the two of them, which made her wonder if Langford would attend tonight in that very box. She refused to acknowledge the little flutter her heart gave at the thought of seeing him.

Hollingsworth escorted Aunt Vivian inside while Emmeline and Lilly followed behind. Once they climbed the numerous stairs to his box, he seated Emmeline on the end, followed by Aunt Vivian, Lilly, and then himself.

The beauty of the Opera House, glowing beneath the candle-light, impressed Lilly. It was opulent, done in shades of cream with red accents, and fairly took her breath away.

"It is a beautiful theater, is it not?" Hollingsworth said, his voice deep and strong. He leaned slightly toward her and she caught a whiff of his musky cologne.

"Yes. I've been here several times with . . . Henry . . . my deceased husband." Her tongue had gotten tied up. Referring to Henry as *deceased* always pained her. "I never tire of admiring the grandeur and style."

"Neither do I." He leaned closer and lowered his voice for her ears only. "Before I forget, I invited Blackstone and Langford to share the box. I know they each have their own, but I wanted to give Mrs. Fitzpatrick time with Blackstone."

So he knew. "That is very kind of you. Though I didn't think it was so obvious about them."

"It isn't. But I remember her first Season and Blackstone, then the Earl of Quincy, and Mr. Fitzpatrick both vying for her attentions. It appears Blackstone never lost his feelings for her."

Lilly had a feeling the night would be interesting in more ways than just by watching the opera.

When the two gentlemen arrived, seats were moved. Langford sat on the end where Emmeline had been. Emmeline and Blackstone sat behind the four others.

Lilly envied their privacy. Langford would look forward around Aunt Vivian and glare at her every so often. What did he think she would do, strip naked and do a dance for Hollingsworth? *Why on earth did I think such a thing?* She wondered what had happened to Langford's good mood from that afternoon. Her heart had certainly taken notice of the change, though that was clearly premature. Then again, perhaps Langford in a good mood wasn't good for her. The last thing she needed was to develop strong feelings for him.

The curtain to the private box closed, and the lights extinguished, draping them in semidarkness. The curtain to the stage opened, and Lilly found herself sitting forward in her seat, leaning against the railing. Everything around her vanished as her entire being was drawn into the opera. She wept, she smiled, and she sighed. At intermission, she dried her eyes and relaxed into her seat, inhaling as her body tingled. "That was haunting," she said to no one in particular.

Hollingsworth's hand covered hers on her lap. "Yes. Haunting and beautiful." Her eyes fell to their touching hands. He pulled his away.

"Forgive me. I have something to ask. Langford permitted me to court you. Are you favorable to that?"

She frowned. "You don't need his permission."

"He feels it's his duty. I respect that." He looked at her inquiringly. One brow raised. "You didn't answer."

"I'm agreeable to courting and getting to know you." The words came easy to her lips, but would courting him be easy? She hadn't a clue how courting worked. Except perhaps she did a little. It was probably no different than tonight or dancing attendance at a ball, taking a ride in Hyde Park or going to Gunter's for ices.

He reached for her gloved hand, turned it over, brought it to his mouth and placed his warm lips upon her exposed inner wrist. She shivered from the intimate touch. His warm brown eyes looked deep into her soul. Or at least that's what it seemed. "Thank you," he said.

Lilly knew at the moment she would have to be careful with Hollingsworth. Getting to know him was fine, but she didn't want to raise expectations she wasn't ready for. And she suspected she was right about him seeming like a rakehell. If he didn't have a reputation as a rogue, he should.

The moment was broken when Langford cleared his throat. "Hollingsworth, may I have a word with you?"

"Stay here," Aunt Vivian interrupted. "The ladies and I will visit the retiring room."

Lilly couldn't help but look back at the three gentlemen staying in the box.

"Mama, why are we leaving?" Emmeline asked once they exited the box.

"Because I need to visit the retiring room."

"Indeed," Emmeline said it as though it was an odd thing to do. Lilly noticed her cheeks were tinged red.

What had been going on behind her during the opera? Something Emmeline didn't want to be taken away from, even for a quick visit to the retiring room.

⟫⟫⟫⟪⟪⟪

Nicholas, the Marquess of Hollingsworth, had no clue why Langford wanted to speak to him, but he would humor the man. "What is it?"

"I change my mind."

Confused, he said, "You change your mind. About what?"

"You courting Lilly."

"Ahhh, *Lilly* is it?" Nicholas had no intentions of stopping his courting of . . . Lilly. Such a pretty name. "Too late. She and I discussed it and she has agreed. You forfeited your chance with her when you gave me permission."

Langford puffed up his chest. Did he think to intimidate him? Not bloody likely. It was fortunate he admired and liked the man. Otherwise, he'd hit him right on that perfect, straight nose of his, marring his handsome face for life.

"She doesn't interest me," Langford said.

"Keep lying to yourself."

Langford frowned and shook his head from side to side. "Forget I said anything. If you gentlemen will excuse me, I have other commitments."

Nicholas and Blackstone shared a look. Blackstone held up his hands. "Ignore my friend. He's lost his bloody mind."

"And heart," Nicholas grumbled.

Langford could find his own bride. Lady Langford would be perfect for Nicholas, he was sure of it. He had studied all the eligible ladies at the Westport ball, and no others had piqued his curiosity. She may have been married before but was as innocent as they came. He would enjoy getting to know her. She captivated him with her beauty. Being married to her would not be difficult. Nicholas thought she looked alluring and innocent tonight, dressed in a lovely white gown trimmed with gold embroidery and a gold pelisse. She was new to London, and if she was as agreeable to a courtship as she said, it would go smoothly and quickly. They could marry within months—something he needed. What he didn't need was Langford interfering.

Because there was another lady his mother wanted him to marry. She was stunning in her own right, but Lady Pricilla Amesbury's silliness had him wanting to smother the daftness out of her, even though her silliness was an act. Not to mention the fact that she was like a sister to him. If he didn't get engaged to Lady Langford soon, he knew that with his mother's slyness and the chit's mother's help, they would no doubt set up a scheme that had the two of them being found in a compromising situation and forced to marry. He also didn't put it past them to simply make something up and leak it to the gossip rags.

He couldn't imagine his mother giving birth to him. She was such a harridan. Nor could he imagine how his father had put up with her, though he was never in her company when he lived except to produce three offspring—two sons and one daughter. Nicholas tried to love his mother, but she wasn't lovable. Neither of his siblings cared for her, either. But they did fear her, which was why he was trying to marry Lady Langford. No, he *needed* to marry her and send his mother to the dower house so he wouldn't have to see her again. Or, at the very least, not have to live in the same house as her and see her bitter face every day. He sometimes felt a little harsh when thinking about his mother, but she was at the very least too meddlesome by far. He needed to see the end of her scheming.

If Langford was determined to intervene, he would have to devise an alternative to Lady Langford. Time was of the essence. He could always whisk the countess away to Gretna Green. That would solve all his problems. But he hated to resort to that. He rubbed his chest and ignored the feeling of guilt that was growing there at using Lady Langford.

THE LADIES RETURNED to the box just as intermission came to a close. Lilly took her seat and wondered where Langford was—not that she cared. She leaned forward, became mesmerized by the opera again, and clasped her hands to her chest when the curtain fell for the last time. Hollingsworth escorted them home and asked for a private word with her, setting her nerves on edge. Aunt Vivian and Emmeline went inside and up the stairs while Lilly entered the drawing room with Hollingsworth following close behind. She left the door wide open.

"Please have a seat," Lilly said as she sat on the settee, her pulse speeding up when he sat next to her.

"Langford changed his mind."

Her eyes widened. "About what?"

"About us courting."

Her insides hummed with anger. "Be that as it may, I agreed to a courtship." She looked him in the eyes. "I haven't changed my mind." What right did Langford think he had to control who she courted and who she did not? He could say it was his duty and he owed it to Henry, but there was something else behind his behavior and she would not stand for it.

"That is good to know, Countess."

"Please call me Lilly in private."

"Only if you call me Nicholas."

An awkward silence followed as Lilly waited for Nicholas to say something, *do* something.

He stood. "I will see myself out."

"Nonsense. I'll see you to the door." Lilly rose and followed him into the entry hall. "Good night, Nicholas." His eyes studied her face, and she could feel herself blushing under the intensity.

"Would you care to join me for a ride in the park tomorrow?"

"That would be lovely." She smiled, hoping the awkwardness of this conversation would end soon.

He touched her cheek with his hand and smiled gently. "May I kiss you?"

She blinked several times. "You may."

Besides his hand on her cheek, he didn't touch her anywhere else—just her lips with his own. They were warm, soft, and gentle, and the kiss lasted only a second or two before he dropped his hand and stepped back, bowing. "Until tomorrow."

When the door closed behind Nicholas, she removed her gloves and touched her lips. The warmth from his lips was still there.

As she climbed the stairs, Lilly found Emmeline waiting in the hallway. "So?"

Lilly couldn't help herself, she touched her lips again and smiled. "He kissed me."

"Yes. I heard."

Lilly gasped.

"Not the kiss, silly. I heard him ask."

"Mmmhmm."

"It's true. Anyway, tell me how it was."

Smiling, Lilly said, "It was nice."

"Nice?" Emmeline frowned. "You mean to tell me the handsome marquess didn't pull you into his arms and kiss your breath away? His tongue tasting the inside of your mouth, causing you to grip his arms for support as your knees threatened to buckle and your throat makes soft purring sounds?"

Lilly could feel her cheeks warm. "No. His tongue? My goodness, purring. I never."

Emmeline sighed wistfully, her eyes taking on a faraway look. "You haven't been kissed properly until tongues are involved. And mewing and weak knees."

"Henry was not much for kissing." Lilly frowned. "Oh my, I have so much to learn."

After Daisy helped her undress, Lilly climbed into bed and thought about her time at the opera with Hollingsworth. Her belly didn't tingle with butterflies when she thought of him as it did when she reflected on that dreadful man, Langford. They were both handsome. One kind, one not. One insulted her, and one did not. Both looked at her with desire. At least, she interpreted it as desire. But what did she truly know about desire? Langford tempted her anger and made her furious; at times, she couldn't speak. Hollingsworth—she should think of him as Nicholas—didn't anger her. Life would be simple and easy with Nicholas. At least what she knew of him made her think so. Now she just needed to figure out if that was what she wanted.

CHAPTER NINE

AFTER LEAVING THE opera, Edmund, feeling the worst mood descend on him, hired a hack and headed into St. Giles. It was a clear night, the perfect weather for looking for Annabelle. Well, not Annabelle per se. Rather her husband who frequented taverns. From what Edmund and the baron had learned about him since Annabelle had left with him all those years ago, the man had a propensity to tavern life. It made Edmund wonder what Annabelle was doing when he was gone.

The closer the hack got to St. Giles, the tighter his stomach became. He didn't know how much good he could do, but he felt he owed it to Baron Winslow to look for his daughter. The baron had also had professionals looking for Annabelle for the past ten years, but it was to no avail. Every lead seemed to turn up empty. Edmund couldn't imagine how the baron went on day after day alone. His wife had passed and his daughter had disappeared. The man was heartbroken and Edmund, now that he was back in London to stay, couldn't stand by and do nothing. He would comb through the slums until he either found her or died trying. But tonight, as with other nights, turned up nothing helpful which only added to Edmund's bad mood.

He walked several blocks over before he was able to wave down another hired hack that took him to Brooks's. He liked White's but Brooks's even better, especially when he was in a dismal mood, such as tonight. He made his way toward the back, beelining to a chair in front of the hearth, when he noticed Blackstone sitting alone with a half-empty drink in his hand. "Rough night?"

"Perhaps . . . perhaps not," Blackstone said with a grin. "What about you? You left the opera abruptly."

He sat and signaled the waiter. "Brandy." He tugged on his cravat trying to loosen it, then gave up and untied the bloody thing along with unbuttoning the top button on his linen shirt. It was choking the hell out of him. "I went looking for Annabelle's husband."

"Any luck?"

"No. I wish I could find her to give Baron Winslow peace. But I'm beginning to believe it will never happen."

"I know it seems hopeless, but don't give up just yet."

Edmund ran his hands through his hair. "On a different topic, I don't think I can stand the idea of Hollingsworth with Lilly."

His friend chuckled. "You're just figuring this out now?"

"No." He sighed deeply and took a sip of his drink the attendant had just set down next to him, enjoying the slow burn down his throat and then continuing on to heat his belly. "She hates me."

"You could compel her to marry you."

"How?" He groaned. "Never mind. I'd never subject her to that. I want her. I don't want her to hate me."

Blackstone signaled for a refill. "I spent four years watching one of my closest friends being married to the woman I wanted. And honestly, did I not secretly, during some dark times, wish him dead so I could have Emmeline for myself? Then, when he died, I struggled with guilt for years because I felt responsible for his death. And because I'm a bloody arse, I blamed her for his death. And now she is free, and so am I, and I'm still conflicted. You know what rabbit hole I've fallen down." He drained his glass and placed it on the table beside his chair. "I don't wish for you to fall down that same hole. It's too crowded since I'm still clawing my way out. So take it from me, the last thing you want to do is step aside and watch the woman you care for marry another, whether it ends up being Hollingsworth or someone else."

Edmund pondered this advice, then offered a bit of his own. "Perhaps you should call on Emmeline tomorrow. But keep your frustrations to yourself. Whenever you're around her you practically snarl at her. She undoubtedly thinks you hate her."

Blackstone looked at him and winced. "Of course she thinks I hate her. Several years ago, when I was drinking heavily, I provoked her to hate me. I thought it'd be easier to have her loathe me than to admit the truth."

"Which is?"

"That I'm in love with her."

"We are both making morning calls tomorrow." Edmund's thoughts got lost as he stared into his empty glass. As he was leaving, he noticed Hollingsworth deep in conversation with his younger brother. Edmund hid behind a chair, giving anyone the evil eye if they seemed inclined to say anything, and eaves-dropped, learning some important facts. His melancholy of moments ago was taken over with seething anger.

FLOWERS ARRIVED FROM the same three gentlemen that morning as the day before. "The flowers are lovely," Aunt Vivian remarked as she entered the morning room with a lightness in her step. Obviously, she'd slept well the night before. Lilly hadn't, and she imagined Emmeline hadn't either, if the circles beneath her eyes were any indication. She would request cucumber slices after breakfast. As not to hurt Emmeline's feelings, she would say they were for her and then share.

"Do flowers always mean the sender will make a call?" Lilly asked.

"Not always," Aunt Vivian replied. "But in this case, I believe so."

"Hollingsworth is taking me for a carriage ride in the park this afternoon. Will he still come for afternoon tea?" Why was she not excited to see him? Why was her heart so fickle? If Lilly had known how difficult navigating the social circles of London would be, she might have stayed at Langford Manor. But then, *he* had been there. Life had been so simple when her papa lived and then when Henry lived. At nineteen and alone, how was she to know her heart's desire?

"Perhaps, but not necessarily." Aunt Vivian sipped her tea. "You are quiet and look tired, Emmeline. Is all well?"

Well, there went pretending the cucumber slices were for her. Emmeline ignored her mother's question.

THE SOCIAL HOUR arrived in the blink of an eye, and Lilly, Emmeline, and Aunt Vivian found themselves in the same spots as yesterday, awaiting their callers. Lilly wore her new green day dress, which had arrived from the modiste that morning. It matched her mother's pendant and brought out the color of her eyes. Emmeline wore a lovely pale blue, which made her eyes positively glow. Aunt Vivian wore navy blue with her usual turban. Truthfully, Lilly didn't know what color her hair was or if she even had hair, as she'd never seen her without a turban.

Harrison entered and announced Blackstone and Langford. Lilly had trouble meeting Langford's eyes. Was it because she'd kissed Nicholas? It was certainly none of his business that she had. When he bowed in greeting, he took her hand in his and brushed his lips across her fingers. His intense brown eyes were flecked with amber and they never left her. Her insides vibrated, and her breath caught in her throat. His look unsettled her, and she didn't know what to make of it. Would he be pleasant like he was during yesterday's call or rude as he was at the opera?

"How was the rest of your evening last night? I hope Hollingsworth was a gentleman and escorted you ladies home at a reasonable hour." It was odd that nothing he said or in his looks gave her any inclination he was not happy with Hollingsworth wanting to court her. Yet, she knew he had rescinded his so-called permission.

Her face broke into a wide smile. "It was wonderful. The opera was sad, sensual, and utterly beautiful. You should have stayed."

She looked directly into his eyes and tried to look like a woman in love, like Emmeline when she thought about Blackstone. And if she was showing false love for the marquess, that was her choice. "Hollingsworth was a perfect . . . *gentleman* during our time alone in the drawing room." The pause between her words had the desired effect on Langford. He narrowed his eyes and studied her intently. She would love to know what he was thinking.

"Is it possible to have a word with you in private, Lady Langford?" he said with a clipped, do-not-refuse-me tone.

Standing, trying to hide her annoyance with him, Lilly said, "Please excuse us. Langford would like a word." As if they had not heard his request. No. Not a request. More of an order.

He stood when she did and followed her out of the drawing room and up the stairs to the family's private drawing room. Her hand quivered as she moved it along the banister. The heat from his eyes bore into her. No doubt the rakehell was staring at her backside, planning his seduction of her. She hadn't forgotten his actions at the Westport ball.

After they entered, she left the door ajar. She still didn't trust him. "Please sit."

"I prefer to stand." He moved to the front of a large window looking onto the street below.

Lilly sat because her knees threatened to buckle.

Langford pivoted, looking at her, studying her with softened eyes, and her heart twitched. She preferred him when angry or frustrated instead of appearing as though he really had feelings for her. She feared she would fall for him quickly if he showed kindness, compassion, and warmth toward her. Sometimes, she wanted to think he cared for her, and his abruptness toward her was only him acting out his frustration at having feelings for his uncle's widow—his aunt, technically—which could be deemed scandalous.

"I would prefer it if you did not see Hollingsworth again."

His words had her shaking her head. Not that she was surprised by them after Nicholas had told her he had rescinded his approval. But the way he spoke now, this was not a demand like he usually used with her. He wasn't ordering her not to see Hollingsworth. How unlike him. He was an enigma—stern and bossy one moment and almost thoughtful the next. Did the man not know his own mind? She was suffering from emotional strain trying to keep up with him.

"I'm riding with him in the park this afternoon."

"Please cancel. Please tell him you have a migraine."

"I will do no such thing." She didn't like this softer side of him. She preferred his indifferent side. That way, she could be angry at him in peace and ignore the way her pulse raced when he spoke to her gently.

At her refusal, his eyes now turned a dark brown void of amber flecks as he glared at her, his thoughtfulness spent.

She closed her eyes briefly, then stood ready to do battle. Her spine was straight, her shoulders back, and her eyes pierced his. "I may not be twenty yet, but I am far from innocent and naïve. I was married for a year and mourned for one. When I lived with my papa, I was in charge of his household. I am much older and wiser than my years. Therefore, I am perfectly capable of making decisions for myself." Her hand flew up as he opened his mouth. "Do not interrupt me. I appreciate your stated desire to look out for my well-being and reputation; nevertheless, it's unnecessary." She flashed him a teeth-clenched grin, watching the expression on his face change from annoyance to anger to amusement and back to anger.

His eyes seared her with their intensity as he walked toward her until he stood very close to her. A nerve twitched in the corner of one of his eyes, and his woodsy scent tickled her nose, sending her heart thumping wildly inside her chest. No doubt he heard it.

"Perhaps you are not naïve for someone living in the country, but London and the *ton* are forces to be reckoned with. No one is above scandal or reproach." He placed a finger beneath her chin and tipped her head up, his eyes alight with something resembling humor. "Not even young, beautiful widows such as yourself." He removed his finger. Her head stayed put. Her eyes sought his, her lips parted in an effort to breathe. Her heart paused mid-beat as he continued to speak. "My uncle asked me to look after you and find you a suitable husband, and, by God, I will honor his wishes."

"But—"

He cocked a brow. "You had your turn. Now it's mine. Despite his charm, good manners, and seemingly affable personality, Hollingsworth isn't who you think he is. Even at his age, he fears his mother. When his father lived, he stayed away from them, living in single gentlemen's quarters. Now that he is the marquess and under the same roof as his mother, she is trying to control him. She wants him to marry Lady Priscilla Amesbury, the daughter of her best friend, whom he dislikes with a passion. He will do anything not to make that happen. Even marry someone he just met . . . a total stranger . . . such as yourself."

His large, warm hand cupped her cheek, his thumb sliding across her jaw, causing goosebumps to break out on her skin. "I predict he will ask you to marry him by week's end."

She gasped.

"Otherwise, he knows his mother will orchestrate Lady Priscilla and him into a compromising situation and force their marriage."

"How do you know this?"

He leaned close to her ear, his warm breath tickling her. "I overheard him talking to his brother at Brooks's last night after he brought you home. Do you think it's a coincidence that he sent *you* flowers, invited you to the opera, and to ride in the park? I think not. He chose you because you are new to town and haven't heard the gossip about him."

Lilly's shoulders sagged as she exhaled. Even though she didn't feel a deep sense of longing or connection to the marquess, Langford's words stung. Hollingsworth didn't like her—he was only using her. Against her will, tears pooled in her eyes, and she felt foolish. She swatted Langford's hand from her face and stepped back, putting distance between them. She didn't need his pity or his gloating. "Thank you for telling me. I'll bring it up with Hollingsworth. Now, if you'll excuse me . . ."

Before she could turn around and walk out, Langford's hands gently cupped her face, the amber visible again in his eyes. Right before he lowered his head, she knew what he was about to do, had a second to decide if she wanted him to.

Even though he could be demanding and ill-tempered and inclined to think the worst of her, something about him still called to her in a way she didn't entirely understand. By the friends he kept, she knew he was loyal and honest, and he probably did have her best interests in mind, even if it didn't always appear that way. If she were being honest with herself, she wanted nothing more than to be kissed by him. In this room. At this time. So she leaned forward just a tad, giving him her silent consent.

His mouth was gentle and soft. She made a mewing sound that came from the back of her throat as he enveloped her in his arms, pulled her close to his body, and deepened the kiss. Leaning into him as his tongue entered her mouth, swirling around and around and tasting her. A moan escaped his lips into her mouth.

She skimmed her hands up and down his back, wishing to her own surprise that he had nothing on so she could feel the warm smoothness of his skin, the tightness of his muscles. As she continued caressing him, his mouth devoured her, sipped from her. His tongue pushed in and out, causing heat to flare inside her body and settle between her thighs. Her body trembled. He broke contact, trailing barely there kisses down her neck.

"My God, you taste so sweet," he breathed into her neck. "I want to taste every inch of you." And at that very moment it was something she wanted as well.

The sound of a masculine voice clearing his throat had them pulling back. "Sorry to interrupt," Blackstone said as he grinned at them, one brow raised. "The Marquess of Hollingsworth is downstairs wondering where the countess is." He chuckled. "Shall I say she is indisposed at the moment?"

CHAPTER TEN

BLOODY HELL, BLACKSTONE was enjoying this. And damn Hollingsworth for showing up. Edmund needed to put an end to his charade. Hollingsworth could use some other unsuspecting woman to get out of marrying Lady Priscilla. Over his dead body would he use Lilly, marry her, and ruin her life. Henry had wanted her to have a love match in her second marriage, and Hollingsworth couldn't give that to her. He'd heard from the man's own lips last night that his heart was defective and he was not capable of love or any feelings of empathy or real joy. His life was an act, he'd said, and he should relinquish his title to his brother and join the stage.

He turned his back on Lilly and faced Blackstone in the doorway. "No. I'll accompany you back to the drawing room to give Lilly a few moments to herself." He was almost afraid to turn back around and look at her, afraid of what he might see. Even though she had kissed him back, would she be angry with him? Did she regret the moment they'd shared? He inhaled, held his breath, and pivoted around looking at the vision before him, and exhaled. Lilly's cheeks were pink—from the kiss or from being embarrassed by Blackstone's interruption, he couldn't say. But her shy smile and the softness of her eyes told him everything he needed to know. The knot in his stomach eased as he smiled at her and nodded his head.

As he and Blackstone descended the staircase, his friend said in a quiet, amusing voice, "Quite the intimate party I interrupted."

Edmund snorted. "Yes, well. I needed to wipe all thoughts of Hollingsworth out of her mind by kissing her senseless." He cringed at the words coming out of his mouth. It was pure posturing, and by the look on his face, Blackstone no doubt knew it. The truth was his body hummed at the memory of her lips and the feel of his tongue sliding across the gap in her front teeth. Many more kisses from Lilly and he would be her servant for life. "I tried not to sound like an arse, but she needs to know the truth about him."

Blackstone's shocked eyes met his. "Did you tell her?"

Inhaling deeply, he replied, "No, just about his mother and how she wants him to marry Lady Priscilla. I will save the rest and use it only as a last resort if Hollingsworth doesn't give up this ruse of wanting to court Lilly. I will not let her marry him and forever be miserable in a loveless marriage with no intimacy. I promised Henry."

"You didn't actually promise Henry. He was already dead when you received the letter, but I understand. You feel responsible for the lovely Lilly." He snickered.

As they entered the drawing room, Blackstone was still chuckling at the humor he found in Edmund's life. "The countess will be down momentarily," Blackstone said.

Edmund sat down and pierced the marquess with a cold stare, though his words contradicted his look. "Thank you for the opera last evening. I apologize that I left abruptly. I had business matters to attend to."

"Quite understandable," Hollingsworth mumbled back.

WHEN LILLY ENTERED the room, after making herself presentable after being in Langford's arms, she found five sets of eyes watching her intently. Her cheeks burned, and she averted her gaze to the tea tray. "Aunt Vivian"—*Relax, Lilly,* she scolded herself, *your voice is vibrating*—"would you be so kind as to pour me tea?"

"Of course, my dear." She picked up the teapot, poured tea, and placed the china cup and saucer into Lilly's hands. Pretending her tea was the most interesting thing in the room, she stared at it endlessly until Hollingsworth broke the spell.

"I brought my phaeton for our ride through the park since it's a warm, sunny day. I hope you're still interested in going?" Instead of looking at her, he glanced in Langford's direction. Had he guessed at what had happened upstairs? Then he looked at her questioningly.

Did she want to go for a ride with him? After everything Langford told her about him, was she willing to put her safety in his hands? What would stop him from causing a scandal if he was as desperate as Langford said? All it would take would be for him to kiss her in public. Today, in an open phaeton, he had the perfect opportunity to push for a marriage. Her entire body trembled and her teacup clinked loudly against the saucer, once again having all eyes fall on her. "I'm very sorry, Hollingsworth, but I'm feeling a migraine coming on. Perhaps another day."

Guilt caused the tea to sit heavy in her stomach. She truly hated lying to the marquess. He looked dejected, and it almost made her redact her statement. However, she followed Langford's advice and her intuition and decided that she needed to stick to her excuse unless she wanted to find herself married to the marquess. The next thing she knew, all three gentlemen were taking their leave. She sighed, leaning back into the settee. "I'm mentally exhausted." *Oh dear, had she said that out loud?*

Aunt Vivian and Emmeline looked at her, both with trepidation.

"What happened upstairs?" Emmeline queried in a soft voice, her eyes full of worry.

"I'll let you two talk in private," Aunt Vivian said as she stood.

Emmeline turned on the settee and looked at her, silently waiting with inquisitive eyes. "I can guess, but I'd rather hear it from you."

"I think I'll return to Langford Manor since *he* isn't there anymore." Lilly was as shocked as Emmeline looked when the words escaped her lips.

Emmeline grabbed her hands. "You don't mean that? What would you do?"

Her chest ached. And it turned out she wasn't lying about a migraine. It was fast becoming real. "I don't know. I don't think I'm made for London and the drama and gossip."

"What happened upstairs?" Emmeline asked again.

Closing her eyes, Lilly tried to get her thoughts together. "Langford told me things about Hollingsworth and his mother. How she wants him to marry Lady Priscilla Amesbury." She looked at Emmeline. "Do you know her?"

Emmeline winced. "Yes. A beautiful icicle, self-centered and not very bright. He would hate being married to her."

"So I gather, since he's using me to get out of having to marry her. I don't like being used. I've already been married. When or if I marry again, I want to marry for love. That was Henry's wish for me—to find love and have a family. I won't have that with Hollingsworth, not according to Langford. I had the feeling he wanted to say more about the marquess but held himself back. I cringe to think there is more to his story."

"And you believe what Langford told you?"

"He was quite convincing right up until he kissed me." She covered her mouth with her hands and laughed nervously. "He kissed me as you described last night. A real kiss with tongues." More nervous laughter. She couldn't stop. What was wrong with her?

"Interesting." Emmeline sighed dreamily. "I wish Andrew would kiss me like that. In fact, we have never kissed unless you count his lips on my hand. Even when he professed his love for me ten years ago, he never kissed me." She squeezed Lilly's hands gently again. "Please don't go back to the country. I can't face the Season alone."

"You have before."

"Not really. I have done very little socializing since Aiden's death. I preferred to spend my time with the Ladies' Society of Mayfair."

"I'll stay." She sighed inwardly as her heart dropped even further. What had she just agreed to? She wanted to support Emmeline and help her find happiness, but at what cost? She was being pulled in two directions by Hollingsworth and Langford. Perhaps it was time to put both gentlemen in their place and look elsewhere for the love and the family she desperately desired.

Langford . . . Edmund . . . the man could be so infuriating one moment and then charming the next. And he'd turned her mind to mushy pudding with his mouth. She shivered, thinking about the heat from his hands as they swept up and down her back. She missed his touch.

"We should probably rest," Emmeline said, interrupting her wayward thoughts. "We have the Burlington musicale tonight. I pray their daughters have mastered their instruments during the past year because they were dreadful last season. Their eldest daughter, Lady Emily, has a lovely voice though, which made up for the terrible instrument playing."

Lilly grinned. "Oh goody, my first musicale."

"I CAN'T BELIEVE you're dragging me to a musicale," grumbled Edmund to Blackstone.

Blackstone, sitting opposite him in his ducal carriage, smirked at him. "Do you want to see Lady Langford or not? If you don't keep a close eye on her, Hollingsworth will sweep in and do something to force the marriage. He's a desperate man. Desperate men will do whatever it takes to get what they want, regardless of how it hurts others. He cares not for the countess or her feelings. And she isn't experienced enough to see the man beneath all the finery, charm, and easy smile."

"Don't you think I know that?" Edmund snapped as he raked his hands through his hair. His insides shook with frustration and anger. He'd call Hollingsworth out if he tainted Lilly's reputation. She should be allowed certain liberties, but he knew the *ton* would be happy to wring her through the gossip rags because of her young age. The mothers of the debutantes were not happy to have a beautiful young widow come to London and give their daughters competition this Season. They would be watching her every move and do anything within their power to see her fall from grace.

Emmeline was another matter altogether. Nobody paid any attention to older widows. Except that wasn't true, was it? A duke wanted her. That made her an enemy of every debutante and their title-hunting mama as well.

He should have stayed in the country.

He sighed and looked out the carriage window. If only he could go back to the first time he met Lilly. He would stuff a handkerchief in his mouth and keep himself from accusing her of stealing from his uncle and using him for his wealth and old age, knowing she'd be a young, rich widow. He would befriend her. If he'd done that back then, they could have lived under the same roof, getting to know one another. Perhaps he could have persuaded her to marry him by now, and to hell with any scandal it might cause.

What a dumb arse he'd been. He had nobody but himself to blame for the current situation. It all could have been avoided if he'd tamped down his anger and shock and treated her with the kindness and respect she was due. All he'd seen was a young, beautiful woman, and steam had come out of his ears. Jealousy had stabbed him in the gut, eviscerating him. The lovely creature before him had been married to his old uncle.

He shut his eyes to block out the vision from that time and replace it with her sultry face from today after he'd kissed her, inhaling and exhaling several times to get his body and mind under control. When it was accomplished, he opened his eyes and turned back to his friend.

"You are right. I have to be everywhere Lilly is. Even if she never chooses me, I don't want her to marry Hollingsworth. Nor become the talk of the *ton* in a bad way. There are other gentlemen more worthy of her."

"I'm glad to see your head is on straight. Now if I could only be so lucky with Emmeline. I pray our past and Aiden's death don't pull us even further apart than we already are. I'm not too proud to admit she haunts my every waking minute, not to mention what she does when I sleep."

"You two will work things out eventually."

"I wish I had your confidence," he groaned. "We have arrived." He stepped out first. "You aren't going to like this, but Hollingsworth just arrived with his brother and sister."

"Great." Edmund stepped out of the carriage. "He brought reinforcements. No doubt telling his sister to befriend Lilly and gush about how wonderful her brother is. Hopefully, Lilly will remember what I told her about him. I'd hate to have to divulge his dark secret."

"Me too, if I were Hollingsworth."

"It's a good thing you aren't. Let's go in and find seats. With any luck, there will be open seats near Lilly and Emmeline."

AUNT VIVIAN HAD begged off tonight's musicale, so Emmeline and Lilly came alone. They took seats halfway between the first and last rows. The row was unoccupied but for them. It only lasted for a moment. Lilly wasn't at all surprised when Langford and Blackstone asked to join them. Blackstone sat on Emmeline's right, and Lilly sat next to Emmeline with Langford on her left. To everyone there, they would resemble two couples. All part of their plan, no doubt. She wanted Emmeline to be with Blackstone—they loved each other. But did she want to sit next to Langford? Without thinking, she'd brought her gloved hand to her lips and relived their intense kiss. Of course, he would think she favored his company. After all, she had let him kiss her this afternoon. He would think she wanted him.

Oh dear, what a pickle. She did want him. But did she really *want* to *want* him? She was becoming indecisive where he was concerned.

The Burlington girls' musical talents grated on Lilly's nerves almost as much as Langford's presence did, if only because she was annoyed with herself with regard to him and the feelings he provoked in her. He occasionally leaned toward her, whispering something or another. But she didn't hear a word he said as her ears continued to be pummeled by the sounds of bad violin and pianoforte playing, along with the pounding of her heart because of his close proximity. Reliving their kiss from that afternoon had caused her entire body to warm. She didn't want to think about it. But it was difficult with him sitting and breathing so close to her with his scent wafting her way. She'd believed it to be musk previously, but it was sandalwood, if she weren't mistaken, and it was pulling her in. She wanted to lean close to him and inhale his potent essence. How mortifying.

She refused to glance his way, her eyes centered on the girls—young ladies, really. One had to be her age, and Lilly remembered seeing her at the Westport ball. Perhaps Langford would be interested in her? Hollingsworth sat across the aisle from her and tried several times to get her attention. Lilly politely ignored him, if one could ignore politely. If what Langford told her today was true, she didn't want to get drawn into his life. She refused to be used as a pawn in the disagreement between him and his mother. Nor would she ever want a mother-in-law such as that. She would make her thoughts and feelings known to him at some point tonight and put an end to it.

When the musicale finally ended, the young ladies bowed to enthusiastic applause, most likely due to its conclusion and not the talent of the players. Most of the guests mingled through several rooms getting refreshments. Lilly and Emmeline were no different, only she was exasperated that Langford stuck to her like an unwanted piece of lint.

"Care for some punch?" Langford asked. "I can't guarantee you it tastes good." He dipped the ladle and poured two small cups. "It looks rather watery."

"Thank you." She took the cup he offered. "It looks fine." Though taking a sip, she had to agree with him. It was watery and tasteless. "Perhaps the biscuits will be better," she remarked. Langford handed one to Lilly. She took a small nibble and shook her head. "Stale already. Too bad, they are my favorite." Feeling his eyes on her, she looked at him and frowned. "You don't have to stay by my side. I'm perfectly capable of keeping myself safe around Hollingsworth. In fact, here he is."

"Lady Langford." Hollingsworth bowed, taking her hand in his and brushing her gloved hand with his lips. "It is lovely to see you this evening. Perhaps we could have a private word?" His head swung to Langford. "If your guard will allow it?"

Hollingsworth was forced to take a step back as Langford moved in front of Lilly as though he were her great protector. She placed her hand on his arm. "Langford," she said in her sternest voice, one she'd never heard herself use before. "If you'll excuse us, I'd like a word with Hollingswoth, and I believe Blackstone is trying to get your attention."

Lilly moved around Langford, took Hollingsworth's offered arm, and strolled with him back into the musicale room, where they were afforded some privacy with only several other guests milling about. She waited for him to speak. For the first time in her presence, he appeared uncomfortable and tense.

"What has Langford told you about me?"

His words surprised her. She didn't expect him to come right out and ask. But he deserved the truth. "Something on the lines that your mother wants you to marry Lady Priscilla Amesbury."

He visibly cringed. Did he dislike Lady Priscilla that much? "That is true. But the decision of whom I marry is mine and mine alone. My mother's wishes don't factor into it."

"I've been told you need to marry posthaste. If you don't, your mother is the type to force the situation by using subterfuge."

He chuckled. The sound was deep and held not a speck of amusement. "You are correct. Langford has good spies. Nonetheless, you are your own woman and can make your own decisions." He took both her hands into his and stared into her eyes. His were pleading with her, desperate in their intensity. She truly felt bad for him. But not enough to marry him. "I want to marry you. Please say yes." His words were whispered and she shivered because of how they were said, as if his very life depended on her answer. And then he added. "I know we have only just met, but I ascertain we will suit perfectly. You will never want for anything and have the freedom to do as you choose. I would never try to control you."

"Langford also said if I allowed you to keep pursuing me, he would divulge certain secrets of yours to me." She pulled her hands from his and instantly his eyes darkened and became guarded. So he truly had secrets. "I'm terribly sorry, but I must refuse."

He bowed, his expression one of rejection and something else. Possibly wariness. "I hope you find the man you are looking for."

With his parting words, he left Lilly, her insides hollow and her eyes stinging with sadness for the marquess. Somehow she would force Langford to share his secret with her. Even though she was confident she'd made the right decision regarding Hollingsworth, she wanted to know what put that guarded and haunted look in his eyes.

That eventual conversation notwithstanding, she needed to stay away from Langford as much as possible. He was also not the gentleman for her even if she wanted him at times. She had several years before she would be considered past her prime. And she had no mother or father breathing down her back. However, her heart pained at the thought. She would give anything to have both her parents still alive.

In any case, it wasn't imperative that she marry anytime soon. No need to settle on a gentleman until she knew she loved him and he loved her in return.

Seeing Emmeline standing with Blackstone in the refreshments room had her making her way to their side.

"I surmise you turned Hollingsworth's offer down. He left rather abruptly, looking distraught," Emmeline said softly for their ears only.

"Yes. I can't marry a man I hardly know or love. Nor is there any hurry to marry. I'm still young." She glimpsed the sadness in her friend's eyes and knew she'd said the wrong thing about being young. Wisely, Blackstone kept his eyes averted and pretended not to hear.

As the guests started leaving, Blackstone said, "May I escort you lovely ladies to your carriage?"

Lilly had to swallow the words she wanted to ask Blackstone before they escaped her lips. She wanted to ask where Langford was. But it was none of her business, and the more he stayed far away from her the better.

Emmeline took his offered arm. "Thank you." After stopping at the door and retrieving their cloaks and Blackstone's cape and hat, they went down the stairs and to their waiting coach.

Once inside the carriage, Emmeline leaned back and sighed. "Thankfully, that is over. I believe my ears still hurt from the music."

Lilly found herself laughing. "That was music? I never would've guessed."

Emmeline joined in the laughter, then turned serious. "We

need to go home and change. The Duchess of Greenville handed me a note requesting us to deliver medicine to a sick baby tonight. He is quite ill and she's afraid if he doesn't receive the medicine immediately, he will not make it through the night. She's sending a carriage and driver. I hope you don't mind going with me. I know nighttime trips can be frightening, but the duchess wouldn't ask if it weren't imperative. And the young mother will not answer her door to strangers in the middle of the night. Perhaps at some point they will trust Mitchel and Flynn, but for now it must be someone from the Ladies' Society."

"I don't mind at all. I wasn't going to be able to sleep tonight, anyway, after witnessing Hollingsworth's expression of dejection," Lilly said as her heart ached for the marquess. "I feel awful for him. He must be desperate to ask a near stranger to marry him."

"I agree," Emmeline said as their carriage came to a stop.

CHAPTER ELEVEN

THE DUCHESS OF Greenville's driver was waiting outside Emmeline's townhome when they arrived home. Lilly and Emmeline both picked up their skirts and hurried up the stairs to change clothing. After Daisy helped Lilly out of her evening dress, she sent her away and quickly dressed in a plain day dress, a black cloak, and sturdy boots. When she met Emmeline in the entry hall, she was dressed similarly. They left the house making haste to the unmarked coach.

"Good evening, ladies," said the driver, Mitchel, as he helped them inside the old but sturdy vehicle. He was one of the men who drove for the cause, a man the duchess trusted implicitly.

"Good evening, Mitchel," Emmeline said as she sat beside Lilly.

"We are on our own this evening. Flynn couldn't make it."

Emmeline and Lilly glanced at each other. It was first time they had gone on an assignment without an escort as well as a driver. She told herself it would be fine, even though her heart beat like a drum inside her chest. Emmeline had been doing this for years and never had an encounter with any unsavory men. She just had to concentrate on the poor sick baby who needed what was inside the large bag sitting on the floor by her feet.

Lilly had only gone into St. Giles during the night a few times but didn't believe she would ever feel comfortable doing so. As the carriage left the respectable neighborhoods of London and traveled farther and farther into the poor, unsafe areas, the more Lilly's heart pounded. She was afraid to look out the curtained window, knowing what she would see.

"I can see the panic on your face," Emmeline said as she touched her hand. "Everything will be fine. We've been to this tenement before. When we arrive, do what you always do. Keep your hood up and don't make eye contact with anyone—except for the poor mother. And you will recognize her—her name is Jane."

Before Emmeline could say anything else the carriage jerked to a stop and Mitchel opened the door and lowered the steps. "Be quick."

Lilly should have kept her head down. Instead, she gasped at the people milling around. Women—prostitutes—scantily dressed and dirty. Filthy men, drunk and swaying through the streets. Lilly gagged at the stench and her gloved hand flew to her mouth. Emmeline knocked and knocked on the door. Jane, the haggard-looking young mother, finally opened it just wide enough for her to hand over the bag and wish her well.

They hurried back inside the coach, Mitchel snapped the reins and sent the horses onward. Lilly leaned back against the squabs with a deep sigh. "I don't believe I'll ever get used St. Giles in the night. It is so eerie. Everything appears heightened. The sounds of the prostitutes and their customers, the drunk men, the awful smell." She shivered.

"It is bad. The poor mother having to live in such squalor," Emmeline said as she hugged herself.

They rode the rest of the way in silence. Lilly listened to the clop of the horses' hooves, the creak of the carriage wheels, and the occasional yelling coming from the street. When they arrived home, she bid Emmeline goodnight and went to her room, undressed down to her chemise, and scrubbed the smell from her body with the pitcher of water and soap left for her by Daisy. No matter how hard she scrubbed, her skin still crawled with imagined filth. Eventually, Lilly conceded that she'd done the best she could.

Instead of climbing into bed, she took a blanket and lay on the chaise longue. Her mind wandered to the many unanswered questions floating around inside her brain.

Langford.

She questioned his motives where she was concerned. How could she know if he truly cared for her when his actions traveled from one extreme to the other? He frustrated her to no end. If she allowed herself to see his handsome face in her mind and remember the feel of his lips on hers her insides melted. A warmth curled around her heart, threatening to take over her entire body. He threatened her peace of mind. He was so contradictory he made her head spin from their first meeting to their last.

And they called *women* fickle.

Even now, her heart pounded and her body trembled. Her fingers skimmed across her lips, causing her to sigh deeply. Whatever was happening between them had to end. She didn't want to live in a state of uncertainty.

As for Hollingsworth, she sympathized with his plight but was glad his attentions would no longer be set on her. She truly hoped he found someone to marry and love.

Edmund sat in a quiet corner of White's after leaving the musicale, enjoying his snifter of brandy. His thoughts got lost in the amber liquid when Hollingsworth darkened his vision.

"How dare you threaten to divulge my secrets? And how do you know I have any?" Hollingsworth's voice was dark and menacing. Edmund had never heard or seen him so angry.

"Relax, I only said I would tell Lady Langford if you continued forcing this courtship. Which I gather from your actions tonight you won't be?"

Hollingsworth grabbed him by his jacket lapels, hauled him to his feet, swung back, and punched him right in the jaw. Edmund, caught off guard was shocked when his arse fell back into the chair after being on the receiving end of the man's fist. His drink and glass fell to the carpet with a muffled thud. He rubbed his jaw and smirked. "I hope you got satisfaction in that hit because it's the only one you'll get. Sit. Have a drink. You need one."

Edmund was shocked when Hollingsworth sank into the chair closest to him. "A brandy, please, and another one for my friend," he said to the waiter who had hurried over at the commotion.

Before either took a sip, Blackstone joined them and nodded his head. "Gentlemen." He sat in a vacant chair. "I'm glad I don't have to break up a brawl."

Hollingsworth held up his glass. "It's early yet."

"That it is," Edmund added.

"Dare I ask what that was about?" Blackstone grinned at both men.

Hollingsworth snorted. "Use your imagination."

This time Blackstone laughed. "But words are so much more interesting." His laughter cut off abruptly. He reached into his jacket pocket and removed several folded pages of paper. "I ripped out the betting pages regarding Mrs. Fitzpatrick." He tossed sheets to the other men. "Look at some of the names and amounts. What a bunch of degenerates. Betting on who will bed the poor widow first. And the dates go back five years."

Edmund didn't miss Blackstone's look when he said *five years*. Obviously, he was happy no one had won the bet. "There's a lot of money riding on this. When the pages are found missing, someone's head will roll."

Blackstone stood, retrieved all the pages, walked to the hearth, tossed them into the fire, and watched them burn. He turned around and shrugged his shoulders. "What pages?"

The three men shared a chuckle. "So," Blackstone said as he

sat back down and signaled for a drink, "when are your nuptials to Lady Priscilla taking place?"

Hollingsworth choked on his drink, having just taken a sip. "When Lord Swenson sires an heir."

"So never. The man must be ninety with no willing wife in sight," Edmund said with a grin.

Hollingsworth groaned. "You really had to be an arse and sabotage my chances with the countess?"

Edmund stared into his glass again, seeking answers in the amber liquid. "I had to. My uncle asked me to help her find a husband who loves her, someone she loves back."

"Love," Hollingsworth scoffed. "An overrated emotion. A drain on one's heart."

"Yes, well, if anyone deserves to be loved, it's Lady Langford." His eyes were still lost inside his glass.

"I'd say she is loved," Hollingsworth said, matter-of-factly. "Have you seen the way you look at her? It's a wonder you both don't go up in flames."

Edmund shrugged. "As you said, love is an overrated emotion."

Blackstone inhaled and exhaled loudly. "Langford's a lost cause. Hollingsworth, why don't you marry Lady Priscilla?"

"I can't. I know I complain about how silly she is and how she drives me crazy, but the truth is she is smart, funny, and kindhearted. The rest is an act when she's out socially. She believes gentlemen of the *ton* prefer their wives to be simpletons. She believes that no one would want her if she showed her true self. And for that reason, I can't marry her. She has always been like a sister to me, and I want her to be happy. I can't use her. She even knows about the rumors, and she would marry me anyway. She says she would rather marry me than marry someone she hardly knows. I appreciate and admire her for that, but I can't be the man she deserves."

"I'm shocked," Edmund said. "If she's only been fooling everyone all this time, she should be on the stage. Perhaps I should consider her myself."

Hollingsworth glared at him. "Do I need to punch you again so soon? You are already spoken for."

"Hmmm. Not really." He didn't realize his feelings for Lilly were so transparent. He would have to be careful from here on out. She may have enjoyed the one kiss they shared, but the look in her eyes this evening told him she was also still leery of him. And how could he blame her after his behavior since they met? The trouble was he couldn't stay away from her. She was quick becoming the sunshine and air he needed to live.

"So, if you can't marry Lilly and won't marry Lady Priscilla," Blackstone began, "and over my dead body will you get close enough to Emmeline to even ask, who can you marry?"

"That's my trouble," Hollingsworth said. "There is no one. The mothers all keep their daughters away from me. The old rumor about me from five years ago is still circulating. Even the wallflowers snub me. It's most degrading."

"Even Lady Grace and Lady Faith?" Blackstone asked.

"No. Not them. They are kind, but their mother is entirely another matter. She makes my mother appear saintly."

Listening to the conversation go on around him had Langford thinking he needed to make amends to Lilly. He had much to atone for and didn't want to find himself snubbed as well.

"If you gentlemen will excuse me, I owe someone an apology."

Losing no time, he walked briskly to Emmeline's townhome, not realizing the time until he'd already knocked on the door. The butler opened the door, his eyes wide with shock. "My lord, the hour is late."

Entering the hall, Edmund said, "I apologize, but I must speak with Lady Langford."

"But, my lord . . ."

"Could you at least tell her I'm here and let her decide if she wishes to see me?"

Several minutes later, he came back with a disapproving look. "Lady Langford will see you in her rooms. Come this way."

Edmund followed the protective butler up two flights of stairs and down the hall to a door on the right. "You may go in. She is expecting you."

In truth, she should not be admitting him at all. It was well beyond inappropriate.

Entering the door and closing it shut behind him, he squinted in the dimly lit room until his eyes fell upon her sitting on a chaise longue wearing her night clothes. His feet ate up the distance until he stood in front of her. The picture she presented had his insides jumbled up with desire. "I'm sorry to disturb you so late in the evening."

"This could not wait until tomorrow?" she said with surprising clarity. Perhaps she'd been having trouble sleeping and hadn't gone to bed yet.

"No. It could not wait. I've been an arse. You have every right to hate me, and I don't blame you." Dropping on the chaise longue beside her, he wondered how to articulate the jumbled-up mess inside his head. Instead, he turned and gazed into her green eyes and time suspended. Her eyes dipped to his lips, then back to his eyes. She took her bottom lip between her teeth. His body tensed with desire.

He jumped back up and paced the room. "I came to apologize for my treatment of you since the moment we met." His fingers combed through his dark hair. "From the second I saw you, I felt something inside me shift, something I didn't understand, and I took my anger and frustrations out on you. And to be honest— and I'm embarrassed to admit this—I was jealous of Uncle Henry."

"Jealous?" She hugged herself. "How could you be jealous of a dead man?"

"Easy. He had you."

"But how could you have felt all that? We had just met."

"I can't explain it." He stopped pacing and looked at her, instantly wishing he hadn't. Her cheeks were flushed, her light hair loose and falling in waves across her shoulders. The white nightgown made her look young and innocent, and his heart accelerated. "Anyway, I'm sorry I barged in so late. I had no idea of the time. Forgive me."

She stood and went to him. "Edmund, you're acting so strangely and you seem flushed. Are you feeling unwell?" she asked, her eyes studying him.

"I'm fine." His eyes dropped to her lips. "Except that I want to kiss you. So very much." He breathed in slowly as he cupped her cheeks with his large hands. "May I?"

She smiled nervously. "You've never asked before."

He smiled back. "That was the arrogant me, thinking only of what I wanted without regard for the consequences of my actions." He pressed his lips to hers briefly. "Tonight, I want *you* to want *me* to kiss *you*."

"Kiss me, please."

EDMUND WRAPPED HIS arms around her back, holding her close, kissed her again and then deepened the kiss. She opened her mouth on a moan and his tongue slipped inside to tangle with hers. The kiss intensified, and her body hummed with what she believed was desire. When she could no longer breathe, and every nerve in her body was overwhelmed, she broke the kiss and nestled her head against his neck.

His hands caressed her back. They stood that way for several minutes before Edmund stepped back holding both her hands in his.

"I should go." He dipped his head and kissed her cheek. "Good night."

She grabbed his hand. "Stay."

The next thing she knew she was swept up into his arms and gently placed on the bed. She moved the covers aside and sat against the pillows, waiting for Edmund, who stood watching her intently. "Is this what you want?"

She felt uneasy for just a moment, wondering if he would be

able to tell she'd never lain with a man before. But she pushed her doubts aside and whispered, "Yes." She was feeling reckless and in need of a loving touch. Even if it was just this once, she wanted that loving touch to be from him.

He sat on the edge of her bed and removed his boots, then stood again and removed his coat and waistcoat. He locked his passionate eyes with hers as he untied his cravat, pulled his shirt over his head, and removed his breeches. Naked and unabashed, he stood, letting her take him in. She trembled with excitement and trepidation. His manhood jutted out, engorged and large. She swallowed down her nerves. Since he was naked, she inhaled and removed her night rail, then sat back against the pillows again and closed her eyes up tight.

The bed dipped and she knew he'd joined her. Still, she didn't open her eyes. She was afraid and nervous and shy and embarrassed. No man had ever seen her body unclothed.

His fingers skimmed down her cheek and her body tingled. "Open your eyes. You don't have to hide from me." His voice was deep and vibrating. Relaxing her facial features, she fluttered her eyes open to find his face close to hers and unease in his eyes. "Do not be nervous."

She shook her head. "I'm not."

One dark brow rose. "I don't believe you." Then he wrapped his hands around her by the waist and pulled her down so she lay flat and he came down on top of her and claimed her lips. She forgot why she was nervous as he devoured her mouth with his tongue. Breaking the kiss, he placed barely there kisses down her neck, causing her to break out in gooseflesh. His lips continued down to her breasts, and she arched her back and gasped as he sucked her nipple into his mouth, causing pleasure to throb between her thighs. Every time he sucked, she felt a pulse of pleasure down there.

He moved to the next breast and gave it the same treatment, and she thought she would lose her mind if he didn't stop. Sensations were flooding her, overwhelming her. She didn't know whether to scream from pleasure or frustration.

And then he moved, kissing his way down her stomach, his tongue circling her bellybutton. Dear God, she was going to die. He nudged open her legs, and then his mouth was there. Shock had her trying to close her legs, but his voice was low and inviting. "Relax and enjoy. You will love this, I promise."

He licked and sucked her womanhood and moaned out loud while he did so. She reached down and buried her fingers in his thick hair, needing something to anchor herself to as she felt out of control. She was on the edge of a great precipice and afraid she would fall to her death. A pleasurable death, but death nonetheless.

When he slipped a finger inside her body where no one had ever been before, not even herself, she almost sprang up off the bed. Instead, she reached out with her free hand, fisted the sheet tightly, and tossed her head from side to side as something inside her exploded. Her legs shook uncontrollably as sounds she'd never made before escaped her lips and reverberated around the room.

Edmund kissed his way up her body, one hand still between her legs and her body wiggled shamelessly against his hand. And then it was gone, replaced by his hard member as it nudged against her opening, and she tensed. His mouth took hers, and he tasted different, earthy but not unpleasant. She lost herself in his kiss as his member slowly penetrated her body. She broke the kiss and gasped at the fullness of his invasion. He'd barely entered her and she wondered how he would fit.

He buried his head in her neck. "You are tight. You feel so good. Open your legs wider and let me in."

She did as he asked. He thrust his hips against her hard. She gasped and swallowed the pinch of pain as he filled her completely and then he froze, lifting his head and looked at her with concern. "You are very tight. Am I hurting you?"

"You're not hurting me." By this point, the sting was easing, so she let the coming together of their bodies, a rhythm as old as time, work its magic, and she rolled her hips, reached for his face, and kissed him as he'd kissed her before. This time, she tasted him and bit his lip as he pumped himself in and out of her pliant body.

He braced one arm beside her head and moved the other between them and touched her, sending her spiraling over the ravine into the abyss. Edmund arched his back; a loud groan escaped his lips as his face tightened, and she felt the warmth of his seed spread inside her.

He pulled out and rolled onto his side, taking her with him. Her back nestled up against his front. He reached down for the covers, drew them up and held her in his arms. His head nuzzling the back of her neck.

EDMUND'S HEART CONTINUED pounding as he held Lilly close to his chest and inhaled her rose fragrance. A fragrance he smelled in the sitting room between what were Henry and Lilly's chambers the first time he'd been to Langford Manor after his uncle's death. Unfortunately, his mind wouldn't relent and let him sleep.

He felt bad leaving her in the middle of the night after they had made love, but there would already be enough talk in the morning among the household. If he could ease the situation by leaving now, he should. He would hate to make Lilly uncomfortable with unnecessary gossip.

He walked home. It took only thirty minutes, and he made his way into his study and poured himself a brandy, his mind still swirling with thoughts of Lilly, of her marriage to his uncle, of his own feeling of being drawn inexorably toward her.

When he'd first returned to London, he'd found two sealed letters in a false bottom drawer he was probably never meant to find. Across each, in Henry's handwriting, was written *For Henry's eyes only.* He had respected his uncle's privacy and left them where they were unopened. But he reflected now—most desks that he knew of had a drawer like that, so Uncle Henry must have known he would find it someday.

He ignored the tingling feeling on the back of his neck and broke the seal to the first letter. It was a handwritten note.

In case anyone has the whither all to question the marriage between Henry Weston and Lillianna St. Claire, the marriage took place on 10 April 1814 and was consummated on that very night.

His uncle and Lilly had both signed it at the bottom. Edmund found it odd, to say the least.

He cracked the second seal and unfolded the other letter. It was a document drawn up by Mr. Beauregard, and as he read it, Edmund's eyes widened in shock. Why had his uncle set up a trust in Lilly's name with such an exorbitant amount of money? As his uncle's widow, Edmund was obligated to pay Lilly a certain allowance. Did Henry think he would not take care of Lilly? Had he thought so poorly of him that he believed Edmund would not do his duty by her?

In a flash of memory he recalled asking Lilly if she was receiving her monthly allowance from him, and she'd said yes. Why had she never mentioned the trust? Even if he had known about the trust, she was still entitled to the funds from him, and he would continue to pay her what she was due. But why had she kept this truth from him?

His heart began to pound, he began to sweat, and he found it hard to take a deep breath.

Did she have more secrets? Had she told him any outright lies? Was this Annabelle all over again, a connection doomed to end in sorrow?

No sooner could he finally see the possibility of making a future together with Lilly, than his heart was ripped from his chest.

What else was she keeping from him?

CHAPTER TWELVE

LILLY AWOKE TO an empty bed where Edmund had been. Her body was a little sore from their lovemaking, but she was glad to be a virgin no longer. Keeping it hidden from everyone, including Emmeline, was exhausting. She was always afraid she would slip up and say something telling.

She was nervous for when she saw Edmund again. They had no understanding between them, and she didn't know what to expect. She rang for Daisy and requested a bath. Once inside the rose-scented hot water, she sighed with relief as her body relaxed and her soreness eased. Her mind went back to last night and Edmund. It was a night she would never forget, and she wondered if he thought of her this morning. As much as she was disappointed he hadn't woken her up before he'd left, she had to believe he'd done so because he didn't want to disturb her sleep.

Later in the morning, Lilly and Emmeline went to the Duchess of Greenville's home for their Ladies' Society of Mayfair meeting. During the carriage ride, Lilly told her about sleeping with Langford, but it seemed she'd already suspected.

"Harrison expressed his apprehension at letting Langford up to your chambers and came to me," Emmeline said, watching her closely.

Lilly's face heated. "I never thought about the household knowing."

"They don't—not really. Only that he visited. I told you when you moved in that my servants were very loyal to me. They may gossip among themselves, but it doesn't get outside. At least not that I've ever been aware." Emmeline grabbed her hand. "How are you feeling? Do you think there is a chance for you two?"

Lilly inhaled and let it out slowly. "I don't know. We made no commitments. It wasn't planned—it just happened. I'm glad it did, even if nothing comes of it. I certainly don't want him to marry me out of some sense of obligation. I want the person I marry to love me."

"You and I are agreement when it comes to marriage."

Lilly sighed with relief when the carriage came to a stop. Dwelling on last night and what may come of it would only cause her concern. She was grateful for the Ladies' Society meeting and the distraction it would provide.

The duchess's salon was a crush of members when they entered. "Welcome, Mrs. Fitzpatrick, Countess," Her Grace said. "Mitchel reported that all went well last night. I thank you for going out on such short notice."

"You are welcome, Your Grace," Emmeline and Lilly said as they curtsied in unison.

The duchess laughed. "No need to curtsy. You know I don't go with formalitics during these gatherings. We are all equals here as we try to help the less fortunate. Speaking of which, Mrs. Fitzhughes visited Jane this morning and learned the baby is doing better."

"What a relief," Lilly said as she started filling baskets with supplies piled high around the drawing room—dry goods, blankets, medicine, clothing, and such. She never inquired as to where the supplies came from. She presumed the duchess had her servants shop for them since it was once every fortnight they made deliveries, except for when there was an emergency such as last evening. Each of the ladies who belonged to the club donated money monthly, including her and Emmeline. Sometimes, anonymous donations were made, but Emmeline guessed those funds came from the duchess herself. Her husband, the duke, was a very wealthy man, and the duchess had a soft spot for those less fortunate.

The duchess's soft spot was assumed to have grown out of a family connection of her own. Lilly, like the other women here, knew the duchess had had a younger sister who found herself to be with child when she was still unmarried. The father of the child, a viscount, refused to marry her, and she was ruined during her first Season. The sister had apparently been so ashamed that she'd run away with what little pin money she had saved and ended up in a tenement in St. Giles. It was rumored that she and her unborn baby soon died of sickness, and the duchess and her parents didn't know her whereabouts or about her death until months later. What was known was that shortly after their quiet funeral for her, the duchess had started this organization.

Lilly's heart broke every time the duchess referred to her sister, Miss Amelia Benedict. The duchess had a heart of pure gold. If not for Henry, would Lilly have faced a similar situation sans the pregnancy? If Henry hadn't married her, anyone could have taken advantage of her in her precarious situation of being an orphan and homeless.

Emmeline grabbed her arm. "Are you well? I thought for a moment you were going to faint. You swayed on your feet."

Blinking several times, she put those visions out of her mind. "I'm fine. We can talk later."

Later came around faster than Lilly wanted. An hour later they were walking back home when Emmeline broached the subject.

"What happened back there?"

Lilly wrapped her arm through Emmeline's. "When my papa died, what if Henry hadn't married me and kept me safe? I had visions of living in a situation comparable to the duchess's sister only without the pregnancy. Although it could have happened to me. A local gentleman might have befriended me and taken advantage. Just thinking about it, my head swarmed with dizziness and my entire body went numb. It was the oddest feeling."

"You don't ever have to worry about anything resembling that happening to you," Emmeline said as she patted Lilly's arm linked with hers. "You have money and a title. Your life is secure and safe."

"I know. But it didn't make it seem any less frightening or real. It must be the anxiety from this business with Hollingsworth and Langford. I've not been sleeping well. And then last night . . ." Her entire body trembled. "I can't find the words to describe what bombarded my heart and mind when I saw the look on Jane's face when she saw us. Not to mention the conditions she lives in. My heart hurts even now remembering it."

THAT AFTERNOON THEY had a garden party to attend at the Marquess and Marchioness of Devens's home on the River Thames. As Daisy put the finishing touches to her hair, Lilly hoped Langford and Hollingsworth would not be in attendance. She could use a reprieve from having to deal with either of them. And she would ignore the squeeze to her heart at missing Langford after what they'd shared last night. It still bothered her that he'd left without a word.

Aunt Vivian and Emmeline were waiting for her in the front hall, dressed for the outdoor party. Thankfully it was warmer today and sunny. Lilly wore a lovely peach day dress with matching spencer and a wide-brimmed white hat trimmed with ribbons and flowers the color of her dress. The wide ribbon tied into a perfect bow off-center beneath her chin. Her white parasol had matching peach flowers and ribbon. Emmeline was dressed almost identically, although in a lovely medium blue. Aunt Vivian was dressed in lilac, complete with a turban and a wide-brimmed hat. Which had Lilly once again wondering if Emmeline's mother had any hair.

The carriage ride was pleasant as they pulled down the wide sweeping drive. After greeting their hosts, the three made their way through beautiful gardens, down a large expanse of green grass to the bank of the Thames. Along the riverbank, tents, tables, chairs, and blankets were spread all around. Guests were milling about, some sitting in small circles and others playing Pall Mall. She didn't know where to look. It was her first outdoor garden party, and she hummed with excitement. She hadn't seen Langford yet, but by the feeling she was being watched, she knew he was somewhere in the crowd.

"Mrs. Fitzpatrick, Countess." A young, handsome gentleman Lilly remembered meeting the night of her very first ball bowed in front of them: Viscount Redford. "Lady Langford, I would be honored if you would join me for a walk."

After last night with Langford, she did not want to encourage the viscount, but not wanting to hurt his feelings, she said, "Thank you. I would like that."

She opened her parasol to shade her face from the warm sun. She didn't take his arm as they strolled on a path wide enough for two through the grass and several small gardens with benches placed here and there. The roses and other flowers delighted her with their light scent. Mixed with the smell of the water, the grass, and flowers, the quality of the air was soothing. Lilly stopped at an exceptional red rosebush bursting with blooms. "This smells amazing."

Redford took a knife from his boot, cut off a stem, removed the thorns and bowed as he held it out to her. "My lady, a beautiful flower for an even more beautifully enchanting lady."

Heat kissed her cheeks. She didn't know what to make of this viscount. "Why, thank you for your generous gift."

"Shall we rest on the bench over there?"

Lilly found herself escorted to a wooden bench where the roses ended and neatly trimmed evergreens took over.

After they sat, he turned her way and grabbed her hand, the one not holding the rose. "I've wanted to attract your attention since the Westport ball, but between Hollingsworth and Langford, I never had the chance after our introduction." He paused and looked deep into her eyes. Lilly noticed several things at once. His face was classically handsome. However, his nose looked as though he'd broken it at one time. His sandy brown hair was thick, and he had long sideburns, which was the current style she didn't care for. His clothing was impeccable in pastel shades she normally disliked, but on him they looked fitting. His pale-blue eyes were an unusual shade. They appeared guarded.

"You may call upon me during the social hour," she said, wondering if she actually wanted to encourage his interest in her. Did she really believe she could ignore her feelings and the pull she felt toward Langford, especially after last night?

Even if that feeling were her heart dropping. Not a note. No flowers. No acknowledgment of what they'd shared. Had it meant nothing to him? Well at the very least his silence let her know with certainty that she couldn't put all her coins in one fountain. Thinking beyond Langford was necessary. They had no understanding between them, she reminded herself sternly, and that one night might be all they would have.

"With your permission, I would like to call on you tomorrow," the viscount was saying.

"Yes," she replied, bringing herself back to the present. But something in the depths of his eyes caused the back of her neck to tingle. Or perhaps it was just a chill in the air. "I believe I should like to rejoin the party."

Redford stood and held out his hand. "As you wish."

When Lilly took his gloved hand with hers, nothing happened—no shock, no heat, no connection, nothing.

CHAPTER THIRTEEN

ONCE BACK AMONG the tables and other guests, Redford bowed off. Lilly joined Emmeline at the food table to fix a plate of sandwiches, cheeses, bread, and fruit.

"You disappeared with Redford quickly," Emmeline said with an inquisitive look.

"Yes. We strolled down the path to a lovely small garden with a bench."

"And?"

Lilly exhaled. "Nothing. He talked very little, as did I. I'll admit he is handsome, but he seems rather dull. He is calling on me tomorrow. Perhaps there is more to the man than meets my eye."

"Perhaps." Emmeline agreed. "I wish I could help, but I have never met the viscount before. Nor have I heard much about him. I could inquire as to his nature with Blackstone if you would like."

"There is no need. I'll learn about him myself tomorrow."

They found an empty blanket and sat down carefully, keeping their ankles covered with their skirts while they nibbled on their refreshments. When Lilly's sun disappeared, she looked up and nearly choked on the grape she'd just popped in her mouth. Langford stood beside her, a plate balancing on the palm of his hand. "May I join you?"

How did he show up out of nowhere like that? And why did her insides heat up when he locked his creamy-brown eyes with hers? His wavy hair, with one wayward curl falling over his forehead, made her fingers itch to push it aside. To feel the silken threads between her fingers. The urge to moan out loud had her swallowing it down instead.

"Yes." Was that her breathy voice?

"Hello, Langford," Emmeline said as she placed her empty plate beside her. "Is Blackstone in attendance?"

Langford sat next to Lilly, his legs out straight with his plate balanced on his thighs. He hit Emmeline with a knowing smile. "Yes. He's playing Pall Mall with Caldwell and several others." Langford put a whole cucumber sandwich in his mouth. It was tiny, after all. "I'll need about ten of these to quench my appetite."

Giggles escaped Lilly before she had time to stop them.

Langford looked at her, one eyebrow brow raised, his lips quirked up into a smile.

Heat started inside her chest and unfurled to encompass her entire body. She would blame it on the warm sunshine rather than on what had transpired in her bed with him. Even though seeing him reminded her of the pleasure her body was capable of. "Sorry. Everything being served today is small in portion. It's perfect for the ladies but not for gentlemen with voracious appetites."

EDMUND ALMOST SPIT out the piece of cheese he'd put inside his mouth when Lilly said "gentlemen with voracious appetites." Bloody hell, those words could refer to all sorts of things. Innocent *and* indecent. And the first thing that came to his mind was gentlemen's sexual desires, specifically his sexual passion related to Lilly after all they shared beneath her sheets. Even now, her rose scent invading his nose and the close proximity of her lush body awoke such a need inside him that he considered moving his plate higher up his lap to hide his erection. His cock strained against his breeches, and with their tight fit, he wouldn't be getting up anytime soon. Then he remembered his uncle's papers he'd found in the hidden compartment of his desk. His heart had better freeze up because he wasn't yet sure if he could trust her and wondered what other secrets she still hid from him. He hated to admit it, but he had a suspicious nature and would question her honesty in all things, knowing she'd already withheld information from him so easily.

He was so lost in his thoughts that he didn't immediately realize Caldwell and Blackstone had joined them on the quickly filling blanket. There was hardly room for the five of them.

"How was Pall Mall?" Edmund asked. "Who won?"

Blackstone chuckled. "Lady Priscilla Amesbury. She stomped on Hollingsworth's pride as he came in second. Those two play cutthroat. You'd think they were fighting to the death. The rest of us hadn't a chance."

Edmund was surprised when Lilly said, "Perhaps Hollingsworth has found his match with Lady Priscilla even though he denies it."

He wanted to laugh, but he held himself back. "Perhaps he has. Only time will tell."

"Caldwell, when, pray tell, are you going to stop traveling to faraway lands and marry a nice young lady?" Emmeline asked.

"I'm not ready to settle down."

"One day, Caldwell," Emmeline said, "when you least expect it, some lovely debutante will catch your eye. You will be smitten and running to the Archbishop of Canterbury for a special license."

Everyone laughed except Caldwell. He looked at Edmund and then at Blackstone. "I won't be the first gentleman to do so."

Edmund's muscles tightened at Caldwell's hint. He would not be running off to get a special license—certainly not to marry

Lilly after what he uncovered. Yes, part of him understood the papers he found were private and pertained to Henry and Lilly's marriage and had nothing to do with him. But another part of him felt betrayed at the implication that neither of them had trusted him to do right by Lilly.

As the conversation went on around him, he studied Lilly to see if she would act differently after what they'd shared last night. She appeared the same, except now and then she glanced his way shyly and looked away quickly. He tried not to think too much about what it meant nor about the pieces of paper folded inside his jacket pocket.

When the gathering ended, earlier than planned as it looked as though a passing shower was going to come through, Edmund approached Lilly. "May I have a quick word with you?"

Her eyes moved to Aunt Vivian and Emmeline before landing back on him. Her green eyes sparkling in the remaining sunlight did strange things to his insides. He felt as though she could see all his thoughts and dreams. "You can walk me to our carriage," she answered.

They walked side by side. She hadn't taken his arm and he tried to not feel snubbed. No sense waiting any longer to bring up what he wished to discuss. He reached into his coat pocket and pulled forth several pieces of folded paper. "I found these in a hidden drawer in the desk in the study. Care to explain?"

Lilly took the papers from him. While she looked them over, her eyes widened and her cheeks pinkened. She handed them back. "I had nothing to do with these. That is my signature on the paper regarding our marriage, but I don't remember seeing it before now. As for the trust, Henry insisted on it."

"So he didn't trust *me*." His stomach knotted in agony at the realization.

"Trust had nothing to do with it."

"How can you say that? The proof is in the papers." He bristled. "What other lies are you guarding that are waiting to be unearthed? What else are you and Uncle Henry hiding from me?"

Her footsteps faltered. "Nothing."

"Forgive me if I don't believe you." He handed over another piece of paper. "I took the liberty of writing down the names of several eligible bachelors worthy of you."

"I see."

"Don't be angry with me. I just want what's best for you."

"Of course you do," she murmured. "Because last night meant nothing to you."

He tamped down his anger because he needed to keep his voice low. "It's because of last night that I made the list."

Her eyes met his, tears forming in hers, and he told himself the list was for the best, but he knew it wasn't true. He could lie to himself until the end of time and the truth would be the same. All he really wanted to do was burn the list and make Lilly his.

But pride was a bloody stubborn emotion.

SHOCK RIPPLED THROUGHOUT her body at his reaction to finding Henry's papers. No matter what he believed, she'd never lied to him. She may not have volunteered the whole truth on some things, but she'd never outright lied. And it was clear to her now that what they shared last night meant nothing to him. Except it had not felt that way at the time. He had truly seemed to care for her. Was that something men did? Could they make love to a woman and have it not affect their heart? Their emotions? Their morals?

What a fool she was. One day. That was all it had taken for him to dismiss what they'd shared and supply her a list of marriageable gentlemen. She hadn't expected him to swoon or propose marriage, but was a bit of kindness too much to ask?

Inside the carriage, Emmeline asked, "What did Langford want?"

Lilly refused to acknowledge the hurt having taken over her

heart. "He gave me a list of potential suitors."

"How very considerate of him," Aunt Vivian said with all seriousness. "Is his name on the list?"

"Mama," Emmeline scolded, "you know it will not be."

"It should be. The room heats up from the way his eyes devour Lilly when they are in close proximity. I had nothing else to do today but watch you girls socializing with your gentlemen—"

"Aunt Vivian," Lilly interjected, feeling sick to her stomach, "they are not *our* gentlemen." Langford was only hers last night and never would be again.

Aunt Vivian waved her arm. "Regardless of what you both think, I watched Langford hunger for Lilly today. Anyone with one working eye could tell he has deep feelings for you. As for Blackstone, my dear daughter, the man looks at you with reverence. Give them both time to come to their senses. Men can be so blind and stubborn at times, it's infuriating."

Lilly looked at Emmeline with wide eyes, and they both burst out laughing. Aunt Vivian had at least one thing right—men *could* be blind, stubborn, and infuriating.

Right after dinner, Lilly went to her room, looking forward to spending the night at home, as they had no commitments that evening. Lilly, dressed in a night rail and robe, fell back on the chaise longue in her room with a deep, contented sigh. The freedom her body had from not wearing a corset felt heavenly. She breathed in and out letting her chest expand and contract. It was not natural to stifle a woman's breathing with a corset enhanced with whale bones.

Soft knocking on her bedroom door had her answering, "Come in."

"I hope you don't mind," Emmeline said as she walked over toward the chaise. "I thought we could give that list from Langford a once over."

"Whatever your mother thinks, it's not thoughtfulness on his part. Langford found private papers belonging to Henry and never meant for anyone else's eyes. Today he accused both

Henry and me of lying and not trusting him to do his duty by supporting me after Henry's death. He said he could never trust me now. Whatever happened between us last night will never happen again. Hence the list." Lilly swiped at the annoying tears sliding down her cheeks.

Emmeline opened her mouth to speak, then shook her head. "I'm sorry. Langford is being a fool in so many ways."

Lilly ignored the pain in her chest and forced Langford from her mind. Earlier, she'd tucked the list into her robe pocket. Pulling it out, she unfolded it and stared at the five names scribbled in Langford's flowy but messy handwriting. "Number one is the Duke of Stanton." Lilly furrowed her brows. "Do I know him?"

"Not that I'm aware," Emmeline said. "He stays mostly in the country with his two children since his wife, their mother, died of a fever two years past. As far as I know, he never comes to London."

"Then why did Langford put him on the list?"

"I haven't a clue. Perhaps he knows something. The last time I saw him was during my first Season. He was unmarried, handsome, and a total rakehell. He'd just come into the dukedom and was not ready to settle down. He eventually married the American daughter of a whaling tycoon. How sad she passed on so young."

Lilly frowned. "Yes. How sad. He must be looking for a replacement mother for his children. Does Langford see me that way? I want children someday, but most certainly not now."

"Who is next?" Emmeline asked.

"Mr. James Caldwell. Langford needs a physician for his brain if he thinks Caldwell is interested in me or I in him. The man just today professed to love his status as a bachelor. We would never suit."

"I agree. Next."

"The Earl of Dunston," Lilly answered. "I remember being introduced to him before the opera. If I recall, he had his mistress on his arm and he looked besotted. Is this list a joke? Is Langford just making fun of me?"

"I don't know," Emmeline said with a soft voice. "Who are the last two?"

"The Viscount Redford." His handsome face flashed in her mind. "He is handsome and seems affable. He has odd eyes, though."

Emmeline giggled. "Odd eyes. Whatever do you mean?"

"They are such a light blue. I've never seen eyes so light. They almost glow. Perhaps it was the sunlight altering the hue."

"Anything else wrong with him?"

"Not that I can think of. Not that I actually know him, of course."

"Final name."

Lilly stared at the paper. Her eyes had to be deceiving her. It was bad enough that Caldwell's name was on the list, but to also have his brother, the baron, was plain stupidity. Neither brother had shown any interest in her or in marriage. "This one is as laughable as his brother."

"Let me guess." Emmeline huffed. "Baron Latham?"

"Langford's an idiot. The baron is even more of an enigma than his brother, Caldwell." Lilly jumped up and sat down at her writing table, took out a piece of parchment, opened the ink bottle, and dipped the quill.

Dear Earl of Langford,

While I appreciate your efforts in compiling a list of potential suitors, I must decline to consider all but one. The only name on the list that is worth considering is Viscount Redford. The others I strictly decline to even contemplate. Not that I am truly considering Redford, either. I simply couldn't think of a reason to cross off his name. Yet. Perhaps you should leave my future life and husband to me. I'm capable of making good decisions most of the time.

Very truly yours,

Lilliana Weston, Countess of Langford

"I wrote him a note," she said to Emmeline. "I wonder what he'll think when he reads it. Not that I care. The faster I get him out of my life, the better." She hoped he'd understand the added significance of the last sentence. As the hours ticked by, she regretted the events of the previous night more and more.

They were interrupted by a knock on the door.

"Yes," Lilly called out.

Harrison entered. "I'm sorry to bother you, but this just arrived for you both." He handed Emmeline a note from the Duchess of Greenville.

"Thank you, Harrison. Lady Langford and I will be going out." Emmeline turned to Lilly, "I'll meet you downstairs in ten minutes."

CHAPTER FOURTEEN

S ITTING INSIDE THE dark carriage, Lilly asked, "It is another sick baby?"

"No. The note said it was a woman in labor. The duchess sent her own physician to her aid. But it appears there is some difficulty, and the physician requests help in keeping her other children occupied. That is where we are to help. Do you have any knowledge of children? Because I certainly do not."

"I do. I would on occasion help the women in our village with their offspring. Keep them entertained during my papa's sermons."

"Thank goodness. My stomach is in knots. I wasn't convinced we would be able to help at all."

Inhaling deeply, Lilly fought her nervousness at actually going into one of the dilapidated buildings in St. Giles Rookery. She had grown up privileged, living in a cozy, well-cared-for, four-room cottage provided to the vicar. She'd never wanted for food or gone to bed with a painful hunger in her belly as she imagined the people of St. Giles did. She'd even had several serviceable dresses. She had been very happy and content living in Kent with her papa. Of course, they'd had poor people in their village, and she and her papa helped them as best they could using donations to the vicarage. But none of that compared to the rookeries in London.

Since marrying Henry, her eyes had opened to the vast differences between the classes. But it wasn't until she'd witnessed the harsh conditions of the families living in the back slums of London that she truly understood what real poverty entailed. What little Emmeline and she did along with the Ladies' Society of Mayfair wasn't nearly enough. When the carriage stopped in front of a precariously leaning three-story wooden tenement, Lilly's heart dropped down to her toes.

"Oh, dear," Lilly murmured. "The place looks ready to fall sideways into the next building."

"Indeed," Emmeline said nodding her head in agreement. "We may as well go inside and pray for the best."

"Yes." Lilly held tight to a portmanteau Emmeline had brought that contained things for the children as she exited the carriage. "Where are we meant to go?"

"The duchess's note said to enter the building, climb to the top floor to number six, and knock." Emmeline led the way inside and up the rickety stairs that moaned and creaked with each and every step. Whatever was coating the stair treads stuck to Lilly's boots with each step. With her free hand, she covered her mouth from the stench of urine and other things she didn't want to know. Her heart broke again at the conditions these families lived in.

The sound of Emmeline knocking on the wooden door that was barely hanging on its hinges snapped Lilly out of her musings. A child, a thin girl around the age of eight or nine, opened the door, her eyes wide. The whites of her eyes were stark against the dim interior lit with one near-guttered candle. The hearth had burned down to nothing. Lilly surveyed the small room. One mattress sat on the uneven wooden floor with two small children huddled beneath a threadbare blanket. The child who had opened the door joined her siblings. None of them spoke a word.

Reaching into the bag, Lilly pulled out a blanket and covered them. Reaching her hand in again, she took out several carved, wooden toys and placed them beside the children. A sudden scream, coming from behind the only door other than the one they'd come through, tore through the air and Lilly yelped, locking panicked eyes with Emmeline, who looked equally shocked.

Handing the bag to Emmeline, Lilly said, in a shaky voice, "I have been present during several births. Perhaps I should go in and see if the doctor needs help."

Emmeline looked ready to flee or cast up her dinner, Lilly wasn't sure which. "I've never . . . I don't think . . ."

"Do not worry. I'll go help." Her eyes went to the door and back to Emmeline. "There is food in the bag, is there not? Give it to the children. They look starved." Another scream pummeled the stale air, and Lilly found her feet taking small, hesitant steps across the small room and opening the door with a loud creak. "It is the Countess of Langford, Dr. Smith. I'm here to help in any way I can."

"Good. Come in. I could use another pair of hands," said the tired-sounding doctor.

Her eyes traveled around the tiny room. The doctor stood at the end of a bed where a frail-looking woman with dark, tangled hair and a large protruding belly lay naked and propped up by pillows. Her eyes were closed and Lilly believed she had passed out from the pain. Her knees were bent up and her legs open. Births were not for those who had a weak constitution, which fortunately, Lilly did not have. It was true that she witnessed several births, and Lilly knew right away that something was wrong by the number of blood-soaked towels lying around the physician's feet.

"The baby was breech. I tried everything, but the babe no longer lives," said the exhausted-looking older doctor. "The mother is dying as well. She's lost too much blood." He wiped his blood-soaked hands on a used cloth. "I have given her laudanum to make her comfortable. It is only a matter of time. I have already sent word to Mrs. White and she should arrive shortly to take the children until a permanent placement at a foundling school can be arranged. When I leave I will send word to the local undertaker, and he will see the mother and her babe are buried in the paupers' burial site."

"But . . . what . . ." Lilly had trouble speaking.

"There is nothing else I can do." He handed her a vial. "If she regains consciousness again, give her this to ease her suffering." He picked up his black valise, nodded his head, and left Lilly standing there with her eyes wide and her mouth open.

Emmeline hovered in the doorway, her hair mussed and her face smeared with dirt and looking as though she'd seen a ghost. "Why did he leave?"

Closing her eyes and taking a deep breath, regretting it immediately as the metallic taste of blood bombarded her, Lilly said, "The baby was breech and died. The physician can do no more. We need to stay until she passes and a Mrs. White comes for the children."

"I'm sorry," Emmeline whispered.

"For what?" Lilly questioned.

"I can't seem to move forward into the room."

"I understand. Just see to the children." Emmeline stepped back and closed the door, leaving her alone with the poor mother who was dying.

A soft moan came from the young woman. "Please come close."

How could she refuse? Lilly approached the side of the bed and gasped. If she ignored the sweaty, matted hair and pale skin and malnourished body, the woman had fine features. In health, she must have been beautiful.

"Please send word to my father, Baron Winslow, that I have died and left him three grandchildren." She gasped and cried out.

"The physician left this for you." Lilly held up the vial, and the mother shook her head from side to side.

"Not yet. I need to tell you. I fell in love with my father's valet. He died a fortnight ago. Killed during a tavern brawl. Tell my father I'm sorry." She gasped for breath and blood trickled from her mouth. "Beg him to take my children in."

Lilly grabbed her cold hand. "What is your name?" For some reason that became most important to Lilly. She needed a name to put with the face and person dying right before her eyes.

"Annabelle." She gasped and gurgling noises came from her throat as she took her last breath. The hand Lilly held fell to the bed.

Lilly covered her mouth, tears stung her eyes, and she found herself sobbing for the poor woman who had grown up privileged, fallen in love with a servant, and died in squalor. Would the baron take her children in? Would he come for her body and bury her in the family plot?

She covered the body with a blood-stained sheet she found on the floor, the only option she had, and hurried into the other room. "Emmeline, I'm going to find Mitchel. I have to send a message."

She ran out the door, down the dark, dangerous stairs, and burst out the door to the street her eyes darting around looking for their carriage. It was a little way down the road outside a rowdy tavern. Lilly pulled the hood up on her cloak, which she'd never taken off, and hurried to their conveyance. "Mitchel, I am so relieved to see you. I need to get a message to Baron Winslow and the duchess."

"Lady Langford, where is Mrs. Fitzpatrick? And what about the mother?"

"Oh, it is so sad. The mother and baby have died. But the mother was the daughter of Baron Winslow. We must get word to him so he may come and rescue his grandchildren and take his daughter's body home."

"I cannot leave you and Mrs. Fitzpatrick here unaccompanied."

"Please." She grasped his hands. "You must at least go to the duchess and relay my message. She will contact the baron, and then you can come back for us."

"The duchess will have my hide if anything happens to you or Mrs. Fitzpatrick."

"Go. We will be fine."

He nodded reluctantly and nudged the horses into movement. Lilly took a moment to watch the carriage maneuver through the crowded streets. Not crowded with vehicles but with people, mostly drunk. Just as she turned, she gasped. Was that Langford exiting a hack? It was dark, and he was dressed in respectable clothing though not of the finest quality he usually wore, but she would recognize that face and swagger anywhere. She ducked into the nearest doorway and watched, her heart pounding, as he made his way toward her. What was he doing here? As he neared her, she pulled her hood lower to shield her completely and swallowed her gasp—it truly was him.

When he ducked inside the nearby tavern, Lilly hurried back to Emmeline, wondering what Langford was doing in St. Giles this late at night or at any time. Of course, he could wonder the same about her if he recognized her. Her entire body shivered. It was a good thing he hadn't seen her.

"Shhh." Emmeline met her at the door. "Fredrick, Sophia, and Anna are finally asleep."

Lilly shut the door as quietly as possible once she was inside.

"What are we to do now?" Emmeline asked.

"I've sent Mitchel with messages for the duchess and Baron Winslow informing him of his daughter's death and of his grandchildren."

"Baron Winslow?" Emmeline looked as though she'd lost her mind.

Lilly told her what the mother, Annabelle, had confided in her.

EDMUND, FEELING AS though he needed punishment for his less

than gentlemanly treatment of Lilly, hired a hack to take him to a tavern in St. Giles, the last place the baron said his man had spotted Thomas Dane, his erstwhile valet who had run away and married his daughter. Though the baron had been hunting for them for years, it seemed they'd moved often, evading him. The poor baron had been heartbroken when his daughter left. As shocked as he had been to learn she had fallen in love with his valet, he never would have turned his back on her or thrown her out. Unfortunately, he hadn't been given the chance to have that conversation with her.

At the time, Edmund had been courting Annabelle Brown and thought perhaps they had a future together. Edmund fancied himself in love with the beautiful, delicate debutante. When she ran off with Thomas, Winslow spiraled into such a desperate state that he reached out to Edmund for help. Edmund had swallowed his pride for the sake of the old man and searched high and low for Annabelle and Thomas to no avail. Winslow finally hired an investigator after hunting for a solid year, but the investigator's luck in locating them wasn't any better. These days their leads amounted only to an occasional sighting.

Tonight, Edmund, dressed shabbily, entered the tavern and sat at an empty table in the back facing the door so he had eyes on everyone who came and went. Winslow had told him that Thomas had been seen in here recently. That led Edmund to think Annabelle and Thomas lived nearby—there was no reason to travel far just to have an ale. But his insides clenched up tight at the thought of Annabelle living in one of the dilapidated tenement houses in the area. They barely looked habitable for animals, never mind people. Was she even still alive? Had she succumbed to disease like so many living in such squalor?

Tears stung his eyes, and he fought them off. Annabelle hadn't wanted him. Yet somehow, he felt some sort of responsibility to her and the baron. Why else had he spent so many nights in the back slums of London whenever he was in town searching for her? She was all the baron had left and Edmund wanted to bring her home to him.

After pretending to sip on the bitter-tasting ale for what seemed like an age and seeing nothing useful in his hunt, he tossed a coin to the man behind the bar and left. The stale, sour stench from inside the tavern was even worse outside as it combined with the slop tossed onto the street. One had to watch where one stepped. There were no hired hacks around, so he walked down the street, his eyes scanning from left to right and occasionally behind himself as well. There were prostitutes, drunks, and thieves filling the road. Still scanning the area, he spotted someone small in a dark cloak, hood up, huddled in a doorway. Deeming the person not dangerous, he kept walking until the road opened up, and he walked some more. If he didn't find a hack soon, he'd be walking all the way to Mayfair.

Out of nowhere, he suddenly heard the sound of horses' hooves, the crack of a whip, and yelling. Then there was an excruciating pain, and then nothing.

AN HOUR OR so after Lilly sent her message, the duchess herself arrived with an older gentleman, shocking Lilly. She never thought the duchess traveled into St. Giles. "Countess, Mrs. Fitzpatrick, Mitchel is downstairs waiting for you. I will take it from here."

"Yes, Your Grace," Lilly and Emmeline said in unison.

As the duchess had told them, Mitchel and the carriage awaited them right out front. They hurried inside, and Mitchel took off quickly. Not long into the ride, Lilly and Emmeline were both thrown suddenly against the side of the coach and into each other. Horses were screeching, and people were shouting.

"Are you hurt?" Emmeline asked Lilly as she pushed herself off the coach's floor and off Lilly.

"I banged my head, but I'm all right. I think." Lilly touched her temple, and her glove came away wet. "I think I'm bleeding." Though it was a little hard to tell in the low light.

The door swung open, and Mitchel stuck his head inside, looking positively panicked. "Are you ladies hurt?"

"The countess cut her head, but otherwise, we are unhurt. What happened?"

"A carriage lost a wheel and was coming straight at us." Mitchel stuck his head inside. "I veered off, and the other driver crashed into someone. I must go help. Please stay inside. I'll be right back."

Lilly met Emmeline's eyes and they both hurried out of the carriage and into the chaotic street. People were running about. Mitchel was barking orders to several men as they attempted to lift a small vehicle off what looked like a person. Icicles traveled up her spine and her insides chilled. She didn't want to get closer to the accident. Her feet, however, did not listen to her.

"Lilly," Emmeline yelled, "where are you going?"

"I need to see . . ." Yes, she had seen Langford recently, and he would travel on this very road to go home, but what were the odds it was him? She just needed to be sure it wasn't him, that's all. She just needed to be sure.

"My lady," Mitchel said, his voice strained from struggling with the carriage. "This is not something you should see. Please get back in the carriage."

"I can't." Her body refused to move. Her eyes focused on the unmoving lower body she could see pinned beneath the wheel. The men heaved again, grunting loudly, and finally, the carriage was lifted off the person enough that another man pulled the injured man out by his one good leg, and her heart stopped. Her body tried to tell her with the icy chills. Even her feet moving without her knowledge was a warning.

Even by the light of streetlamps and carriage lanterns, it was clear. The man, broken and battered on the ground was Langford.

She yelled at the top of her lungs to be heard over the commotion. "Easy! Be very careful!" With strength she never had before, she shoved several people aside to reach Langford. She dropped to her knees and cradled his head in her lap. "Edmund, can you hear me?" The sound of him groaning had her heart beating once again. He was alive. That was good, wasn't it?

"Mitchel, I need your help," she called.

Their driver pushed his way to her side. "My lady?"

"This is the Earl of Langford. Please try to get our carriage as close as you can. We need to get him to Mrs. Fitzpatrick's home and call the physician. Although I'm afraid to move him, we must." One of his legs was bent at an odd angle and blood was seeping into his tan breeches.

Between Mitchel and several other men, they placed Langford as gently as possible on the floor inside their coach. The sound of his moaning and, at one point, bellowing out in pain had Lilly clenching her teeth and swallowing hard so as not to be sick. She climbed inside the coach with Emmeline. Lilly knelt on the floor, her hand gently stroking his face and his hair as she spoke soothing words to him. "It's Lilly. I'm going to take care of you. You have nothing to worry about. I'm here." She didn't know how she managed to keep the panic out of her voice as her entire body trembled uncontrollably.

The ride felt like it took forever. Every time the carriage jarred and bounced, Langford groaned. Her eyes never left his face which was etched with agonizing pain. She wanted to check for other injuries but was afraid to cause him more pain. The one thing she knew was that his leg was at an odd angle and most likely broken. She prayed he had no internal injuries. Dear God, what would she do if he died? The only family she had left was Aunt Vivian, Emmeline, and him, even if the familial connection was by marriage only. Even if she was madder than Hades at Langford for tossing her aside so carelessly, she could not imagine life without him.

As soon as the carriage stopped and Mitchel opened the door, Emmeline was hurrying up the stairs and into the townhome, rousing servants and barking orders as she went. Immediately, a footman ran down the street, presumably to the mews to get a horse and fetch the family doctor. Along with Mitchel and three other servants, they gently and carefully carried a moaning Langford into the house, up the stairs, and to a guest bedroom.

It was a good thing he wasn't conscious of the amount of damage done to his body. If he had been alert he would have been screaming at the jostling of his person up the stairs and onto the bed.

"Countess," Mitchel said, his face full of alarm. "I will leave you now and report what happened to the duchess. Please send word if you need anything."

"Thank you, Mitchel. You have been most helpful." As Lilly pulled a chair close to the bed and slumped into it, she could barely remember what had brought them to St. Giles in the first place. Then it all rushed back and tears slid down her face when she remembered Annabelle's death and the death of her unborn baby.

With tears silently streaming down her cheeks, she stared at Langford, willing him to live. "We have unresolved issues. Don't you dare think about dying on me, you infuriating man."

CHAPTER FIFTEEN

"How is he?" Emmeline asked as she stood at the foot of the bed.

"I don't know. I'm afraid to touch him and make his injuries worse. I do hope the physician hurries. He looks pale, lifeless, and broken. I'm afraid for his leg." She sobbed loudly. "Oh God, he can't die. Not like this. Not when he has so much life ahead of him."

"Mrs. Fitzpatrick," said Emmeline's family physician, Dr. Bailey, as he hurried into the room carrying his valise. "Please tell me what happened."

Emmeline explained what she knew of the aftermath of the carriage accident to the doctor while she and Lilly lit all the candles and lamps in the room.

"The coach wheel was on top of him, pinning him by his legs," Lilly added. "He is the Earl of Langford, doctor. Please help him."

"I will do my best," Dr. Bailey said as he ran his hands up and down Langford's body checking for injuries. "Your head is bleeding. As soon as I see to Lord Langford I will look at your head. Has he been conscious?"

"No," Emmeline answered.

"His leg is broken at the thigh and his shin bone pierced through the skin and is causing blood loss. I need to set both bones and hope infection doesn't set in. I would hate to have to amputate it. His shoulder is also dislocated and will need to be put back into place. I will need some strong footmen to hold the earl steady while I set his leg and pop his shoulder back in. No other bones appear to be broken, but I'm worried about internal injury." He began cutting off Langford's clothing until he was left in his breeches. "You may want to avert your eyes as I'm also removing his breeches."

Emmeline, wide-eyed and nervous, met Lilly's eyes, and they both turned their backs.

"In fact, while I set his leg you may want to vacate the room."

The last thing Lilly wanted to do was take her eyes off Langford, even just to turn around. Part of her believed that if she was seeing him alive and breathing, then he would stay alive and breathing. Nevertheless, she hurried from the room with Emmeline, calling for two footmen. Moments later two came running down the hall. "Dr. Bailey needs your help inside."

"I'm frightened," Lilly said as she leaned against the wall out in the dim hall, her eyes focused on the shape of the closed door.

"Me too," Emmeline said. "I had Mother send messages to both Blackstone and Caldwell. They will want to be here."

Deep screams pierced the air. They went on for a time. They sounded animalistic, even though Lilly knew they came from Langford. Her hands covered her ears, and she mumbled, "It's going to be fine. He's going to be fine."

"Lilly." Emmeline's voice sounded far away. "Does your head hurt?"

"What?" It was then Lilly realized she was kneeling on the ground, holding her head and shaking all over. Even her teeth were rattling. "No. I don't know what happened. When he screamed . . ."

The doctor opened the door. "You may come back in. I've set the bones in his leg, sutured, and splintered it. With luck he will keep the leg and only walk with a limp. His shoulder popped back in easily. He also has a nasty bump on the back of his head, but I don't detect any internal damage, which is a miracle considering what happened. I'm hoping he will regain consciousness soon. I left a vial of laudanum on the night table. See to it he has a teaspoonful once every four hours. For several days, it's imperative to keep his pain at bay. I will be back tomorrow afternoon to rebandage the stitches. Pray infection doesn't set in."

"Dr. Bailey," Lilly spoke. "Thank you so much for taking care of Langford. I hate to ask, but can you look at my head?"

"Oh, my dear, I'm sorry I forgot." He waved to a chair. "Please take a seat."

Lilly sat in the chair next to Langford and winced when the doctor cleaned her cut.

"You do not need stitches. It is more of a scrape than a laceration. I'm putting a bandage on it. I will check it when I return."

Emmeline walked with the physician. "I will see you out."

When Lilly was left alone with Langford, she stood and walked around the bed holding a lamp to see his injuries close up. The side of his face was scraped and raw but not bandaged. She could not see the bump on the back of his head, nor would she feel for it. If she touched him she was afraid she would cause him pain. His left arm was bandaged, and the cloth wrapped around his midsection so he couldn't move his arm or shoulder.

She hesitated to move the sheet to look at his leg since she knew he was naked beneath the thin sheet. Her cheeks heated at the thought of being in a room with Langford in a state of undress. It didn't matter that she had seen him naked before—these circumstances were much different. But then her curiosity got the better of her, and she slid the sheet aside just to get a peek of his lower leg. Not that there was much to see as it was bandaged. She didn't dare move the sheet up to see how far the bandage went. She presumed to the top of his thigh.

Once again, her cheeks heated. At any other time, she may have admired his muscular physique, but it didn't seem right now.

Sitting back down in the chair, the lamp beside the bed illuminating his features which were drawn. Every once in a while, he groaned and gritted his teeth. Even unconscious, he was overwhelmed by the pain. Her fingers went to her temple and realized it was sore to the touch and there was a dull ache across her forehead. But it was not enough to take her away from Langford's bedside.

Mullens, Edmund's valet, and Mrs. Lewis, the very capable housekeeper at the Langdon townhouse, had just arrived and were settling into chairs to watch over him. Lilly wondered absently who'd had the presence of mind to send for them. She was grateful someone had. Lilly expected Blackstone and Caldwell would arrive at any moment, as well, provided they were at home to receive the messages.

After all the commotion when they arrived home, the house seemed eerily quiet now.

Every so often, Lilly's head fell as she nodded off. Her mind and body were exhausted from the night's events. From the poor mother and baby dying, leaving three small, orphaned children, to Langford getting run over by a carriage. She had often thought about how dull her life was, especially during her year of mourning. Well, she would live with dull if the alternative was what had transpired tonight. She never wanted to go through such a thing again, ever.

Her head bobbed down again at the same time Langford groaned. "Where am I?"

Lilly jumped up so fast, the room spun, and she had to grab onto the chair to keep from falling. Mullens and Mrs. Lewis also startled and now stood at his bedside. "You are at Emmeline's townhome," she said quietly, willing her heartbeat to resume a normal pace.

"Why?"

"There was an accident. You don't remember?"

She watched as his brow furrowed. "No. Why is my head foggy? My body hurts everywhere. It even hurts to have my head on the pillow."

"Dr. Bailey gave you laudanum for the pain. You were pinned beneath a carriage that had lost a wheel. You have broken your leg in two places and dislocated your shoulder."

He coughed several times. "Is that all? It feels as though I broke every bone in my body."

Was he trying to make light of the situation? "Dr. Bailey said you were very lucky not to have internal injuries."

"Hurrah for me. I need to . . . you know . . . use a chamber pot." He used his good hand and pointed to the noticeable bulge between his thighs.

Heat burned up her neck to her face. He obviously hadn't noticed Mullens standing at the other side of his bed. "Mrs. Lewis and I will step outside, Mullens."

They hurried out the door and into the hallway. "It is a very good sign he is awake," Mrs. Lewis said even though her expression was one of worry.

"I hope so," Lilly replied.

Mullens came to the door after a moment. "You may come back in, my lady."

She approached Langford's bedside. "How do you feel?"

"I'm tired. My eyes don't want to stay open, which is good because if I'm sleeping, the pain will go away."

"Sleep," she whispered. "I'll watch over you."

"You don't . . ." He didn't finish. His chest rose and fell in deep, even breaths.

"My lady," Mullens began. "Go get some rest. Either Mrs. Lewis or I will stay with his lordship. We will not leave him alone for a moment."

But Lilly couldn't bring herself to leave. Though Mullins was right—it was silly for all three of them to remain. "I want to stay. You go get some rest and I will send for you if I need anything. I'm sure you will be much needed in the morning."

After she was alone, she played the head-dropping and twitching awake game. It became tiresome. The bed Langford slept in was large enough for two. If only she could lie down for just a few minutes . . . But no. She was afraid she would roll over and bump his shoulder or leg. Not to mention what a shock anyone entering the room would get finding the two of them sleeping in the same bed.

No. She would stay on the wooden chair, her behind hurting and her cloak wrapped around her for warmth.

"Lilly?"

The sound of a man calling out her name while she slept puzzled her sleepy mind. Why on earth would a man be in her room? Unless she was dreaming about Henry. But no, that wasn't his voice. The voice was similar, but it wasn't Henry. Struggling to break through the fog keeping her tethered in sleep, she managed to breach the mist and open her eyes.

"Langford." She gasped as the events of the accident played through her mind triggering her concern. She stood from the hard chair, every muscle in her body protesting. "How do you feel?"

"Horrible."

"Oh dear." Lilly took the brown vial off the bedside table knowing it was well over four hours since he'd had the laudanum since the sun was poking between the seams in the curtains. "It's time for laudanum. It will help with the pain."

"I hate the stuff," he grumbled.

"Please do as the doctor says and use it until the pain abates."

"Fine."

Lilly opened the stopper, poured a small amount onto a teaspoon careful not to spill even a drop. She leaned over Langford. "Open." Somehow he managed to take the liquid without getting any on him.

"When will the doctor be back? I have some questions for him."

"Sometime today. Meanwhile, can I get you something? Perhaps some broth or toast?"

He snorted and looked annoyed at her. "I'm injured, but I'm not an invalid. I would love some strong coffee, buttered toast, and jam. Could you put the pillows against the headboard so I may sit up?"

Sit up? Did he have any idea how much pain that would cause? She readied a pillow and watched wide-eyed and winced as he tried to use his one good arm to hoist himself up.

"Bugger all." He breathed heavily not making much head-way. "Can you assist me?"

Lilly looked at Langford's bare chest and swallowed. "In case you haven't noticed, you have no clothes on beneath the sheet."

"I bloody well know that. I don't care. I want to sit up." His brows raised. "And you've seen me naked, or have you forgotten already?"

She would ignore his snapping at her—this time. He was in a great deal of pain, and she knew it made people lash out. "How do you suppose I can help?"

"Carefully climb on the bed and straddle my hips. Do not, and I repeat *do not*, bump my bad leg. When I say go, you put your arms on either side of my waist and lift me up and forward at the same time as I use my good arm."

Lilly finally removed the cloak she'd kept wrapped around her through the night for warmth and draped it on the back of the torturous chair she'd slept on. Her backside was going to ache for days. She hitched up her skirts flashing her pantaloons to Langford, but at a time like this, there was little call for modesty. As he reminded her, she had seen him naked. And he had seen her naked as well. She kneeled on the bed and swung one leg over Langford's thighs, careful not to jostle his legs or touch him. "Tell me when you are ready." When she looked down, thinking about using his waist to aid him, she realized his arm was wrapped up and pinned to his stomach. Where on earth would she put her hands? And even if she pulled at his waist, she didn't believe it would work. She needed to get her arms beneath his arms and lift him that way. If she was even strong enough.

She lifted her eyes to his and he said, "Is there a problem?" The laudanum was affecting him as his eyes looked glazed and he slurred his words.

"I can't use your waist to lift you."

"Use my hips then."

She opened her mouth to speak twice before she closed her lips and contemplated his hips. As far as she could tell, his hips would offer even less leverage than his waist, and jostling them would only result in more pain. "I'm sliding my arms through your armpits. That's the only way it will work. I'll count to three."

When he didn't answer her, she opened her eyes and found his closed. "Langford. Are you awake?"

No answer. Just as she was about to gently climb off him, the door opened and Emmeline, Blackstone, and Caldwell entered the room.

"Lilly," Emmeline gasped, "what in heaven's name are you doing?"

"Will someone help me get off him?" she said, more than a little disgruntled.

Caldwell started to move forward. "I'll help. But I must say I'm shocked. I didn't think you were the kind of woman to take advantage of an unconscious man."

Lilly gasped.

Emmeline threw out an arm, stopping Caldwell. "You are not helping." She moved toward the bed and very carefully helped Lilly off of Langford and onto the floor.

Lilly rolled her eyes and exhaled. "He wanted help sitting up. That was all we could think of to aid him, but then he fell asleep in the middle of the attempt, since I had just given him medicine for his pain. Now, perhaps you two fine gentlemen can help him while I retreat to my room so I can die of embarrassment."

All three of them laughed. They *laughed* at her.

She huffed. "I don't see what is so funny."

"Oh, it was funny," Emmeline said. "Thankfully, it was only the three of us who entered the room. Anyway, how is he?"

The four of them stood around Langford's bed while he slept

fitfully, much as he had last night.

"He woke up once last night, and I told him what happened because he didn't remember anything. Then he awoke a short while ago, I gave him the laudanum the doctor left for him, and he fell asleep again."

"Both Caldwell and I stopped by in the middle of the night, and Mullens met with us and assured us that Edmund had awoken and was resting and the doctor had set his leg. We opted not to disturb him and went home. He didn't explain the extent of his injuries, though. What did the physician say about his leg?" Blackstone asked as he lifted the sheet exposing Langford's injured leg to his mid-thigh.

"That hopefully it will heal and not get infected. He will most likely walk with a limp."

"He's not going to like hearing that." Blackstone replaced the sheet over his leg and then lowered it to his waist. "How is his shoulder?"

"He dislocated it. The doctor put it back." Lilly didn't know exactly what that meant, but it sounded positive. "The doctor said it will heal nicely."

Blackstone's face was pale and his eyes looked worried. "He could've been killed." He then looked at Lilly and Emmeline, his brows drawn. "Emmeline mentioned the accident happened in St. Giles. I know why Langford ventures into St. Giles. He's looking for someone he once cared deeply for. But what in bloody hell were you two doing there? The place is dangerous in the daytime, but at night, it's . . ." His body shivered. "All three of you are fortunate to be alive."

CHAPTER SIXTEEN

LILLY STAYED SILENT as Emmeline explained. "We belong to a ladies' club. We help the less fortunate. Most of the time we travel there during the day, but last night a woman was in labor and needed help."

"I hope it was worth risking your lives and you helped her," Blackstone said, clearly exasperated.

Tears trickled down Lilly's face. "She died. The baby was breech and couldn't be born. They both died. Her husband had recently passed, and she left three young children."

"I'm sorry," both Caldwell and Blackstone said.

"Then what happened?" Blackstone inquired.

Lilly continued. "Apparently, the mother, Annabelle, was the daughter of a baron. The baron arrived right before we left."

Blackstone and Caldwell exchanged an intense look. "Which baron?" Blackstone asked.

"She said her father was Baron Winslow." Lilly looked at Emmeline questioningly. Why should the two men grow so somber at the name? But Emmeline looked as confused as she felt.

Blackstone looked at Langford, closed his eyes, and sighed. "Annabelle is the one Langford was looking for. I trust you to keep the information about her and her death to yourselves until Langford recovers. I don't want this to interfere with his healing.

When he is better, I will tell him."

Lilly and Emmeline exchanged wide-eyed looks.

"Who is she to him?" Emmeline asked. "I never heard her name mentioned, and I have known Langford for ten years."

"She is someone from his past. That's all I can say, as it's not my story to tell," Blackstone replied in a monotone voice. His eyes went to Langford once again.

Lilly excused herself. She needed air and she couldn't get any into her lungs—the room was suddenly closing in around her. Her chest constricted while her heart ran wild. After exiting the room, she hurried to hers, poured water from a pitcher into the basin and splashed it on her face. She breathed in and out several times, hoping to get her heart and breathing under control. What Blackstone said about Annabelle, God rest her soul, had strange things happening to her. Had Langford loved Annabelle? Blackstone made it sound as though he had. And now poor Annabelle was dead, a baron's daughter dying in the slums of London. Why? How? Except Lilly knew the how and why. Using her dying breath, Annabelle had told her, but it didn't make it any easier for Lilly to understand. How could she feel a love so deep and strong that she would leave the safety and security of her home and venture out into the world penniless, all for the love of a man?

What would a love like that feel like? Lilly splashed water on her face again and patted it dry with a cloth. She met her reflection in the mirror and didn't recognize the stranger looking back at her. She was pale, her hair a bird's nest, her clothes wrinkled, dirty, and bloody, and her eyes were sad and lost and very innocent. She'd been sheltered her entire life right up until she moved in with Emmeline. She didn't know if she could be the woman she needed to become in order to survive, a woman with real knowledge of the world around her. There were so many things she didn't know or understand. It was good she had Emmeline, Aunt Vivian, and the Ladies' Society of Mayfair members. One could never have too many friends at their side.

Not that she ever really had any friends before, but it was nice to know she did now.

She'd almost begun to consider Langford a friend, too. But after what had happened the other day with the documents he'd found, would he ever be again? Would he even still feel obligated to Henry and honor a dead man's wishes and see her settled into a happy marriage? If he chose not to, it wasn't as though Henry would know.

Regardless, for the time being, she would take care of his health and well-being. She would speak to Emmeline and find out if Langford could stay here until he was healed. It would be much easier than Lilly having to travel back and forth to his townhome, even though it was a short walk away. She would feel better being in charge of his recovery, especially with Mullens and Mrs. Lewis here to help as well.

She would simply learn to ignore her feelings for him and help him heal. If she didn't help him recover she just knew she would feel guilty, even though she had no reason to feel that way.

EDMUND'S MIND STRUGGLED through the dense fog trying to keep him trapped. He wanted to wake up, but his mind refused because when he was coherent everything hurt. He supposed it was his brain's way of keeping the pain at bay.

He had a feeling this was what being drawn and quartered felt like, right before your limbs were ripped from your body and you bled to death. Death. He did remember Lilly saying he was lucky to be alive. It didn't feel that way. What he wouldn't give to feel nothing. He may have been sleeping or unconscious when his friends were talking—he couldn't really tell—but somehow he'd heard what was said. Now his heart joined the unbearable pain slicing through his body.

Annabelle was dead.

Edmund, Quincy, Caldwell, and Fitzpatrick were young, privileged gentlemen of the ton *enjoying a London Season. At eighteen years of age and attending university, none were in the market for a wife. The Marriage Mart mamas left them alone, knowing it wasn't worth their time to fawn over them and foist their daughters on them—not yet. But that didn't mean the young friends didn't enjoy their time and quickly become rakish. Some more than others.*

Edmund enjoyed a brief liaison with a widow. Unfortunately, she became possessive of his time, and he wanted to enjoy his freedom. That was until he met Miss Annabelle Brown, daughter of a baron. She was making her come-out at the tender age of seventeen. The moment Edmund managed an introduction, he was lost in a haze of infatuation. He called on her daily. Sent flower arrangements from a hothouse several times a week. Danced with her as much as was proper. And when she was dancing in another's arms, he stood on the side seething. Quincy was worried for his friend, for he noticed Annabelle wasn't as taken with Edmund as he was with her.

That bothered Quincy, but whenever he mentioned it to Edmund, they argued, and it put a strain on their friendship. Never had Quincy thought a lady would come between them.

As the Season went on, Edmund spent more and more time at Annabelle's townhouse, monopolizing her time. Even though Edmund had begun the Season with no intention of getting married so young, he could not let Annabelle marry another, and she had many other suitors. He requested an audience with her father, the baron, and asked for his permission to propose marriage to his daughter. The baron favored Edmund. It was evident in the conversations they shared. He believed Edmund was young to marry but gave his permission nonetheless. Even without a title yet, he was an heir to a prosperous earldom.

Edmund retrieved his mother's sapphire ring, the one his father had given her when he proposed. The baron invited Edmund to dinner that night, and the three of them had a lovely dinner and retired to the drawing room after. The baron excused himself, leaving Edmund alone with Annabelle. His heart pounded inside his chest and his hands sweated at the seriousness of what he was about to do. He loved Annabelle with all his heart and had convinced himself that he was ready, that he couldn't wait to be married. As he got down on one knee and held out his mother's ring, the look on Annabelle's face, shock and disbelief—and not of a favorable sort—eviscerated his insides. Her head turned from side to side.

Edmund jumped up, blinded by the rejection. He fumbled out of the room into the hall, looking for his hat and cloak. The butler handed them to him, opened the door, and Edmund ran outside and down the street and kept going, ignoring all the stares, until he couldn't take in another breath of air, bent over, and lost the contents of his stomach in someone's bushes.

He walked the streets of London in a stupor for hours, finding his way to the docks on the banks of the Thames, which were bustling at all hours of the night, loading and unloading cargo from large and small shipping vessels.

As he stood there taking it all in, he wondered if he should jump into the Thames and drown himself, making the agony splitting his heart in two go away. He couldn't imagine going on living in such immense pain. And that didn't even take into account his mortification and embarrassment. How could he ever face Society or Annabella again without feeling like a worthless fool? He had contemplated leaving Cambridge when they married. Now he couldn't wait to get back to his studies. He would hide from the world and bury his heart so deep inside himself that it would never be found. He would never love another for as long as he lived.

A strange mixture of dream and memory buffeted Edmund as he struggled back toward consciousness. But when he finally achieved it, he regretted it immediately as immeasurable pain from his leg and shoulder bombarded him. Closing his eyes, he concentrated on breathing through the pain he felt deep inside his bones. When he believed he could ignore the pain and speak, he opened his eyes to find Blackstone and Caldwell standing at the end of his bed.

"Are you two going to gawk at me," he paused, taking in air and ignoring the pain throbbing in his shoulder and leg, "like I'm a newly painted Rembrandt?" Edmund laughed—tried to—which resembled a cough as he tried to make light of his situation.

"Ah, so you have decided to join the living and grace us with your presence." Blackstone's laissez-faire attitude didn't fool

Edmund. His features were drawn. "You do realize Rembrandt died in 1669?"

"By both of your sour looks, you'd think someone besides the esteemed painter had died."

Both his friends coughed and glanced at each other, and their worried eyes fell on him.

"Stop the pitying looks. I'm not dying. I've been run over by a carriage. It could be worse. Such as Annabelle dying in childbirth." The part of his heart that still belonged to her cried out in silent agony. The other part, resigned to living without her a long time ago, ached as though he'd lost a good friend, but nothing more. Progress. "What about her father?"

"He knows. How did you?"

"Come, Blackstone, I was under the influence of laudanum, but I heard every word you four said."

"We didn't want you to find out that way. I know how much she meant to you."

His heart lurched. "Meant is right. I got over her a long time ago. I was doing a service to the baron by searching for her whenever I could."

"Yes, well," Caldwell began, "I imagine the baron is heartbroken."

Edmund could very well imagine the baron's pain. His only child, whom he hadn't seen in over ten years, was dead after having lived in the hellish slums of London by choice. "Someone give me a dose of laudanum so I can go back to oblivion."

⊱⊱⊱⊰⊰⊰

BLACKSTONE AND CALDWELL left in the early afternoon, making Lilly promise to send word if he took a turn for the worse. Dr. Bailey came shortly after they'd left and went again after rebandaging Langford's stitches on his leg and leaving another vial of pain medicine. Lilly should have felt better after he left, but her insides were a jumbled mess. Even though Langford was under the influence of the pain medicine, he'd seemed overly distant and somber whenever he was awake, though that wasn't often or for long. Blackstone had told her that Edmund knew about Annabelle's death, and she supposed that must be what had him in such a somber mood. She left him in the care of Mullens and Mrs. Lewis as it was teatime, and she remembered suddenly that she was expecting a visit from Viscount Redford.

Dressed in a yellow muslin day dress trimmed with blue ribbon and embroidery, she made her way downstairs to the drawing room and found Emmeline and Aunt Vivian sitting beside one another on the settee entertaining the viscount. Lilly frowned. She was right on time, and the viscount was overly prompt.

He stood as she entered the room. "Lady Langford." He bowed. "How lovely you look today."

She curtsied. "How nice to see you again." She swept her hand toward a side table and a bouquet of pink roses. "The flowers are beautiful. Thank you."

A confident smile broke out on his handsome face. "Beautiful flowers for a beautiful lady."

Lilly blushed. Compliments always caused her cheeks to heat, no matter who delivered them. "Thank you again. Please sit." She took the chair beside him, separated by a small round table, and took in his appearance in black-and-tan riding clothes. He did present a handsome picture. It was a shame he didn't cause her insides to flutter—perhaps when she got to know him better.

"I hear Langford was in a terrible accident. How is he?"

The viscount genuinely appeared concerned for Langford's well-being, though she didn't believe they were well acquainted. "The doctor is hopeful he will recover if he can avoid infection and says that he is fortunate to be alive."

"No doubt. I surmise most people would die immediately after being run over and pinned beneath a carriage wheel." He paused and shook his head just a tad. "But not Langford."

"No. Not Langford," she agreed, not caring for his expression or the tone of his voice. "May I offer you tea? A biscuit?"

"No, thank you. Although, I wouldn't mind something stronger if you have it?"

It wouldn't be the first time a gentleman caller had asked for liquor. Lilly went to a sideboard across the room and splashed a healthy amount of brandy into a crystal glass.

"Here you are," she said as he took the offered drink from her hand.

"Thank you." He took a sip. "Very nice and smooth." They sat in genteel silence for a moment before he spoke again. "Lady Langford, would you care to join me for a ride in the park tomorrow afternoon?"

Her first inclination was to refuse—she felt so tired and worn after last night—but if she wanted to marry and have children some day she needed to allow men to court her. And perhaps she would feel better tomorrow. "I would like that very much."

He stood and bowed. "Until tomorrow, then."

"He seems like a fine gentleman," Aunt Vivian said once the viscount was gone. "Do we know much about his family?"

Lilly looked to Emmeline for the answer.

"His title is an old one, but I believe he came to it by a convoluted turn of events. The viscountcy belonged to a cousin whose wife birthed only daughters and who then tragically perished in a stable fire. Quite recently as I recall."

Lilly and Aunt Vivian both gasped. "How terribly sad." Lilly could only imagine the heartbreak the family was going through. She hoped Redford was being kind and generous with the deceased viscount's family, as they were at his mercy unless the cousin had been smart and set up money in trust for them, much as Henry had done for her. She would make a point of inquiring as to their well-being during their ride tomorrow.

"Emmeline, Aunt Vivian, I'm going to take my leave and visit Langford and see if he would like me to read to him. For someone used to being in the thick of his business and running the earldom, he must be bored silly."

When she swept into the room, her nose wrinkled at the smell of antiseptic and laudanum. Langford was propped up on pillows, his eyes closed, and his handsome features were soft in his sleep. His partially covered chest, sprinkled with dark chest hair, rose and fell. Seeing him relaxed in rest, looking young and handsome, had her almost wishing they could be together. Shaking her head, she tiptoed farther into the room and sat on a comfortable upholstered chair someone had brought in. She was grateful for it—she could not face spending any length of time again on the hard wooden chair as her backside still ached from spending many hours sitting in it last night and this morning.

When she realized she'd brought nothing into his room to occupy her time, having thought he'd be awake and she would read to him from one of the several books resting on the nightstand, she decided to rest her eyes for a spell. She hadn't slept much last night, and certainly not well, worrying about Langford. Henry had asked him to look after her future by helping her find a worthy husband, and she could only think he would want her to look out for his nephew now in his moment of need.

CHAPTER SEVENTEEN

THE RUSTLING OF the sheets had her eyes popping open. Langford's body flinched several times, and she knew it could be caused by the laudanum, or perhaps he was in terrible pain. Either way, he was sleeping fitfully when what he needed was a nice, calm rest. When the twitching in his body finally abated, she closed her eyes and sank into the back of the soft chair.

"You don't have to watch over me."

Her eyes flew open again. She knew he was addressing her since she'd sent Mrs. Lewis and Mullens to get something to eat and she was the only other occupant of the room. "I know I don't. But I want to. I thought perhaps you were bored and might want me to read to you."

"Maybe later. With the throbbing in my head, I'd prefer silence."

"Oh." She sighed. "I'll take my leave then." She started to rise.

"Please stay. I didn't mean it that way. I don't mind you talking to me, just not reading a book I have to pay attention to."

Lilly smiled.

"That's not what I mean either. Forgive me. Did you or Emmeline have any callers today?"

"Viscount Redford called upon me and invited me to join him

for a ride in the park tomorrow."

His heavy-lidded eyes met hers. "What was your reply?"

"I said I would like that very much." His eyes widened, then drooped again. He was still sleepy . . . or something else. Lilly gave up trying to decipher his moods, injury or no injury.

"Since he was the only name on my list you said interested you, I am not surprised you accepted his invitation." He paused and closed his eyes, his face scrunching up in what she recognized as pain.

"Let me give you laudanum."

"No. I've had enough of it. It makes my mind fuzzy, and I have trouble knowing what's real and what's not. It makes me do nothing but sleep and the dreams it causes are dark and troubled to say the least."

Lilly tucked the vials into the drawer of the side table just in case the pain turned unbearable and he changed his mind later.

"So, tell me what you think of Redford," he said, his voice soft and tired sounding.

What did she think? "He's handsome and appears affable. I only spent a small amount of time in his company at the garden party at the Devens's. Do you know much about him?"

"Not much. Just what I heard at my club when he inherited the title."

She was shocked he didn't know more about him since his name was on that list of potential suitors. "Why did you include his name on the list if you couldn't vouch for him personally?"

"He appeared taken with you."

And that was reason enough? She didn't want to talk about Redford or about herself any longer. "Tell me about Annabelle."

He shut his eyes, and a sound resembling a groan came from him. It wasn't just the sound that took her by surprise. It was the sadness that took over his features, which had her heart aching for him and his loss of the lady he once loved—and, to be honest, a bit jealous as well.

"We met during her first Season. I was eighteen and she was

seventeen. When I think back now, I was clearly too young and green to be contemplating marriage. I had barely sowed my oats. Yet I wanted her, loved her, and knew the only way I could have her was to marry her.

"I was drawn to her immediately and called upon her daily. Unfortunately, I was too immature to see the signs and warnings that she didn't have feelings for me—at least not the ones I had for her. I asked for her hand. She refused. It was as simple as that. The following day, she ran away with her father's young valet." His eyes met Lilly's, and she shivered at the longing she saw in his deep-brown eyes. "Tell me about last night."

Lilly understood what he was asking. "Emmeline introduced me to the Ladies' Society of Mayfair run by the Duchess of Greenville. We provide goods and services to the poor families living mostly in St. Giles, but we will help anyone less fortunate. Last night, the duchess asked us to assist her physician in delivering a baby. He needed help keeping her other children occupied." She paused, wiping tears from her eyes as she relived the memories. "I had been present during several births in the country when my papa was vicar. I thought I knew what to expect. It wasn't until after we arrived that we were informed the baby was breech and couldn't be delivered. The babe had already died and the mother was following. The doctor tried everything." Lilly was shocked to find her hands covering her ears. If she closed her eyes, she could hear Annabelle's screams loud and clear even now. "I'm sorry. This must be hard for you to hear."

"Please continue." His voice was barely a whisper. It sounded as though his throat was clogged with unshed tears.

"Annabelle had lost too much blood, and the doctor gave her a large dose of laudanum to make her comfortable. It wasn't long before she succumbed. Before she died, though, she told me who her father was and that her husband had died a fortnight before in a tavern brawl."

"Thank you."

"Do you still love her?" As soon as the words left her lips, she wanted to take them back. Between Annabelle's rejection, death, and his accident, hadn't he been through enough? He didn't need her adding to it by making him say painful words out loud.

"I loved the person she was before she refused my proposal. I don't know the person Annabelle became, although my heart hurts because of how she ended and for her children."

"The duchess sent Emmeline a note—her father has her children. He's going to raise them."

"That is good. Whenever I was in London, I looked for her. Not for myself. For the baron. He'd gone into a deep, dark place after she left. I felt I owed him. I felt partially responsible for her running away. In my mind, if I hadn't asked for her hand, she would have stayed home and continued to love her father's valet in secret."

"You know that isn't true. It would not have been secret for long. And if you hadn't asked for her hand, someone else would have, and the chain of events would have played out the same."

"I understand, but still . . ."

"Is there anything I can do to make you comfortable?"

"Could you tell Mullens that I would like to clean up?" He rubbed his hand on his jaw with his good arm. "And a shave. When will I be able to go home?"

"The doctor doesn't want you moved for several weeks. It's not even been two days. I'm afraid you're here for the time being." Lilly exited the room, went down the stairs and asked the butler to pass on the message to Langford's valet.

LILLY DRESSED FOR her ride in the park the following afternoon in a lovely cream-and-green day dress with a matching pelisse and a cream bonnet trimmed with pretty green ribbon. The sun hid behind white clouds and there was a chill in the air, but overall the day was pleasant enough for a ride. She waited patiently in the drawing room as the hour to see and be seen in the park arrived. Viscount Redford was prompt. He helped her into his mid-rise phaeton pulled by two horses. When they were both settled, he gave the reins a snap, and they entered the road in the direction of Hyde Park.

"It is a lovely day for a ride. Cloudy but not raining," Redford said as he handled the horses perfectly.

"Yes," Lilly replied as they passed several carriages, curricles and other phaetons, the occupants nodding in greeting.

There was a queue to enter the park, and Lilly wasn't surprised. As long as it wasn't stormy, people flocked to the park on dry days in open carriages. The ladies and gentlemen could proudly display their fancy wardrobes and hats out in the open for all to see. Lilly always thought it silly to parade in the park in front of one's peers, each hoping to outshine the next person. Though of course, on reflection, that was also what they did in the evenings when attending one event or another. And tonight they had an intimate dinner affair at the home of Mr. and Mrs. Hadley. They were close acquaintances of Aunt Vivian and no doubt she'd had a hand in the guest list.

"Do you have plans for this evening?" Lilly knew it was forward to ask, but she did anyway. She would rather be prepared if she would be spending time in his company tonight.

"Why yes. I'm attending a dinner party hosted by Mr. and Mrs. Hadley."

"What a coincidence. So am I, and the Dowager Baroness Connolly and Mrs. Fitzpatrick also."

He turned his head and smiled without showing his teeth, his silvery blue eyes taking her in. "What a pleasant surprise to know you will be in attendance. I shall hope we are seated next to one another. Perhaps I will have a word with Mrs. Hadley."

They finally entered the park, and the line of riders, carriages, and open-air vehicles traveled at a snail's pace. But at least it was preferable to stopping and starting as the jarring caused the back of Lilly's neck to ache and her stomach to dip.

"I was hoping to have a word with Langford about getting his permission to court you exclusively."

Was Lilly ready for exclusivity? "You don't need his permission, but should you prefer it, the best way to communicate with him would be by note. He is not up to visitors as of yet."

He looked at her and frowned. "I realize he is recovering from serious injuries at Mrs. Fitzpatrick's home—his accident is all anyone is talking about around town—but is it proper for a single gentleman to reside in a home with three widows? Two of which are young and of marriable age?"

His words and the way he said them annoyed her. "Why ever not? He is confined to bed and a relative—at least by marriage—to all who live there. Besides, the doctor said he cannot be moved for several weeks. When that time comes, he will go and finish his convalescence in his own residence. I will not allow him to be moved and risk him being an invalid for life because his healing leg is damaged beyond repair during an unnecessary move."

"Forgive me for interfering in family matters." He sounded sincere, but she could tell he did not like the situation.

"You are forgiven," she said as they exited the park. Several minutes later, they were pulling up to Emmeline's townhome. They had ridden the last portion of the journey in uncomfortable silence.

He assisted her down from the carriage, he raised his top hat, bowed, and said, "I look forward to seeing you tonight."

"I do as well." Lilly curtsied, picked up her skirts and entered the house when the door opened. The butler was always on duty. "Thank you, Harrison."

That evening, dressed in a cream evening dress with matching cloak, Lilly gripped her cream reticule so tight she had to force her fingers to relax as they were cramping.

"You seem tense, my dear," Aunt Vivian remarked with a disquieted look on her face.

"I do? I am, but I don't know why."

"Did your ride go well with Redford?" Emmeline asked, her

face also looking troubled.

"The weather was dry, the park was crowded, and the company was fine, I suppose. But that isn't what's troubling me."

"Then what it is?" Aunt Vivian asked as she leaned forward and patted her gloved hands.

Her insides vibrated with awareness and worry she could not explain. "I just have a strange feeling. My heart and mind are unsettled, but I cannot say about what."

"Perhaps the dinner will take your mind off whatever troubles you, and you can relax and enjoy the night," Vivian said as she leaned back against the navy, tufted squabs.

Once inside the Hadleys' lovely townhome, Lilly found herself relaxing. She conversed with the other occupants of the small dinner affair in the large drawing room as they awaited the announcement for dinner. Redford sought her out and bowed. "Lady Langford, you look positively radiant this evening. I trust you enjoyed our ride in the park this afternoon?"

"Thank you. I enjoyed the ride, the company, and the fresh air very much." Redford, the handsome gentleman that he was, looked splendid in shades of blue and cream. It was a bit much, but she'd learned from the short time of their acquaintance that he was a slave to current gentlemen's fashion. He was the epitome of a dandy.

"May I inquire on Langford's recovery?"

"He is the same as earlier today. But his spirits are high, which is very important in aiding his recuperation."

"Having never been injured, I will take your word for it."

"Since my papa was a vicar, I helped many of the village occupants during times of need and sickness. I sat at many bedsides, and I can tell you that those who kept a positive outlook healed faster than those who wallowed in self-pity or just couldn't muster enough energy to fight for their lives."

He dipped his head and looked contrite. "Forgive me. I hadn't realized you had experience with the sick and healing. Tell me, what was it like being a vicar's daughter?"

Her eyes studied his, looking for any sign of judgment, but she found none. "There were days I was kept busy helping Papa with his duties and aiding the villagers in one way or another. Other days were quiet, and I enjoyed the fresh country air."

"Do you miss it?"

Surprised by his question and his interest, she answered truthfully, "Yes. I miss my papa and the people from the village that I grew up with. Even when I married I still lived nearby. And I miss my husband and the person I was then." Melancholy gripped her chest, and she breathed deep to ease the ache. Lilly was shocked that the emotions buried beneath the surface had chosen this moment to emerge. And that a conversation with Redford, of all people, had caused it to happen.

"I'm sorry about your losses. It must be difficult for someone of your tender age to deal with."

"Yes, well, thankfully, I have Mrs. Fitzpatrick, Dowager Baroness Connolly, and Langford. They are now my family, even if only by marriage. Speaking of which, I meant to express my own condolences during our ride today on the death of your cousin and inquire about his wife and children's well-being."

"Thank you regarding my cousin. Although, to be truthful I'd only met him a few times when I was a young lad. His wife and children are safely ensconced in my country house. They do not care for London." A touch of sadness briefly took over his unusual silvery-blue eyes and then it was gone with the blink of his eyes. "Ah, the dinner gong." Redford appeared relieved at the interruption to their conversation. "May I escort you into the dining room?"

As it was an informal affair, people were flowing into the dining room in no particular order. "Yes. That would be nice." Lilly placed her hand on his arm as they strolled into the large room with a long, elaborately decorated rectangular table set for twenty. Lilly noticed she was sitting beside Redford. Was it coincidence, or had he spoken to Mrs. Hadley as he'd said he would? It didn't matter, she supposed. Directly opposite her was

Emmeline with Blackstone beside her. She was thrilled for her cousin. Perhaps this extra time together would knock some sense into the duke.

The table was set with elaborate cream, burgundy, and gold-edged china. The silverware was polished to a shine so bright and clear that Lilly knew if she picked up a spoon, she would see her reflection.

The first course was served, starting with a creamy turtle soup. It was delicious. Lilly had grown up in the country with simple food, and Henry had also enjoyed a simple diet. Since arriving in London, she had been acclimating her palate to the rich and creamy foods served at meals, but she preferred the heavy cream sauces to be served separately, which was how it was done at Emmeline's home.

As the meal progressed, dishes and courses came and went, and she found it difficult to follow the numerous conversations going on around the table. Finally, Redford stopped conversing with Blackstone across the table, which was a faux pas during formal affairs but perfectly acceptable during small gatherings such as this, and turned to her.

"Are you unwell? You have hardly touched your food."

Shocked that he'd noticed she replied, "I'm afraid I'm not very hungry this evening." She glanced around the table, her face flushed, hoping nobody else had noticed. But most everyone else was either eating or talking, and not another person around the table paid any mind to her. Even Emmeline and Blackstone appeared to have become quickly engrossed in an intimate discussion. And Aunt Vivian had the attention of an older gentleman Lilly hadn't the pleasure of being introduced to. By the pink of Aunt Vivian's cheeks, the twinkle in her eyes, and the rapt attention she gave the man, she seemed quite taken with him. And why not? Falling in love was not just for the young. Aunt Vivian was still a strikingly attractive woman at fifty-five. And Lilly knew firsthand, since having married a man in his sixties, that age didn't define a person. How wonderful would it be if

Aunt Vivian found another husband or companion to spend the rest of her years with?

While her attention had been elsewhere, the third course of delicious-looking desserts—creamy custards, jellies, confections, and fruits—was served. Lilly nibbled on fruit and a confection filled with sweet blueberry jam.

Afterward, the ladies retired to the drawing room while the gentlemen remained to have port and cigars.

Emmeline wrapped her arm through Lilly's and whispered, "Redford appears quite taken with you."

"Indeed. He is kind and considerate."

"That doesn't sound promising for the viscount."

"Whatever do you mean?"

"That is what someone might say about an acquaintance, not about a suitor. Do you feel anything for him?"

Lilly looked around and exhaled with relief that nobody was paying them any attention. "I've never been truly in love, even though I loved Henry. How do I know what to expect? How does one feel?"

Emmeline sighed. "I imagine it feels different for everyone. But for me, being in love is all-consuming. The one you love is all you think about day and night. When you least expect it, something they did makes you smile, or blush, or both. You daydream when you are meant to be doing something else. Your feet barely touch the ground. And at other times, they annoy and aggravate you so much you want to scream." She shook her head and laughed softly. "You will know. That is all I can say. Even if you fight the feelings, eventually you won't be able to."

"Yes, well, I feel nothing resembling any of that for Redford, yet." But one maddening gentleman's face did flash in her mind—Langford. But it seemed he only wanted to marry her off to someone else, anyone else. She needed to transfer her feelings for Langford to Redford. Or anyone, really. Simple. Easy.

Tell that to her heart.

"Redford is handsome, though," Emmeline whispered. "And

he is not interested in anyone else but you as far as I can tell. He is a catch, and you could do so much worse."

"He is a catch and I'm trying to give him the chance to win me over. I just need some time to get to know him better. If it doesn't work out I still have time."

"I suppose, in that respect, you are fortunate to be so young." She paused and frowned. "Me, I'm running out of time if I want to have a family. If Blackstone won't come up to snuff, I will become a lonely, childless old widow." She blinked several times fast. "If I cry, I will hate myself."

"Blackstone loves you. Anyone with vision can see it. Would you like me to nudge him along? I could pretend you have some handsome, rich new suitor to make him jealous, so he'll stop shuffling his feet."

Emmeline laughed, her hand going to her mouth to stifle it. "That might work." She paused and her face fell. "Unless he bows out of the picture all together like he did with Aiden."

"Never. It was different with Aiden—they were best friends. It would only work again if Langford or Caldwell loved you. Not if it was essentially a made-up suitor."

"True. Do not look, but Blackstone and Redford are coming this way."

"Ladies," Blackstone said with a dip of his head.

"Blackstone," Lilly said as she curtsied.

"Mrs. Fitzpatrick," Blackstone said. "If I recall, you enjoy chess. Can I convince you to play a game?"

"Why, yes. I would like that."

Lilly watched as Blackstone helped seat Emmeline at a table already set up for a chess match and then took the other seat opposite her. She squinted trying to see if she could recognize his love for Emmeline in his eyes. He was obviously guarding his emotions, because she couldn't see the usual yearning.

"Would you like to take a stroll in the gardens, or at the very least step out onto the veranda for some fresh air?" Redford asked.

"Fresh air would be lovely." She placed her hand on his forearm, and he led them out of the drawing room and down the hall.

"I have it on good authority that the library has doors opening onto a veranda and the gardens beyond."

Her first inhale of crisp, fresh night air caused her body to quiver from the chill, and she was glad she'd had the foresight to grab her cloak from the butler. "The moon is beautiful tonight with the thin, wispy clouds moving by."

"Yes. It is," Redford agreed looking intently at her. He reached out, cupping her face with both his hands and turning her to him. "But you are more beautiful than the moon and the sky." His eyes dropped to her lips, then back to her eyes. The gray of his eyes darkened to near black. "There's something I've been wanting to do since the night we met."

Her lungs refused to work as she swallowed. "There is?"

"May I kiss you?"

Words escaped her as her heart beat a fast staccato. Before she analyzed her emotions too closely, she breathed out. "Yes." She leaned forward, meeting him halfway as his soft lips made contact with hers. His kiss seemed nice. It was not the all-encompassing experience she had shared with Langford, the one where his tongue tasted her, and he devoured all she had to give. The viscount's lips tasted of port and his breath smelled faintly of smoke.

He stepped back and dropped his hands. "Thank you."

She fluttered her eyes open and found him grinning at her. "You are welcome." What did one say after being kissed? Especially one that had no effect on her at all. She wanted her head to tingle, her heart to stop, and her toes to curl. Perhaps next time if he used his tongue, which made her think. And before she could tell herself why thinking was a bad idea, she cupped his face with her hands, leaned into him and touched her lips to his. Then parted her lips and licked his with her tongue. Redford moaned, wrapped his arms around her back and thrust his tongue inside, sweeping it around and around. He didn't hesitate in deepening it even more, and Lilly had trouble keeping up, especially when his hands began to roam down her back and got close to the curve of her behind.

Gasping, she pulled away, stepped to the railing, and leaned against it, breathing heavily.

He joined her at the railing. "Forgive me."

The kiss had been nice. She was breathless, but was she breathless for the right reasons or just because she needed air? And why didn't her body tingle? Would these feelings come to her in time? Could she make them come?

"Perhaps you could escort me back to the drawing room."

CHAPTER EIGHTEEN

O N THE CARRIAGE ride home, all was quiet until Emmeline queried, "Tell me about Redford and where you two disappeared to."

Heat suffused her cheeks, and she looked at Aunt Vivian, who was thankfully sleeping. "We went out on the veranda for fresh air."

"And? Don't keep me in suspense."

"He kissed me. It was pleasant. Lips only."

Emmeline sighed. "Don't gentlemen know how to kiss?"

"Well, after he broke the kiss, I practically grabbed him and kissed him properly."

Emmeline gasped and covered up a giggle with her gloved hand. "No."

"Yes. I need to know If I have feelings for him. If I desire him. The kiss was nice until his hands drifted a bit low and I jumped away. For now, I'm going to continue enjoying his company, and hopefully, I'll develop feelings for him before he asks for my hand—if that is what he plans to do. Perhaps he is looking for a dalliance with a widow and nothing more. If that's the case, he will be sorely disappointed as I have no intention to dally with anyone."

Before the conversation could continue, they arrived home. Lilly hurried up the stairs and made her way to Langford's room to check on him before she went to bed. His door was ajar, and a candle flickered on the nightstand. Entering the room, she nodded to Mrs. Lewis who was doing some mending as she sat watch in a chair across the room, and she quietly tiptoed toward the bed, not knowing whether Edmund was asleep. If he was, she didn't want to disturb him. Standing at his bedside, she startled when she saw his eyes were wide open and watching her intently.

"Oh." She put her hand to her chest. "I thought you'd be sleeping."

"I'm not tired after sleeping almost all day. And I'm bored. Tell me about Mr. and Mrs. Hadley's dinner party."

She was surprised he'd want to hear about it and that he was actually being cordial. "Truly? You want to hear about a dinner?"

"Yes. Anything is better than spending more time alone in this room and counting the pink roses in the wall covering."

"I see. Mrs. Lewis," she said, turning to the older woman, "I will sit with Langford for a spell if you would like some fresh air."

"Thank you, my lady, but it's not necessary. I only arrived a few minutes ago and relieved Mr. Mullens."

Lilly nodded and sank into the comfortable chair beside his bed and adjusted her skirts. "Well, there were twenty for dinner. Do you want to know everyone who was in attendance?"

"Good lord, no."

"Well, Blackstone was there in any case and sat beside Emmeline for dinner, and they played chess afterward."

"How nice. Did he finally profess his undying love for her?"

"Not that I saw. Perhaps soon." She clasped her hands together on her lap, suddenly nervous. "I sat beside Redford for dinner, and we went out on the veranda for fresh air."

"Was it cold out?"

"Yes, there was a chill to the air, but the bright moon and the cloud formations were beautiful."

"Did he finally kiss you?" His voice had dropped several octaves and seemed gruff.

So he wasn't as unaffected about her and Redford as he made

it seem. "He did."

His head turned and he pierced her with his eyes. Eyes that looked angry, sad, and curious at the same time. "How was it?"

She humphed loudly, coughed, and shook her head. "I'm not telling you."

"Why not?" His lips curved up into a grin, and his eyes shone with mischief.

"You don't really want to know, do you?" Surely he was jesting.

Now he coughed. "No."

"Good. Because I'm not telling you." She rose. "Goodnight, Langford."

As she shuffled her tired feet toward the door, she heard his deep voice say, "Goodnight, Lilly." Her breath caught in her throat at hearing him use her given name.

⟫⟫⟩⟨⟨⟪⟪

WHEN DAISY KNOCKED and entered her room the following day, Lilly buried her head beneath the covers. "Surely it cannot be morning already."

"Yes, my lady. It is half nine," she replied as she swung open the curtains, letting in light. "What dress would you like to wear today?"

Lilly knew the viscount would be calling on her, so she should put on her most flattering day dress. "The mint green one, as it will complement my eyes nicely."

After she was dressed and Daisy had confined her hair to a neat coil, she made her way to the morning room and found Emmeline and Aunt Vivian breaking their fast.

"Good morning," Lilly said as she took a plate and studied the offerings on the sideboard.

"Good morning, my dear," Aunt Vivian replied as she rose from her chair at the table. "I'm off to visit the Marchioness of

Rutherford this morning. I received word that the marquess died early this morning after a fall down the stairs. The young dear must be beside herself with grief."

"Please give her my condolences," Lilly said, her heart hurting for the marchioness. Letitia was in her mid-twenties. She was the daughter of one of Aunt Vivian's dearest friends, Mrs. Cambridge. Letitia had married the marquess, who was thirty years her senior, during her second Season. Lilly wondered if their match had been at all like hers and Henry's, though it couldn't be entirely similar. Letitia had birthed a baby boy not six months ago.

"Yes," Emmeline added, "please give her my condolences as well. Lilly and I will pay our respects tomorrow."

Lilly sat at the table, draped the cloth napkin on her lap and took a bite of her toast with jam. "Poor Letitia. To be widowed so young and with a baby."

"Yes. Well," Emmeline said with sadness in her eyes, "we both know what that is like. Except neither of us has a baby to care for and love."

"Perhaps when she is up to it, we can introduce her to the Ladies' Society of Mayfair."

"That is an excellent idea," Emmeline said.

After breakfast, Lilly thought to check on Langford and tell him of the marquess, but when she approached his door, she heard masculine voices coming from within, voices she recognized as Blackstone and Caldwell. Instead of interrupting, she backed away. She would visit Langford later in the day.

LILLY'S MIND WANDERED to Letitia several times during the day, and it brought back her own pain and anguish from Henry's death. She sat now in the drawing room beside Emmeline on the settee, awaiting Redford's visit. A tea tray sat on the coffee table, waiting to be served. "Did you know Blackstone and Caldwell visited Langford right after we had breakfast?"

"No, I didn't. It is amazing what goes on in my own home that I'm unaware of."

"I'm sorry. Do you think he'll come back to call on you?"

Emmeline's answer was a long time coming. "I don't know. He said nothing about it last evening. Besides, if he wanted my company, he could've sought me out when he was here earlier. I'm tired of saying this, but I think I may need to look elsewhere for a husband and soon."

Lilly placed her hand on Emmeline's, which was on her lap. "I hope not. Perhaps I could speak to him—"

"No," Emmeline said quickly. "No. If it is meant to be, it will be."

Harrison entered the room. "Viscount Redford."

Redford swept into the room, clutching his hat and bowing. "Ladies."

"Please have a seat," Lilly said, indicating the chair facing her.

After sitting down, he said, "Clouds are coming in. I think it's going to rain soon."

Lilly's lips curved up into a smile. Perhaps someday soon, another drawing room topic would replace the weather. It was so silly and tedious it actually amused her. "May I pour you tea? Or would you prefer brandy?"

He met her with a wide smile. "You know me so well already, Lady Langford. Brandy, please, if it's no bother."

"No bother at all." She made her way to the sideboard and splashed the amber liquid from the decanter into a cut crystal glass, filling it one-third of the way. She made her way to him and held out the glass.

"Thank you. You are most kind."

Lilly perched herself on the edge of the settee and poured tea for both her and Emmeline, who looked sad and lost in thought. Pretending to sip her tea, Lilly studied Redford over the rim of her teacup. He was handsome, well-dressed, and had impeccable manners. He had a pleasant personality and always treated her with kindness. His strange eyes were something she would have to get used to, though. They were such an unusual light shade of blue, which made it hard for her to get a sense of what he was feeling. She shook herself mentally. She was being silly picking on his eyes when the rest of him appeared nearly perfect.

After half an hour of light conversation, Redford stood to take his leave. "I'm traveling to my country estate tomorrow. I could be gone several weeks. When I return, I hope we can pick up where we are today."

"Yes. Of course," Lilly said.

"I will send word when am back in town. Good day, ladies." He bowed and exited the room.

Lilly found herself sinking into the settee once he'd exited the room and sighing loudly. "What will I do while he is gone? It's not going to solve how I feel about him if I can't see him."

"You can take all the time you need to develop feelings for Redford. You are in control this time. You choose who and when you marry. You are so lucky in that respect, as am I."

"You are correct. Perhaps my heart will grow fonder for Redford during his absence."

CHAPTER NINETEEN

EMMELINE, LILLY, AND Aunt Vivian visited the widow Rutherford after breakfast the following day. The drawing room was full of people paying their respects. Lilly's throat scorched in pain as she remembered the days after Henry's death and how an endless stream of people from the village came by with their condolences. She'd never felt so alone in those days, even though she was surrounded by people. Looking at Letitia, her face pale, her eyes swollen, no doubt from crying and lack of sleep, Lilly wished she could take all her anguish and pain from her loss away. However she knew from experience it would take a long time before she felt even half herself again. Fortunately for her, she had a baby boy to give her love to and to occupy her time.

When they returned home several hours later, Harrison greeted them at the door.

"The doctor is here, Lady Langford. He asked if you would come to the earl's chamber when you returned."

Lilly's stomach plummeted. "Is the earl feeling worse?"

Harrison looked concerned. "Best to speak to the doctor."

Lilly removed her pelisse and bonnet and handed them to the butler. Ignoring Aunt Vivian and Emmeline's worried looks, she picked up her skirts and hurried up the stairs, a knot of worry eating at her insides. The door to Langford's room was slightly ajar, and before she entered, she listened and peered through the opening. Langford seemed to be moaning while the doctor was trying to soothe him with words and his hands on his chest.

"What has happened to Lord Langford?" Lilly demanded as she entered the room, making eye contact with a troubled-looking Mrs. Lewis and Mullens hovering to one side as she made her way directly to his bedside. She was afraid to look too closely at Langford. Afraid of what she would see.

"He has developed a fever, Lady Langford. His leg is infected. I removed the splint and stitches, drained the puss, and cleaned and rebandaged the wound. His leg is swollen, hard, and hot to the touch, which is not ideal. I will come back daily to monitor his progress. Meanwhile, the best thing for him is to sleep so his body can fight off the infection. He must get his dose of laudanum every four hours. I gave the cook a recipe for a tea that he must drink every four hours as well. You must force it down his throat if he won't take it willingly—it should help fight the fever. And I mixed up a poultice for his wound that I will replace daily."

"Is there a risk to his leg?"

"Yes. If the infection spreads throughout his entire leg, I fear it will need to be amputated in order to save his life."

By then, Emmeline and Aunt Vivian had joined Lilly in Langford's room, worried expressions on their faces.

When the doctor turned to them, he tried to look optimistic. "Let us pray it doesn't come to that. He is young and strong, and I believe he can fight this. Meanwhile, I would prefer someone stay with him at all times."

"He will never be alone," Vivian said before anyone could speak.

"I will be back in the morning unless I receive word he's taken a turn for the worse."

Five sets of eyes followed the doctor as he left the room. Once the doctor left, the same sets of eyes made their way to Langford. "I'll stay with him now," Lilly said as she stood beside him, watching his body tremble with chills and listening to the moans escaping his lips.

"I will return in an hour, my lady," Mullens said, his face drawn and pale.

"If you must, but I'm not leaving his side until the fever is gone."

When she was alone, she bathed his forehead with a cool cloth. It seemed a contradiction. His body shook with chills while his skin burned up from fever. But she knew from experience a cool cloth helped ease the fever. If his body got too hot, he could die. She sobbed out loud. If she had to, she would stay at his bedside every minute of every day until he was well. She could not let him die. She wouldn't survive burying another family member she . . . cared for.

His moans tore through her heart. Lilly rewet the cloth and bathed not just his face but his neck and what little of his chest was exposed due to his bandaged arm and shoulder. His uninjured leg found purchase and managed to drag the sheet and blanket down to his thighs. She looked away from his soft manhood, feeling as if she was invading his privacy. She covered him up to the waist and continued to bathe him, hoping and praying to bring his fever down.

A knock on the door startled her. "Come in."

"My lady, I have brought the special tea the doctor asked the cook to make," Mrs. Peterson, Emmeline's housekeeper, said as she put the cup and saucer on the night table. "I also brought Mr. Mullens, knowing you would need help sitting his lordship up."

"Thank you."

"Mullens," Lilly put the cloth down in the basin, "can you get him propped up on the pillows?"

"Yes."

Between Lilly, Mrs. Peterson, and Mullens, they maneuvered his body up to a partially seated position—enough that Lilly believed she could get him to take the tea, which the housekeeper handed her with a cloth for any spills.

"Mullens, can you open his mouth for me?"

"Yes, my lady."

Langford fought his valet, his head lolling from side to side. Finally, Mullens managed to open his mouth, and Lilly poured some of the vile-smelling liquid in. Mullens immediately closed his mouth, and Langford made gaging and choking sounds when he was forced to swallow. When they subsided, they repeated the process several times until the tea was gone.

Exhausted physically and mentally, Lilly was relieved when she and Langford were alone again. She collapsed into the chair, leaning forward, watching his every twitch, her ears straining to hear every moan or whimper, every breath he took. She was so afraid to close her eyes and miss any sign of distress. Her body trembled from anxiety, her stomach churned, and her head throbbed.

This went on all day. As the sun set, she went around the room lighting candles, afraid that if there was not enough light, she would miss any signs of trouble. She refused to let him die or his health deteriorate. Determined to break his fever and keep him comfortable, she spooned laudanum into his mouth every four hours. Every hour Mullens brought fresh, cool water so she could continue bathing him. When his sheets needed changing, Mullens, along with several footmen, oversaw replacing them.

What she was doing for him was for a wife or mother to do, not an unmarried widow who'd only seen a naked man once before. But even as exhausted as she was, she didn't want to turn over her watch to anyone else. Somehow, this felt like her task, her responsibility, and she was afraid to leave his side, afraid that if she left, something horrible would happen. Her mind knew that her being with him as opposed to someone else had no influence over his recovery, but her heart wouldn't believe it.

"Lilly," Aunt Vivian's soft voice traveled through the quiet darkness. "You need rest. We don't want you falling ill from exhaustion. Please go to bed. I will take care of Langford as if he were my own son."

She sighed, fighting with herself, knowing Aunt Vivian spoke the truth. Inhaling and exhaling deeply, she pushed herself to stand and stretched, easing her tired, sore muscles. "Thank you. I know you'll take good care of him. In an hour, he is due for laudanum and his special tea." She wiped stray strands of hair from her eyes. "Mullens will help you along with Mrs. Peterson and Mrs. Lewis."

Lilly shuffled her exhausted body out the door. If Aunt Vivian said anything in reply, she didn't hear it. When she reached her bed, she didn't bother with removing her clothes. She climbed on top of the counterpane and fell into a sleep worthy of the dead.

When she opened her eyes after a dreamless sleep, she climbed off the bed and shuffled to a window and threw the curtains open. A miserable drizzly day greeted her. While she stood there it took several moments for her to remember why her mind was foggy and her body ached.

⇥⇥⇥⇥⇤⇤⇤⇤

TWO DAYS LATER, Lilly awoke again with the same body pains and fuzzy mind from more long hours spent caring for Langford. She rang for her maid.

"My lady," Daisy said as she entered the room with a bucket of warm water that she poured into a basin. "Let's get you cleaned up so you can go see Lord Langford."

"Have you heard anything? Has he improved?"

"I'm afraid not. Baroness Connolly, Mrs. Lewis, and Mr. Mullens are with him."

"Please help me get ready. Any day dress will do."

After Lilly was undressed, washed up, redressed, and her hair done up, she hurried out the door, making her way to Langford's room. Rushing through the door, she whispered, "Is he better?"

Aunt Vivian's frown answered her question, and her heart dropped.

"Dr. Bailey just left. He re-dressed his wound and resplinted his leg, saying the good news is that the infection hasn't spread up the leg, which is promising. We just need to get the fever to break. He had tea and laudanum a half hour ago."

"Thank you."

Aunt Vivian made her way to the door. Before she exited, she turned and said, "If you need me, you ring for me. The earl's sickbed is no place for a young lady such as yourself."

Warmth kissed her cheeks. "I'm afraid it's too late for that."

"Indeed, I figured as much. He will be furious when he finds out you have been nursing him during his sickest hours."

No doubt he would be, but she couldn't leave him. She'd forgotten about her anger with him for accusing her of lying to him and for that ridiculous list of potential suitors. She could be angry with him again later when he was well.

Once she was alone with Langford, she bathed his flushed, hot face, neck, and chest. He didn't protest, and she didn't know if that was a good sign or bad that his body didn't react to the cool water. One change she did notice was that his breathing seemed less labored, more even and steady. Instead of moaning in his sleep, he was muttering words she couldn't quite make out. All this gave her heart a bit of hope that he was on the mend.

Later that morning, Blackstone and Caldwell visited. "How is he?" Blackstone asked. For someone who was usually impeccably put together, he was looking quite worried and disheveled.

"Yes, is he any better?" Caldwell asked, his own appearance not faring any better than Blackstone's.

"I think he may be a bit better than yesterday and last night. The doctor was pleased the infection hadn't spread, which is positive news."

Blackstone went to Langford's bedside and lifted the sheet and blanket, frowning as he studied his injured leg. "I can't see anything because of the bandages. If his fever would break, I'd feel more optimistic."

"Me too," Caldwell agreed.

"I see improvement from yesterday," Lilly told them.

"We can sit with him if you would like a respite. Go have tea and something to eat. He'll be fine with us."

"I would appreciate that." Lilly had come right to his room after dressing this morning, skipping breakfast, and at the mention of food, her stomach growled. "I'll be back shortly." She made her way downstairs to the morning room, hoping there was something left of breakfast, but the room had been cleared away of every last crumb. Making her way to the drawing room, Lilly found Emmeline sitting by herself. "I'm going to ring for tea. Will you join me?"

"Pardon?" Emmeline appeared lost in thought. She blinked her eyes several times. "Never mind, I heard you. Yes, tea would be lovely."

"What has you out of sorts?" Lilly inquired as she pulled the bell for a servant.

"Blackstone came and spoke with me before he went up to visit Langford."

"It is good he made a point to seek you out today."

"Yes. Indeed it is." Emmeline paused. "He invited me to the theater tonight."

"That is wonderful news." Lilly had never been to see a play herself, but it sounded like great fun. Perhaps someday.

"It is. With you and Mother seeing to Langford, it will be just the two of us." She rose and paced the room back and forth several times before she stopped. "I'm nervous to be alone with him." She threw her arms out. "This is my dream come true, so what is wrong with me?"

Lilly tried to be encouraging. "You love him. You have waited six years for him. Of course, you are nervous. Anyone would be. And there is absolutely nothing wrong with you besides being a woman in love and hoping for a future with the man of your nightly dreams."

Emmeline's mouth curved up into a knowing smile. "My nightly dreams do indeed involve Blackstone and me together in wedded bliss."

Lilly pondered the words *wedded bliss*. Hopefully, she would experience such a thing one day. "Conquer your fears. Be brave, be assertive, and pursue your duke."

Emmeline smiled wider. "You make it sound so easy."

"With you and Blackstone, it may be that easy since you both already love one another. You just need to find out what is preventing him from committing himself to you, and help him overcome it. Until he does, I fear you both will be miserable."

"How did you get to be so wise in affairs of the heart at your age?" Emmeline queried. "And never even having been in love."

In love? Lilly wanted to be in love, but Emmeline was right—she hadn't been yet. But that didn't mean she couldn't recognize it in others and help them if she could. "I'm not wise, just observant. And your love is easy to see."

She frowned and became lost in her own thoughts pertaining to that elusive emotion. What would it feel like? Would she recognize it if and when it happened to her? What she felt for Langford was strong, but was it love? And what about Redford? Unfortunately, he didn't strike anything resembling love into her heart—at least not yet—which was too bad. On the surface he was perfect for her, if a tad boring. But sometimes boring was good. He wasn't out at his clubs or the gaming hells throwing his money away. Though a niggling feeling unfurled inside her stomach. How did she really know he wasn't doing just that?

Enough thinking about Redford. "What shall you wear tonight?"

A smile lit up Emmeline's face. Her cheeks pinked, and her eyes sparkled. She was getting excited about the theater with Blackstone. "I was thinking of the new ice-blue silk gown from Madam Serena. She outdid herself on it. I don't think I've ever seen anything so beautiful, with the unadorned silk bodice and the flowing skirt of delicate lace overlay. The matching cloak and gloves are just as beautiful. And when the light catches the silk and lace it shimmers."

"He will forget his name when he sees you. With your dark hair and blue eyes, every lady in attendance will envy you both for your looks and for being on the duke's arm."

"It's settled. I'm no longer nervous. I'm terrified."

After partaking in two cups of tea and an equal number of biscuits, Lilly made her way up the sweeping staircase to Langford's temporary room. Her eyes widened in shock when she saw Langford sitting up, his eyes open and listening intently to something Caldwell was saying. She swayed on her feet as relief flooded her body. "You are awake."

"Lilly," when he spoke, Langford's voice sounded hoarse and weak, but it was the best sound she'd heard in days.

Tentatively, she approached his bedside. Why she was suddenly nervous was beyond her. As she studied him, she noticed several things. The redness on his face was gone. His brown eyes, though not fully aware, were no longer hazy from fever. His dry lips were curved up into a grin, and she found herself smiling back. "It is good to see you alert. How are you feeling?"

"I was just explaining to these two that I feel as though I was run over by a coach. And then I remembered that is exactly what happened." He paused and ran the hand of his good arm through his disheveled hair. "I feel lucky to be alive. Devastated for Baron Winslow that Annabelle is dead. And if I can ignore the pain in my head, I'm angry that you and Emmeline traveled into St. Giles . . . and at night no less."

"We already discussed this."

"Please let me finish before I fall asleep, which is going to happen any moment. I understand about your charity, but not about the fact that you are venturing into the back slums when it is dangerous on so many levels. And I would like to discuss it at some length when I've recovered more."

Lilly wanted to protest, but his eyes drifted closed and she knew the exertion of talking had depleted his energy.

"We will take our leave, Lady Langford. I will rest easy knowing he is in your capable hands." Blackstone dipped his head. "Thank you. I am forever in your debt."

"My thanks as well, Countess," Caldwell said as he bowed. "You have brought our friend back from the brink of death."

CHAPTER TWENTY

AFTER THEY LEFT, Lilly sat by Langford's bed and pondered what his friends had said. She didn't feel any responsibility for saving his life. Dr. Bailey's medical care and Langford's will to live had made the real difference in his recovery. As well as the help from Aunt Vivian, Mullens, Mrs. Lewis, and Mrs. Peterson. She had done very little besides sit at his bedside and pray. And pray she had, because it had all seemed out of anyone's hands once the fever set in. Her insides eased with relief as she curled up into the chair and closed her eyes. Her body relaxed, her eyelids fluttered closed, and her breathing slowed as she drifted into a safe, warm, soothing place.

Her dreams were vivid. More vivid and real than her usual dreams. She watched the scenes unfold as an observer from high above, not from within her body.

She resided at Langford Manor in Kent. The air was warm and fresh, scented with lavender from the fields surrounding the large home. Her brows furrowed thoughtfully. When she had lived here previously, there were no lavender fields. Had Edmund planted them? Did he know how much she loved the color and scent of lavender?

The two of them together appeared happy and very much a couple. A married couple. Her eyes squinted, and she gasped when she noticed her belly heavy with child. And then she was in labor with Dr. Bailey standing by her feet, looking sad and worried. His lips were moving, but his words were garbled. He was shaking his head as pain tore through her body, ripping her in two. A scream resonated from deep in her throat and rose up, tearing through her lips and rattling the windowpanes.

"Lilly," Langford's worried voice pulled her from her dream.

"Yes. I'm here." Her voice was still muzzy from sleep.

"You were dreaming."

She blinked open her eyes and met his concerned ones as they studied her intently. "I was."

"You had a smile on your face. It must have been a pleasant dream. But then something happened and you cried out."

"I'm sorry. I didn't mean to disturb you." Her heart pounded so loudly inside her chest that she could count the beats in her ears. She inhaled and exhaled, trying to calm her heart and settle her nerves. She didn't remember the particulars of her dream anymore, although she could recall the warm loving feel at the beginning of it. In the end, all she remembered was pain lancing her body and then darkness. She shivered and hugged herself.

"Are you cold?"

"No. I was thinking about my dream."

"Tell me about it?"

"I can't. All I remember is that it began happily, but it changed and then it was sadness and pain and then nothing but darkness."

"I dreamed strange dreams the past few nights," Langford said. "I was lost in a torrential thunderstorm. The winds were howling, sending the rain sideways, and I didn't recognize my surroundings. When the lightning flashed, it was so vivid it blinded me." The dream still plagued him even now.

During the tumultuous storm, a woman called his name. Ignoring the rain and wind battering his body, he followed the sound of the voice. Several times he tripped on rocks and slipped in the mud covering the saturated ground. The closer he got to the voice, the more his heart pounded inside his chest. She sounded distraught and he knew, without a doubt, she was hurt or in terrible danger. As the woman cried out his name, he struggled to distinguish who it was, Annabella or Lilly. But Annabelle was dead, he knew it. He fought through the storm until he found the person he sought hovering in the middle of a cluster of small trees. Her arms were wrapped around her bent knees, with her head resting on them. Her drenched clothing clung to her body, and her soaking wet hair stuck to her face—a face he so desperately wanted to see.

"You were calling my name. Are you hurt?"

"Edmund," she said with a sigh.

He gasped when he recognized the voice as Annabelle's. Except he saw Lilly's beautiful and frightened face, looking up at him through rain-soaked lashes.

"Edmund?" she said with worry. "You look like you are seeing a ghost."

He shook his head to clear his mind. When he dared to look at Lilly again, his body relaxed as her face stared at him. "Lilly, what are you doing here?"

"I went for a walk and got lost," Lilly replied, now in her own voice.

He held out his hand. "Let me take you home."

"Langford, are you feeling ill?"

Hearing Lilly's voice—her true voice—tumbled him out of his remembrance of his dream.

"I feel fine." He needed to change the subject. "Now, please tell me more about you, Emmeline, and the Ladies' Society of Mayfair."

She blanched. Clearly, this was something she didn't want to speak about, but he was determined. He owed her his life, but he didn't want to ever have to repay the favor in kind. He needed to try to persuade her from traveling into the rookeries of London again. The danger was everywhere, and he shuddered to consider could happen if two well-bred young ladies were kidnapped. They could be sold to a bawdy house and never be seen again, most likely dying at the hands of a customer or from disease. The image his mind conjured up rocked him to his core.

"Are you positive you feel fine? Your complexion is pale and your body is trembling," Lilly asked, her brows furrowed with worry.

"Yes. I'm fine. I was thinking about what could happen to you and Emmeline if you fell into the hands of the wrong person while in St. Giles. Please promise me you will not go there or any unsavory place again."

She closed her eyes and took several breaths before her eyelids fluttered open. "I can't promise you we will never travel into the rookeries. But I promise you we will be careful and never take unnecessary risks. I can tell the duchess that we can no longer travel at night." She looked him right in the eye and batted her lashes. "Will that do?"

Truly? Did she think he would be appeased with that answer or be swayed by the fluttering of her long, thick lashes? She didn't know him well if she thought that was all it would take for him to leave the matter alone. Perhaps for something trivial, but not when her safety was at stake.

"Langford," she said. "These people rely on us. Perhaps you can accompany us and protect us when you recover."

"Capital idea." He huffed. "Except it will be some time before I'm ready for that duty."

"Mayhap you could ask Blackstone or Caldwell to escort us. We don't normally go but once a fortnight."

"I will inquire as to whether they would be willing to escort you both."

"Blackstone is taking Emmeline to the theater tonight."

"Yes. He told me. It's about bloody time, if you'll pardon me for saying so."

She laughed and it was the most beautiful sound. "You have it correct."

"Is Redford accompanying you to the theater as well?" He refused to acknowledge the pit in his stomach as he awaited her answer. After all, this courtship with Redford was partly his idea. He'd rejected her after he'd found those papers and had felt betrayed. Though nearly dying had him thinking more clearly about their situation. He'd been an arse and needed to remedy it. When he made a full recovery things would change.

"No. He has traveled to his country estate."

"I see."

"Besides, you need me."

His cock stirred for the first time since his injury. "That brings to mind who was looking after me while I was unconscious, fighting infection and fever. From what I understand, it was several long days." He could not imagine the dowager baroness letting Lilly care for him in his state of undress, never mind when his body had to perform certain functions . . . Christ, he couldn't even let his mind ponder it. It was too mortifying. But he knew the answer to his unspoken question by the look on her face and the blush reddening her cheeks.

"Aunt Vivian, Mrs. Lewis, Mullens, and I took turns." She looked down at her hands on her lap, twisting her fingers together. "Don't worry, we took good care of you. And if your bedding needed changing, Mullens and several footmen took care of it."

He groaned. "If I get sick again, I don't want you anywhere near my bedside."

She looked at him with hurt in her eyes. He didn't mean it the way it sounded. But the thought of her witnessing his body's weaknesses, unable to do anything for himself any more than a newborn baby could, shamed him.

Before he could apologize, she hurried from the room, leaving him with his guilt for snapping at her.

LILLY DIDN'T KNOW what to think of Langford's hurtful words. Perhaps she'd overreacted by leaving so abruptly. After all, he wasn't feeling well, and she knew people were peevish when not at their best. Still, he could have been grateful for her help. She knocked on Aunt Vivian's door and when she heard her voice say, "Enter," she opened the door and stepped inside. "I'm sorry to bother you, but Langford seems annoyed that I was part of overseeing his care when he was fevered. Do you mind checking on him today with Mullens and Mrs. Lewis?"

"Not at all, my dear."

After that, the day crawled by for Lilly. She spent time in the library reading, but her mind refused to understand anything her eyes read. She strolled through the gardens, but all the usually lovely smells coming from the roses and flowers seemed wrong. They mixed together to form one potent scent that overwhelmed her, turning her stomach against her. Hurrying from the garden, she sought refuge in her room, lounging on the chaise longue and staring into the empty fireplace. No matter that she told herself Langford didn't mean his hurtful words, they pained her heart. Did he not understand that he could have died? And if he had died and she wasn't taking care of him, she would never have been able to forgive herself.

She cared for him. More than she should and more than she wanted to.

Two days after Langford's fever broke, against Dr. Bailey's advisement, Mrs. Lewis and Mullens took him home. He would spend the remainder of his convalescence in his townhouse with all his household taking care of him, and Emmeline's house became suddenly too silent after he left. Lilly found herself wandering the halls with too much free time on her hands. Looking after Langford had given her purpose and something to do during the day. Yes, she'd admit she had been exhausted when he was there; however, taking care of him made her sleep-deprived state worth it.

Weeks went by with only brief notes daily from either Mullens or Mrs. Lewis. Langford's recovery was going well. Moving had done him no lasting damage, there was no more sign of infection, and his leg was healing well. Lilly tried not to be disappointed he didn't write her himself. She also never received a missive from Redford during that time, which made her think that both men had forgotten her. In the evenings, she and Emmeline resumed their regular attendance of social functions.

Emmeline seemed to enjoy herself, but Lilly's heart wasn't in it.

⇒⟫⟪⇐

EDMUND HAD BEEN home for a month and sat in the library with his injured leg resting on a footstool, where he spent much of his time anymore. The leg still pained him when he moved it or walked—with the aid of a cane—but it was healing and getting stronger every day.

Howard, his butler, entered the room, followed by a visitor. "The Duke of Blackstone, my lord."

"Thank you, Howard. Before you leave, please pour brandy for His Grace and myself." Edmund indicated the chair beside his and Andrew sat down.

"Do you realize I have been visiting daily since you returned home and Howard still feels he needs to announce me? And you still ask him to pour us brandy when I'm perfectly capable of pouring."

Edmund studied Blackstone and frowned. "Why the sour mood?"

"I don't know. I woke up this way." He took the glass that Howard offered and downed the contents in one gulp. "Thank you, Howard. Another, please."

Edmund sipped his brandy. He had to be careful not to get tipsy and slip and fall and reinjure his leg. Dr. Bailey had exclaimed just that morning that the bones were healing nicely, but one fall could set him back on his recovery or damage his leg more permanently than it already was.

Blackstone took the refilled glass and sipped this time. "When do you think you'll be able to get out and about around town?"

"Dr. Bailey says soon, but I'm in no hurry."

"All right." Blackstone looked at him with narrowed eyes seeking answers. "Are you going to tell me what happened between Lilly and you?"

"No."

"Why not?"

"Because it's personal and embarrassing. What about you and Emmeline? How is the courtship going?"

Blackstone snorted. "It is not a courtship. I fear we are mostly at odds with each other these days. But I'm hoping to remedy that in time. Are you ever going to forgive Lilly for the papers you found which Lilly didn't create? Your uncle only did what he thought he needed to do to protect her. I'm glad he did and wish other husbands would be so forthright."

"I hired a Bow Street Runner to look into Redford," Edmund said, changing the subject.

Blackstone looked at him, one brow quirked. "And why is that?"

"Call it intuition." He combed his fingers through his hair.

"There is something off about him. I'm glad you did," Blackstone said.

He sighed. "I've only been in the man's company a few times before my accident. But nothing he said or did rang true with me. I never should have suggested him to her. I need to know Lilly will be safe and happy if he proposes and she accepts."

"Do you think he will propose?"

"I know he will. He wrote to me asking for my blessing."

"And did you give it?"

"No. I told him I would think on it." He paused and sighed. "I can't give an answer until I see the runner's report."

Blackstone stood and placed his glass on a tray on the sideboard. "Is there anything you need before I leave?"

"No."

CHAPTER TWENTY-ONE

REDFORD ARRIVED BACK in town a month and a half after he'd left for his estate and called upon Lilly. She tried to be excited by his visit, but she couldn't rally her emotions. He'd never sent word to her the entire time he was gone, and given the length of time he'd been away, she'd come to believe he wasn't interested in her anymore. So when a large bouquet of flowers arrived early one morning with a card apologizing for his absence and begging her forgiveness, she honestly didn't know how she felt. And she had to remind herself that she had planned to give Redford time to court her. Now that he was back, it was time for her to understand how she felt about him and his pursuit.

Aunt Vivian and Emmeline both begged off afternoon tea and Lilly found herself entertaining Redford alone. With the door open, of course. She was still not entirely comfortable with the man. After all the time that had gone by, they were back to being near strangers.

Redford joined her on the settee, and she tried not to fidget nervously. "Did you have a nice visit to your estate?" she asked.

"Yes. Thank you for asking. I must apologize for the length of time I've been away. The scope of things that needed my attention was larger than I initially thought. I did accomplish much of what I set out to do, which was good." He paused. "Meanwhile, I was hoping to escort you to the Greenville ball at

Vauxhall Gardens tomorrow evening. I traveled hard so I would get home in time. I am very much looking forward to it."

"As am I." Lilly was very excited to attend.

"May I escort you?"

"Yes."

"I hope you don't mind me asking, but is Langford still recovering here?"

She had the feeling he had wanted to ask her this when he'd first entered the room but had exercised his patience and waited. She decided she would answer him, even though it was not really any business of his. "No. He left shortly after you traveled to the country." She refused to acknowledge the pain in her chest at the admission. She'd not heard a single word from Langford since he'd left, though thanks to Mullens, she knew he had recently begun walking with a cane to get his strength back. She should be thankful he'd left because if he were still around, she wouldn't be able to think about Redford, and she needed to.

He turned on the settee to face her and took her hands. His thumbs rubbed over the backs of her hands, and she tried to ignore her body tensing tighter than a violin's strings. "I think it is time you called me Peter. May I call you Lilly?"

She formed the word yes, but nothing came out, so she nodded. Hoping to distract him, she pulled her hands away and picked up the teapot. "Care for tea?"

He chuckled. "No. Am I making you nervous?"

"No. Why would you think so?"

"Because your hands are shaking, rattling the cover to the pot."

"Oh." Lilly placed the teapot on the tray and thought it was best not to pour herself any because Redford . . . Peter was correct. Her hands were shaking, as was the rest of her body. He seemed different today; he was more attentive and forward with his touch than he had been during other morning calls. Though perhaps her recollection of their time together wasn't as clear as it could have been. After all, it had been six weeks since she'd seen him last.

"I have something to ask you," he said as he tugged her hands into his once again. His lips curved into a smile and his eyes stared at her intently. "I know this may seem sudden, but I knew the moment I met you that you were the one for me, and I have come to love you." He paused and took a deep breath. "Lilly, will you marry me and make me the happiest gentleman alive?"

If she had been holding a teacup, it would have shattered on the floor. Instead, Peter held her hands, refusing to let them go. Finally, she tugged hard enough that he relented.

"Forgive me," he mumbled.

One hand went to her mouth as she coughed, and the other rested on her heaving heart. Why she was so shocked at his proposal? She had always known that was his ultimate goal for courting her.

He went to hold her hands again, but she kept them away from him. For one second she saw something resembling anger flash in his eyes and then it was gone.

"You don't need to answer me now. Tomorrow night at Vauxhall Gardens will suffice. That way we can celebrate in the privacy of one of the pleasure gardens." He stood and bowed. "Until tomorrow, my dear Lilly."

Instead of seeking advice from Emmeline or Aunt Vivian, Lilly retired to her room for the rest of the day and night having a dinner tray brought to her room. That night sleep eluded her and she spent much of the night pacing and wearing a line in the blue Aubusson rug covering the wood floorboards. When her legs tired, she climbed into bed and burrowed beneath the counterpane, willing her mind to stop creating all these scenarios for why she couldn't marry Peter and instead come up with reasons why she should marry him.

Eventually, she slept and managed several hours of rest before Daisy woke her for her morning ritual and breakfast.

THE THOUGHT OF attending a private ball at Vauxhall Gardens hosted by the Duke and Duchess of Greenville with Redford, Emmeline, and Blackstone had her fidgeting as Daisy finished her magic with her hair that evening. She'd never been to Vauxhall Pleasure Gardens before and looked forward to it. Except that Peter expected an answer to his marriage proposal.

She had promised herself yesterday that she would give Peter a chance and consider marrying him, which she had done all night and day. She thought she could probably live with him being a bit boring—she had enough excitement with the Ladies Society of Mayfair. And hopefully, it wouldn't take long to have children, and she would be otherwise occupied with them. Having a boring husband could be a blessing. He wouldn't demand her time and attention be taken away from their offspring. But what of her determination only to marry someone she loved?

"You are almost finished, my lady," Daisy said as she put the last pins into her perfectly coiffed hair and added feathers for adornment in the same color as her dress.

"Thank you. You may go now."

Lilly stood up and paced the room, the worn line from last night still evident in the rug. If only Henry were alive to give her counsel. Of course, she wouldn't be in this predicament if he were alive. She didn't want to disappoint Henry and fail to find what he wished for her. But the more she looked, the more she realized what a rare commodity marrying for love was.

She met very few married couples of the *ton* who were in love. Many flirted outright in front of their spouse with little regard for their feelings, gentlemen and ladies alike. Had they no shame? Her insides screamed again. Would that be her future if she married Peter? She didn't believe she could ever behave so, but would he?

Suddenly, the last thing she wanted to do was go out. Her only saving grace was that she would be with Emmeline and Blackstone.

A knock on her door startled her. "Enter."

"Blackstone and Redford are downstairs. Are you ready?" Emmeline asked, looking splendid in a ballgown of robin's-egg blue and silver.

Lilly picked up her reticule that matched her ballgown's elegant shade of green. "I'm ready."

"Are you feeling well? You seem out of sorts and pale."

"Peter wants an answer to his marriage proposal tonight." Lilly had confided to Emmeline and Aunt Vivian about Peter's proposal at breakfast that morning.

"Please don't let him force you into making a decision when you aren't ready. Marriage is for life or until death takes one of you." Emmeline reached out and squeezed her hand. "Make the decision on your time, not his."

Lilly felt the knot in her stomach ease. "You are right. If he truly wants to marry me, he will have to wait. He told me he loves me, but I can't say it back."

"Do you love him?"

"I don't, but I think perhaps I could in time. I like him well enough."

"Tell me what you feel when he kisses you."

"His kisses are nice."

"Oh, Lilly, you know kisses with someone you love should not only be nice. They should be . . ." She paused and shook her head. "They should be more."

"I know." And she did know. She had kissed someone once who made her feel more than she wanted to. "We should go. We don't want to keep the gentlemen waiting."

CHAPTER TWENTY-TWO

THE CARRIAGE RIDE to Vauxhall Gardens took time, as carriages clogged the streets in every direction. Lilly fingered her mother's emerald necklace as she contemplated her life and future. The problem was that Peter wasn't in it whenever she dreamed or daydreamed about her future.

On the surface, Peter would make a suitable husband. He'd never asked anything of her. He had odd-colored eyes that didn't show emotion easily, but could she fault him for something he was born with? His kisses were pleasant enough, certainly not revolting. As for the marriage bed, now that she had experienced it with Langford, she wasn't frightened and was sure she could muddle through.

Tears pooled in her eyes, and she willed them to go away. Her heart constricted quite painfully, and an empty feeling took over in the pit of her stomach. A future with Peter didn't feel right. It didn't matter how many good qualities he had; deep down inside her soul, she knew he wasn't the man for her. If she accepted his proposal it wouldn't be fair to either of them.

Her eyes fluttered closed and she heard Henry's voice. "I want you to marry for love and have a family made from love." She whispered in her mind, *I will.* Her eyes popped open and she knew she had the strength and courage to turn down Peter's proposal.

She would refuse his proposal tonight after the ball—no need to ruin everyone's night by doing it before. In the meantime, she would simply pretend all was fine with Peter and enjoy his company and the ball.

Lilly's eyes scanned her outdoor surroundings as they finally alighted from the carriage. The place was positively beautiful, and no amount of money was spared by the duke and duchess to make it resemble a fairytale. The dance floor was set up outside in front of the three terraced building, the top resembling a crown. The orchestra played from the first terrace, and oil lamps illuminated the gardens and the perimeter of the fencing. Informal seating was scattered around for socializing or more intimate gatherings. Her heart pounded at the excitement of it all as they made their way to greet their hosts.

Lilly curtsied. "Your Graces. What a beautiful place to hold a ball."

The duchess whispered, "My dear, please tell me how Langford is."

Her heart dropped at hearing Langford's name. "He is recovering nicely."

"You and Mrs. Fitzpatrick must go dance and have a wonderful evening. I will see you both at my home on Wednesday."

Lilly curtsied again, "Thank you, Your Grace."

When they left their hosts, Peter asked Lilly to dance just as the first strings of a waltz played.

She placed her hand on his outreached arm, and they strolled to the dance floor, already overflowing with couples. It was not the first time she'd waltzed with Peter, but she would have preferred not to be this close to him since she decided to turn down his marriage proposal. His hand on her waist felt wrong, and her hand holding his was awkward. But knowing people were watching, she smiled and looked at him, pretending to be having a good time and enjoying his company.

"You seemed quiet during the ride here. Is all well?" As he spoke, the strange blue of his eyes bored into her soul, causing her to quiver. The intensity of his stare felt invasive. "You shivered. Are you cold? I can retrieve your wrap if you'd like."

He said all the correct things, and his concern seemed genuine. "Thank you, but I'm fine." He twirled her around the dance floor with ease. He was a wonderful and graceful dancer. Better than her. "This place takes my breath away with its beauty."

Peter pulled her closer and whispered, "You take my breath away with your beauty." She fought not to pull away when his hot breath wafted against her ear. His nearness caused her to feel unsettled. How would she ever make it through tonight?

She realized he was staring at her, waiting for her to reply to his compliment. "Thank you. You look handsome and dashing this evening as well." She wasn't used to seeing Peter in black and it suited him.

When the final strings of the waltz concluded, Lilly exhaled with relief, and they made their way to Emmeline and Blackstone who were standing near a tree sipping wine.

"You did not dance," Lilly said, surprised that Blackstone would not take advantage of the opportunity to hold Emmeline close to his heart.

They looked at each other with mischief in their eyes, "We took a quick stroll through the gardens. The smell of the jasmine in bloom is lovely," Emmeline said with a secret smile.

"I love the smell of jasmine," Peter said. He turned to Lilly. "Care to take a stroll?"

Lilly took his offered arm, and they entered the dimly lit, private gardens. She had heard about debutantes finding themselves in compromising situations and ruined by scandal in these very gardens. Lilly was thankful, for the first time, she was a widow and protected from that sort of scandal.

When they found a secluded spot, Peter stopped, turned, and took both her hands in his. "I hope you have good news for me?"

Lilly forced herself to look him in the eye. She hadn't wanted to do this yet, but it seemed there was no avoiding it. She swallowed and cleared her throat, trying to get the words out.

"I'm sorry, Peter. I cannot marry you."

"What?"

"I'm sorry, I—"

"I heard you." His voice deepened, and his eyes hardened as he sneered at her. Right before her eyes his jovial nature changed. His once handsome face twisted up with hatred, and he looked at her with disgust, making him resemble the devil himself. She knew she'd made the right decision if this person was hidden beneath his gentle manners.

The sudden change was startling, and she struggled to understand why he should react so strongly, so angrily. "Why should you want to marry me so?"

"Because I need your money. I'm near bankrupt. Courting you cost me a fortune, one I didn't have. I inherited a poor title and estates. Not to mention the fact that my cousin's wife is spoiled along with her three daughters. And I'm expected to give them dowries and pay for their introduction into Society."

"But why me?"

"You were easy pickings—a young widow, her head in the clouds, looking for love." He spat on the ground. "Love doesn't exist, you stupid, foolish child."

He was beginning to truly scare her. As she stepped back to put distance between them, he stepped forward. His arms wrapped around her back tightly, refusing to let her go.

"How dare you waste my time? If you do not marry me, I will see you ruined. I will tell everyone that we had a tryst in these gardens, and you will certainly look the part." While keeping one hand around her waist, he plucked the pins from her hair and used his hand to disarrange her tresses. "Now let us see to mussing that pretty gown of yours."

"Don't you dare!" she cried out. "Get your hands off me!" Fear penetrated deep inside her being, something she'd never experienced before. Widow or not, he was right—this would be more than enough to land her in the middle of a ruinous scandal. What chance would she have for love then? "Don't you dare . . ."

One moment he was holding her and the next he was gone. Lilly tumbled to her knees and vomited up the glass of wine she'd drunk. When she looked up she saw Langford punch Peter—no, Redford—right in the face, and he dropped like a stone.

"Are you hurt?" Langford's uneasy voice asked as he and Blackstone yanked Redford up off the ground and held him between them.

"How did you find me?" she asked as Emmeline helped her stand and kept an arm around her waist to steady her. Lilly didn't think she could stand alone as her legs wobbled.

"Langford came looking for you with some disturbing news about Redford, and we knew we had to find you." Emmeline hugged her gently. "And not a moment too soon. Do you think you have the strength to walk through the gardens to the street where Langford's coach is waiting? We can't go back through the party without causing a scene."

"Yes." Lilly looked down at her clothing only slightly disheveled. "Do I look that bad?"

"No," Emmeline answered. "But Redford does with his busted nose and blood all over his face and shirt."

"It serves him right." Lilly couldn't help herself. She burst out laughing, then covered her mouth when her laughter turned to sobs.

They snuck away from the ball easily enough without being seen, Emmeline still with a protective arm around Lilly and Redford being dragged along between Langford and Blackstone. When they reached Langford's carriage, Lilly was shocked to find two more men standing there.

"We will take it from here, Lord Langford," one of them intoned.

"Who are these men?" Lilly asked, her mouth suddenly dry.

As the men took a semiconscious Redford to a small coach not far away, Langford said, "They are men I hired to investigate Redford. I'll explain the rest in the carriage."

Blackstone turned to them and said, "We will walk to my

carriage to give you two some privacy." He offered Emmeline his arm, and they walked on.

Langford, leaning heavily on his cane, which Lilly hadn't even noticed until now, helped her inside the carriage. But instead of sitting opposite her, he sat beside her and reached for her gloved hand. "Don't be angry with me, but I hired a Bow Street Runner to investigate Redford. Those were his men. They will see him delivered to a magistrate."

She turned to look at him. "Why did you hire them in the first place?"

"The more I thought on Redford, the more convinced I was that something wasn't right. And I'm glad I looked closer. If you had married him . . ." His entire body trembled. "It was he who set the fire in the barn that killed the previous viscount."

Lilly gasped.

"The viscount had several daughters but no sons to inherit the title, and Redford was tired of waiting for him to die and let the title come to him naturally." He groaned. "If you'd married him, no doubt he would have killed you as well before long to get his hands on your money. Bloody hell." He ran his fingers through his hair. "It's all my fault you find yourself in this predicament for having his name on that blasted list I made you."

She squeezed his hand. "It's not your fault. He fooled all of us." She leaned her head on his shoulder. "Thank you for saving me."

"If anything had happened to you . . . I'm not sure what I would've done."

"I'm fine now, thanks to you."

EDMUND SUPPOSED IN the end that it was a good thing that he'd gone a bit mad from boredom and inactivity during his recovery at his townhome in Mayfair. He'd been mostly preoccupied with visions of Lilly with Redford, that was where his madness lay. It had caused him to lash out at his servants, for which he would forever be ashamed. But Blackstone and Caldwell, who had visited daily, agreed that something was odd and untrustworthy about Redford.

So Edmund had called for a Bow Street Runner he'd worked with regarding their business and had hired him to poke about. It had taken several weeks, but the runner had done his job. Now Lilly was safe and Redford would die in Newgate or hang at the gallows for murder. He deserved no better.

When his carriage pulled up to Emmeline's house, he wasn't ready to let Lilly out of his sight. Still holding her hand, he swiveled in the seat and took her other hand in his as well. "I'm so sorry you had to go through that tonight. Believe me, I tried to reach you as fast as I could, but my leg, well, it still gives me trouble."

Her lips tilted up into a beautiful smile. "You saved me. I thank you from the bottom of my heart."

He leaned forward and pressed a kiss to her forehead. "Good night, Lilly."

Still looking at him, her smile faltered, her expression shy and hesitant. "Would you stay with me tonight? I don't want to be alone." Her gaze lowered and she turned a bright shade of pink. "I don't mean . . ."

He grinned and his eyes softened. "I know what you mean. And, yes. I will stay with you. I owe you for caring for me when I was recovering from my accident."

Her head tipped up and she frowned. "You don't owe me anything. Never mind, I'll be fine alone."

He touched her cheek and smiled. "That's not what I'm staying. Forgive me for saying that I owe you. I will stay because you asked me, as a friend." He knocked on the roof and the door opened and the stairs were pulled down. Edmund helped Lilly exit the vehicle. Harrison had the front door open as their feet hit the top step. He ignored the censuring look from the butler, but

Edmund respected the man for looking out for the three unmarried ladies living here.

Lilly led the way up to her chambers and left him while she entered her dressing room. He leaned on his cane to steady himself and breathed deeply, trying to ease the sexual desire running rampant through his body. It remembered the last time he'd visited these rooms. But he was not with Lilly in her chambers tonight to sleep with her. She'd had a terrible shock and only needed the safety and comfort he could give her. And he wanted to prove to her that he was a good man. Perhaps he was not completely worthy of her, but he hoped to become such a man someday. As for now, he was at Lilly's disposal. Whatever she needed from him, he would supply.

When Lilly emerged from her dressing room in a flowing white nightgown and matching robe, her silky blond hair touching her waist, all the air in his lungs dispersed, and he bent forward, gasping for air.

"Is something wrong?" She was at his side, touching him in no time, her voice laced with concern.

He almost laughed but swallowed it down. Laughing at a time like this would be in very bad form. *Get a hold of yourself, Edmund, you fool.* "No. I'm all right." He stood up and glanced at her delicate hand on his arm. A hand that sent scorching heat curling up his arm through his shoulder and down to curl around his heart.

Her brows furrowed. "You are not acting all right." Her hand went to his cravat. "Here, let me help you. You will feel more relaxed if you shed some of your clothing." She untied his cravat and removed his coat and waistcoat until he stood before her in his linen shirt, breeches, and boots. "Sit, let me help you with your boots." He stifled the groan trying to escape his throat. Did she have any idea what she was doing to him? Once his boots were removed, he wiggled his toes in his stockings and cleared his throat. "Go to bed. I'll sleep on the chaise longue."

She rose up on tiptoe and brushed her warm, soft lips across his cheek. "Thank you."

As he stretched out on the chaise longue with his legs hanging over the end, he heard the rustle of the bed covers and then her sigh. He reached beneath his head for a pillow, covered his face with it and groaned.

After an hour or so, he realized there would be no sleeping tonight with the woman of his dreams so close by and making murmuring sounds in her sleep.

CHAPTER TWENTY-THREE

LILLY AWOKE TO birds chirping and the sound of rain. But there was another sound that puzzled her: snoring—deep rumbling snores. And then last night's events assaulted her memory. She swung her legs off the bed, stood, and silently made her way to the chaise longue where Langford slept. Her heart stopped as she took him in. He was stretched out on his back, his legs dangling over the edge of the chaise longue, one hand behind his head and the other resting on his stomach. His features were soft, and he looked angelic and young. One lock of hair curled down the middle of his forehead and she wanted so badly to push it aside. Any excuse to touch him. She could pretend most days that her feelings for him were trivial, but the truth was that she was utterly and hopelessly in love with him.

"Do you always sneak up on your guests and watch them sleep?" He raised both his arms over his head and stretched, and she couldn't take her eyes off his chest, his stomach, and the bulge in his breeches.

Embarrassed, she adverted her eyes. "Forgive me. I heard you snoring."

He chuckled, "I have been accused of that from time to time." She must have made a face because he quickly added, "From Blackstone and Caldwell as we sometimes share a cabin on one of our ships when we travel."

"I see." She had mistaken his meaning and felt contrite. "Did you sleep well?"

He sat up and patted the cushion next to him, clearly hoping she'd sit. She did, and the warmth from his body radiated into her side where they touched. "I didn't think I would at all, and it took me a while to fall asleep, but yes, I slept well. Did you?"

"I'm shocked to say I fell asleep as soon as my head rested on my pillow. The events of the night with Redford must have taken a toll on my mind and body." She turned her head and looked at him. "What will happen to him?"

He tilted his head and asked, "To Redford? He will be punished. What sort of punishment depends on the magistrate and what can be proven."

She reached between them and gripped his hand. After last night, she felt much more comfortable touching him. "Thank you again for saving me."

"I've been a fool." He squeezed her hand gently. "I hope I have begun proving myself to you, shown you I'm not always an irrational, insensitive arse of a man. And I want you to know I would do anything for you. I'm going to tell you something and I hope you won't be upset. The night I arrived at Langford Manor, I found a sealed letter on my pillow from Uncle Henry."

Her eyes blinked in surprise.

"He asked me to look after you," he continued. "And his greatest wish was for you to marry the second time for love."

"Henry and I talked about it many times. I hadn't realized all this time you knew about it."

"I did, and I'm sorry I kept it from you. What I want you to understand is that, yes, I'm looking out for you as per Henry's letter." His hands cupped her face, his compassionate, warm brown eyes tinged with desire bore into the depths of her soul. "But my feelings for you have nothing to do with Henry and everything to do with how my heart aches for you. My hungry eyes seek you out whenever we are in the same room. My insides don't relax until I know you are safe and well. My hands wish to touch your soft, silky skin at every opportunity, which in my opinion is never enough. Your full, luscious lips call to mine and drive me nearly insane with the need to taste them." His lips brushed against hers, making her entire body quiver. "None of that has anything to do with an obligation to Henry and everything to do with you and me."

Tears silently trailed down her cheeks and Edmund wiped them away. "I pray these are tears of joy?"

Words stuck in her throat, so she nodded her head.

"Thank Christ." Their lips met, their tongues seeking each other's essence. Nothing and no one would intrude on this moment. Without breaking the kiss, Edmund cradled her body to his, stood, and she found herself plopped down onto the chaise longue to the sound of his laughter. "I forgot about my leg. I'm sorry. I can't carry you to the bed."

Standing, Lilly giggled and wrapped an arm around his waist. "I'll help you." They made their way to the bed and Edmund sat down, Lilly hurried to the door and locked it. She knew it was early for Daisy, but she didn't want to risk someone coming in.

What little clothing they wore was tossed to the floor, and Lilly got her first close-up look at his leg and the jagged scar adorning it. Where the stitches had been was raised and purple.

"This healed nicely," she said as she ran a gentle fingertip down the scar.

"It did." Edmund's amber-flecked eyes were intense as one large hand roamed up and down her body, instantly distracting her from his leg. Every touch, every caress, tore moans from her lips, and her hips rose off the bed, hoping his hand would touch her where she craved it most. When his hand cupped her womanhood, her legs opened wider and she almost cried with relief. His fingers sought her entrance, sliding in and out. His eyes locked with hers, and as much as she wanted to look away, she couldn't. As her body tumbled over that elusive precipice, with Edmund watching her, she'd never felt so vulnerable, cherished, or loved.

Before her body had time to recover, he rolled on top of her, placed his hard member at her entrance and slid all the way in with one slow thrust. He took her mouth in a punishing kiss. His tongue mimicked the actions below, and before Lilly could take her next breath, her body exploded once again. At the same time, Edmund arched his back, and his body tensed as his warm seed spilled inside her. They collapsed into each other's arms. Lilly didn't think she could move for at least an hour.

HE'D HAD HIS share of women in his bed, but he'd never had a true emotional and physical connection to anyone until Lilly. He still couldn't comprehend the volcanic eruption he'd experienced with her. It was so intense he'd thought he was going to lose consciousness for a moment there when he released his seed.

"Are you awake?"

"Hmm. Yes," she answered with a sleepy voice, stirring his body again. What he had to say next would douse the flames quickly.

"Tell me about Henry and how your marriage came to be."

It took a while for her to speak, and at first he thought she might be ignoring him. "I had just turned seventeen and Papa thought we would have time to secure a husband and future for me. But then we found out Papa was sick and had very little time left. Suddenly my future and securing a husband for me was upon us. Unbeknownst to me, he approached Henry and asked him to marry me. I was shocked when I found out and shocked that he agreed."

She paused, her body shook. Edmund wrapped his arms tighter around her waist and kissed the back of her neck. "If this is too hard for you, you don't have to tell me."

"No, I'm all right. When Papa told me Henry had agreed to marry me, I was both relieved and frightened. I didn't know what he would expect of me. Would he want heirs? I knew Henry was an honorable and good man, but what kind of husband would he be? We married within days with a special license; hours after Papa performed the ceremony, he died. The next day he was buried, and I found myself in a carriage with my new husband, crying over my papa's death."

"I'm so sorry. That must have been a terribly trying day for you."

"Thank you." She sighed and he knew her fingers were wiping away tears. "Henry was so kind to me during the ride to Langford Manor. He said that we both needed time to mourn and that he would come and speak with me the following day. And when we spoke the next day in his study he told me he didn't want to bed a child, nor did he want heirs. That our marriage would be in name only, he would take care of me and I would take care of him."

Edmund's heart stopped at what her words implied. "That was very kind and noble of him. But I'm not surprised. Uncle Henry was the epitome of a true gentleman."

"Yes, he was."

"Does that mean you were a virgin the first time we made love?" His breath suspended as he awaited her answer.

"Yes."

"I understand why you didn't tell me. But I wish I'd known." Nothing about his behavior at the time would have given her reason to trust him with her secret. Had he been gentle enough with her? He hoped so. "Tell me more. What did you do to occupy your time for that year?" The floodgates of his curiosity opened, and suddenly, he wanted to know everything there was to know about Lilly and her life before they'd met.

"Every day, Henry and I went riding. He kept busy managing the estate, but I was a little bored. We traveled to London several times. I was happy. We talked together about my future and what he wanted and hoped for me. We talked about you." She patted his arms which were circling her waist. "Although there wasn't much to say since Henry hadn't seen you in person for years."

His body tightened. "I will forever regret not having come to see Uncle Henry more often before his death. As his heir, I should've made time for him. I owe him so much, and I can never express my gratitude to him."

"Taking care of his estates and his tenants and being a genuinely kind and caring man would be thank you enough for Henry."

"I promise I will."

She inhaled and he knew she was getting to the emotional, hard part of her story. "The day Henry died, we were riding and we raced. He always let me win, but he could still ride like the wind. But he fell." She wiped more tears away. "I'd just finished my year of mourning Papa, and now I was in mourning again, only this time for my husband. A man who had become my best friend, my confidant, my everything."

Edmund moved his arms and began rubbing her back, hoping to soothe her heartache. "And then I came along and I behaved like an arse."

"Humph. It took you just over two months to arrive. It seemed like a lifetime. And yes, you were a privileged, arrogant, vile man the first time we met. I couldn't get away from you fast enough. Thank God I had Emmeline to save me."

He chuckled, "Do you need saving now?"

She turned around, cupped his cheek, her eyes shining with unshed tears and she smiled. "Now more than ever."

He brought his lips to hers just as someone knocked on the door.

"My lady, it's Daisy."

Lilly stifled her giggles by burying her head in his chest. "Daisy, I'm tired this morning. Come back in an hour."

"Yes, my lady."

"I should go since the servants are up. I don't want any gossip surrounding you."

"Emmeline has the best household. They do not gossip. Nor

does my maid, Daisy. But I agree, you must go so I can start my day."

He kissed her deeply. He didn't want to leave her bed. "Does all this mean you will consent to marry me?" Bloody hell, the moment he uttered the words, he knew it was the wrong time and the worst way to propose to the woman he loved. She was unlike anyone he'd ever met. He felt every muscle in her body tense as she pulled away from him, both physically and emotionally. What a bloody arse he was . . . again.

HIS PROPOSAL SHOULD have made her heart sing. But for some reason a sadness penetrated into the very center of her being. Had he only asked because of what they shared in her bed, twice? She didn't want to spend her life questioning his motives. He'd yet to profess his love, and that was what she needed. He knew that was what she needed.

"I would like you to leave now," she said in a tired voice. "If it's acceptable to you, I would like time to think over your proposal. I'll send word when I've decided. Until then, please don't call on me."

He reached out with his hand to touch her but pulled it back. "Forgive me. I hadn't meant to propose." He ran his fingers through his hair. "What I mean is, yes, I meant to propose, but I wasn't prepared to do so at this time. Bloody hell," he mumbled. "I'm messing this up. Please don't shut me out."

Every part of her body ached, and her mind screamed out, *Yes! Say yes!* Instead, she said, "After Redford, I need time. Please understand."

"I will try," he said as he gathered his things and left.

Lilly lay back in bed, tears sliding down her face as she tried to ignore the pain in her heart.

CHAPTER TWENTY-FOUR

FOUR DAYS HAD passed since Edmund's proposal, and it was the night of the Earl and Countess of Warren's masquerade ball, 25 June 1816, the last major social event in London before the midsummer break and the *ton* made their mass exodus to the countryside to enjoy picnics, hunts, and house parties. Emmeline, Aunt Vivian, and Lilly would be staying in London except for the several house party invitations they'd accepted, since none of them owned country estates. Langford had once offered Lilly use of Langford Manor in Kent at any time, but she couldn't face asking him about it now.

Her courses had arrived again that afternoon, confirming she hadn't conceived the other night. Nothing was tying her to Langford through any sense of duty. She loved him—she knew that now. But she also knew she could not marry him if he did not love her back. She could not be happy in half a marriage, so she would simply have to stitch up her broken heart and go on.

Lilly decided to forgo a specific costume and wear a new gold silk gown with a matching gold chemise. Madam Serena had finished the lovely dress a day ago for this very occasion. The gown had off-the-shoulder sleeves and a low-cut neckline and was quite clingy. The elaborate gold mask was decorated with feathers and beads. Her hair was pinned up with curls cascading over the bare skin of her shoulders and chest. When she was ready, Daisy stepped back and declared her a work of art worthy of a museum, but Lilly felt exposed and thankful for the mask to hide behind. Perhaps she would leave before midnight and the removal of masks.

Emmeline dressed as a Roman empress. The cream and gold costume and plain gold mask were quite flattering on her. Aunt Vivian had chosen not to attend. She said she was too old to parade around in a costume. She warned them that even though it was an invitation-only ball, the demi-monde and unsavory lower-class gentlemen sometimes snuck in and mingled with the upper class, so they should remain watchful and cautious.

Since this was Lilly's first masquerade, she didn't know what to expect, and when their carriage pulled up to the Warrens' well-lit London estate, she couldn't take her eyes off some of the elaborate and revealing costumes. There were pirates, dominos, gypsies, Marie Antionettes, and French musketeers, and those were only the attendees she could see from the carriage. She couldn't imagine what she would glimpse inside the ballroom. Her heart beat wildly with excitement and nerves.

"How do you know who anyone is?" she asked Emmeline as they exited the coach.

Emmeline laughed softly. "You don't—that is the point. Although if you are well acquainted with someone, you should recognize them unless they alter their voice to match their costume."

"Oh dear." Lilly sighed.

"Some take hiding their identity very seriously and will play the role of their costume to perfection until the great unmasking."

"Perhaps I should have declined my invitation." Lilly's head tingled and she felt a little lightheaded. She wrapped her arm around Emmeline's for comfort as she recognized the signs of panic.

"Do not worry. We shall stay together as much as we can. The first thing we do is try to recognize Blackstone, Caldwell, and

Langford."

"Langford." Lilly tried not to groan.

"I know you are unhappy with him. So am I, but he is a good friend to have." She paused and lowered her voice. "I know his marriage proposal, such as it was, disappointed you. But give him time. Men can be dimwitted where women are concerned, especially when it involves a woman they care very deeply about."

Lilly wasn't convinced of that. Well, she was convinced that men could be dimwitted, just not that Langford cared deeply for her.

They greeted the earl and countess on their way into the ballroom—no announcement of names or introductions if the guests were to remain incognito. That suited Lilly fine. She could stand on the outskirts of the ballroom and watch the show. And when she deduced who Langford was, she would stay well away from him and his heartbreaking proposal.

"Come," Emmeline said, "let us take a turn around the room and see who we recognize."

"I've been in London a year and visited only a few times with Henry before that. I don't think I'll recognize anyone with masks on."

"Be that as it may, we can delight in making fun of some of the more outrageous costumes," Emmeline commented.

The tension in Lilly's shoulders eased and she almost laughed out loud at the sight of a court jester dancing around the edge of the dance floor by himself. "Who do you suppose that is?"

Emmeline giggled. "Someone who does not mind making a fool of themselves."

"Caldwell comes to mind," Lilly said with a smile. "Not that I know him well, but he doesn't appear to take life too seriously, although he must at times when it comes to business."

"Ever since I've known him he has been like that. But if you look into his eyes, they do not mirror his easygoing nature. He is hiding something."

"Oh, a mystery to solve." Lilly believed, now more than ever, that most people held much beneath the surface, and so many struggled with some closely held sorrow—perhaps a death, a secret, an unrequited love. She herself had struggled with all of those things.

"I believe I have spotted Blackstone and Caldwell, though I don't see Langford. Near the entrance to the refreshments room there are two men, one dressed as a pirate and the other a ship's captain. Very fitting for them. Let's go and say hello."

"Perhaps it is not them." Lilly hesitated.

"That is the good thing about a masquerade, if we mistake someone's identity, there is no embarrassment or awkward moment."

They approached the two gentlemen, and the ship's captain bowed. "Ladies, how lovely you look this evening. Can I interest you in a sail down the River Thames on my ship this lovely evening?"

Even though Blackstone tried to disguise his voice, Lilly recognized it, and before she could speak, Emmeline murmured, "Another time, perhaps. It seems I am not dressed for sailing."

He held out his hand. "Would you honor me with a dance then?"

Lilly quickly found herself standing alone with the pirate.

"Do not look nervous that Emmeline left you with a stranger." He bowed. "Caldwell at your service. If you don't honor me with this dance, I'll make you walk the plank." He grinned.

As they made their way to the dance floor, Lilly found herself actually enjoying herself. Caldwell was an exceptional dancer, and he didn't miss a step of the country dance. She couldn't say the same for herself. She faltered twice, but she didn't care. No one knew who she was.

When the dance ended, Caldwell escorted her to where Emmeline and Blackstone stood in a quiet corner of the ballroom. Lilly's skin tingled, and she recognized the feeling of being watched. As nonchalantly as she could, she looked around and found someone staring at her. He was tall, his arms were crossed on his chest and he was dressed as a smuggler. Or at least she thought he was. He could have been a gentleman sailor, but something about his glare, mannerisms, and posture gave the impression of a more dangerous man.

"Who is that?" She asked Caldwell.

"Who is whom, my lady?"

"Sorry. The smuggler over by the entrance. He is staring at me as if he wants to do me bodily harm."

Caldwell chuckled, "I haven't a clue, but you have attracted his attention. Would you like me to approach him and inquire about his attention?"

She almost tripped, having caught the edge of her gown with her gold slippers. "Most certainly not. Although, you don't suppose Redford . . ."

"I can't imagine the magistrate letting him out of Newgate anytime soon. In any case, you need not worry. Blackstone and I will protect you."

Did Caldwell's proclamation ease her worry? Not if the continuing pounding of her heart and the shaking of her body were any indicators. She glanced over her shoulder toward where the smuggler stood and exhaled the breath she didn't realize she'd been holding as she saw he no longer stood there. "Thank you."

Standing close to Emmeline she asked, "Did you see the tall man dressed as a smuggler standing at the entrance to the ballroom?"

"No. Why?"

"No reason." She leaned close and whispered in Emmeline's ear, "He was watching me. I couldn't distinguish his face with the black mask, but something about him had me on edge. He looked like he wanted to harm me."

Emmeline gasped. "Do you want to go home? Perhaps this night is too much for you. I have heard some people hate masquerade balls because the costumes and masks frighten them."

"No, that is not it." At least Lilly didn't think so. "Will you accompany me to the ladies' retiring room? I think I need a moment to clear my head."

As they made their way through the crush of bodies, Lilly got separated from Emmeline. Then she nearly screamed as someone grabbed her arm and pulled her behind one of the potted palms scattered around to give guests the illusion of privacy. More annoyed than frightened, she looked up into the face of the masked smuggler and murmured, "You!"

"I'm sorry. I didn't mean to startle you."

"Langford, why are you shadowing me?" She placed her hands on her hips and glared at him. Even if he couldn't tell with her mask on, it made her feel better to stare daggers at him.

"Is that what you think I'm doing?"

Sighing, she relaxed somewhat. "Yes. No." She didn't know anything where he was concerned. Except he still made her heart race. "Please say whatever it is you dragged me behind this plant to say."

He swung his head up and frowned. "Can we go somewhere private and talk?"

Lilly sighed. They did need to talk. But she would rather not have the delicate and emotional conversation at a masquerade ball. "Call on me tomorrow. Is there anything else?" *Take me in your arms and kiss me. Behave like a smuggler and take what you want.*

"Be careful. Gentlemen hiding behind masks tend to be much more forward. Stay with Emmeline. By the way, where is she?"

"In the ladies' retiring rooms where I'm going."

He bowed. "Have a good evening."

He turned and strolled away from her, leaving her alone after cautioning her about staying with Emmeline and being wary of overly forward men. She made her way down the hallway and somehow got turned around, found herself in the card room, and was surprised to see ladies sitting at tables gambling. She stood off to the side and watched with fascination. She'd never been in a gambling hell or a card room. It was surprisingly quiet as the players concentrated on their cards. When a game ended, there were groans from the losers and ecstatic cheers of jubilee from the winner. So engrossed in the card play, she didn't notice the person who came up behind her until a low voice said in her ear, "Come with me."

She was about to reply when he grabbed her arm and dragged her out of the room. Before she could pull away, he had her pushed up against the wall of a dark hallway. It looked like the servants' hallway. "I'm glad to see you again, Lilly."

His voice made her gasp in shock while her heart tumbled. "Redford."

"'Tis I, my lady," he snarled.

"But you killed a man." Lilly's knees almost buckled.

"Mere conjecture. And I was released while awaiting trial, though I don't expect there to be one. My cousin's wife will come forward and swear the fire was set by her husband. She will state the previous viscount was careless regarding the safety of lanterns in the barn."

Lilly was having trouble breathing with his body pushed up tightly to hers.

He stepped back and grabbed her arm again. "Do as I say, and you will not get hurt."

"Where—"

"Be silent. Do not speak until I tell you to. Keep walking or I will sneak into Mrs. Fitzpatrick's home tonight and slit her throat."

Lilly swallowed any other words and was dragged by the arm through the corridors, her feet barely keeping up. Several times she tried to get away, but his hand was wrapped so tight around her upper arm that she would soon sport a bruise. She tore off her mask because she couldn't see, and it wasn't long before she stumbled out a door to an alley, cool air hitting her face. The servants' entrance. No one would pay them any mind since every servant was occupied with the masquerade.

Redford continued pulling her along in the opposite direction of the Warrens' home until she saw a black unmarked coach. Redford headed straight toward it. He opened the door and shoved her inside, causing her to bang her shins, and she breathed through the intense pain. She scrambled off the floor and onto the seat, never taking her eyes off him. He climbed in opposite her and tapped the roof.

The curtains were drawn, and no lantern was lit inside the carriage, so she could barely make out his silhouette. But she could hear his heavy breathing and smell his sweat and stale cigars.

He tossed her a blanket. "Get comfortable. We have a long journey ahead. As long as you behave, I won't restrain you. Try to escape and you will find your hands and feet bound."

The air inside the coach was warm, but her body was chilled, so she covered herself with the coarse woolen blanket. This was not Redford's usual coach. He must have hired a hack.

"Where are you taking me?"

"Come now, Lady Langford, you are brighter than most young ladies of your age. You should be able to figure out our destination."

Her insides trembled because she already had, but she refused to say *Gretna Green* out loud. Instead, her mind went to calculating how long it would take to get there. Two days if they rode hard, three if they took breaks. Where on earth had Redford found the money for this? He had confessed to being broke and needing her money. Had he stolen it? "I thought you were short on funds."

His laughter reverberated inside the coach. "There are many ways to procure funds. Now leave me in peace." Within minutes his breathing changed and she could tell he'd fallen asleep.

Lilly found the hired hack to be poorly sprung, and she bounced around at every rut and rock and dip in the road. Her stomach turned queasy and she hoped she wouldn't be sick. She had a feeling Redford wouldn't take kindly to her casting up her accounts on his boots. She inhaled and exhaled slowly and steadily, hoping to settle her stomach and her nerves. Just then, the carriage dipped, sending her sliding toward the door, and she banged her head. Now she felt even worse. Redford slept through it all.

Her stomach finally settled and, what seemed like an age later, the driver stopped at a solitary roadside inn, presumably to get fresh horses, even though they'd only been on the road for perhaps an hour and a half. Lilly couldn't be sure though.

Since Redford still slept she took the opportunity to get out of the conveyance and take stock of her situation. Her eyes scanned her surroundings. It was dark. The clouds hid the moon and stars and she wondered how the coach driver could see the road.

Her heart dropped. There was nowhere for her to escape. She couldn't run down the empty road—she would certainly be easily caught again. She could try running into the forest—she wouldn't be able to see, but Reford wouldn't be able to see her either. Just as she'd made up her mind to run toward the tree line, Redford came up behind her and put his hands on her shoulders, and squeezed.

"Do I need to restrain you?"

"No," she answered quickly.

"Get back inside the carriage." He took his hands off her shoulders, and he clasped her upper arm, the same one he'd grasped earlier, and she swallowed down the pain as he led her back into the vehicle. It was several moments before they were on the road again. The only good thing that had come of their stop was that the driver had placed a basket of food inside with them.

Lilly rummaged around inside the basket and took out a hunk of bread and a piece of cheese to nibble on. She set the basket beside Redford.

"I expect my wife to serve me."

"It is good then that I'm not your wife." The moment she said the words she wished she could take them back. He reached forward and she jerked back against the squabs believing he meant to hurt her. Instead he grabbed the food from her hand.

"'Tis only a matter of time before you learn to obey me. Until then, you will go hungry."

Her hunger vanished, but her stomach continued to hurt as she wondered if anyone had noticed she was missing. Surely Emmeline knew by now, and she would have sought out Blackstone and Caldwell to help her find her. Tears trickled silently down her cheeks as she prayed for help. It was all she could do not to sob out loud and attract Redford's attention.

CHAPTER TWENTY-FIVE

WHEN EMMELINE GOT separated from Lilly, she hurried back to Blackstone and Caldwell. "Have you seen Lilly? I can't find her."

Caldwell replied, "I haven't seen her since we danced."

"She saw someone dressed as a smuggler and was afraid of him."

Both Caldwell and Blackstone chuckled. "That was Langford."

"Of course it was. But knowing it was him doesn't ease my fears. Where is she?"

"Where is who?" Of course, Langford chose that precise moment to join them.

"Lilly," Emmeline replied, getting more worried by the second. "I got separated from her and can't find her."

She couldn't see his face, but by the tightening of his stance, she could tell he was worried, too. "The Duke of Westport just told me that Redford was set free until his trial. Did any of you see him here?"

Emmeline thought she was going to be sick. How could this be? How could such a man simply be let loose?

"I think we should split up and check every inch of this place," Langford continued. "Emmeline, you stay with Blackstone and check the family's private rooms. Caldwell and I will separate and check all the public spaces and the immediate grounds. Talk to everyone and see if anyone remembers seeing her. Tell them her costume. Someone might know something. We should meet back here in an hour. Because if we haven't found her by then, she isn't here."

BLOODY HELL, EDMUND scolded himself for leaving his cane with the footman at the door as he limped as fast as he could down the hallway opening every door he came to and scanning the room from top to bottom. He soon found himself in the servants' hall, which he believed led outside. Most of the London townhomes had similar floor plans and this was no different. He came to the kitchen and crossed it, taking a candle from the table as he went and continuing down the corridor. If Redford wanted to escape with Lilly unnoticed, this would be the best way.

His foot stepped on something that crunched beneath his boots. He picked it up and his heart tumbled to his knees. The squished, elaborate gold mask in his hands belonged to Lilly. He'd never forget the beauty of seeing her wearing it. He hobbled as quickly as he could and burst out the door into an alley. Breathing heavily, he continued running toward the street, scanning for anything out of the ordinary. Unfortunately, the street was full of parked vehicles, and guests still arriving. He hurried back inside to meet with the others, hoping against hope that they'd found her somewhere without her mask and his fears were unfounded, but when he saw them, Lilly wasn't with them.

He wanted to tear his hair out and bellow at the top of his lungs. If only he had stayed with her earlier, insisting they had their conversation then. His insides had protested waiting until tomorrow, but he'd let her choose the time and place. He needed to ask her forgiveness for his crazed behavior of late, and he needed to say three life-altering words. *I love you.* He rubbed his chest, which ached from exertion and stark terror. He held up her mask.

"I found this near the servants' entrance. Redford must have her."

Emmeline leaned her head against Blackstone, and his arm circled her waist, helping her stand because she looked ready to collapse.

"Blackstone, take Emmeline home. Caldwell and I will go to my house and head out on horseback. I have an idea he's heading for Gretna Green to force Lilly to marry him. We should be able to catch up with him."

Thirty minutes later, Edmund and Caldwell sped off hoping to intercept the coach carrying Redford and Lilly before they traveled too far. Both parties would have to stop at roadside inns along the way for fresh horses. Fortunately for them, Redford would need to travel in a coach with Lilly and wouldn't be able to move nearly as quickly as they could on horseback.

Into the dark they rode, not as fast as Edmund would have liked, but to keep the horses and themselves safe, they had to go slower than during the daytime. Not to mention a throbbing pain lancing up and down his leg causing him nausea.

After twenty miles or so, they stopped to retrieve fresh horses, and as much as Edmund needed to rest his leg, which had gone numb, there would be time after they found Lilly. When Edmund inquired about a man and woman traveling with a driver, his tension eased somewhat. They had been seen. God only knew that Redford had done to Lilly by now, but at least they knew they were on the right trail, and they were only about a half hour behind the carriage. If they pushed the horses harder they could overtake Redford soon.

They quickly switched their saddles, and off they went. For the first time since he knew what happened to Lilly, he breathed deeper, knowing he would find her and she would soon be safe from the bloody blackguard that was the murderous Viscount Redford. And if it was the last thing he did, he would see the man pay for his actions regarding Lilly.

Minutes later, the clouds parted and the moon illuminated the road. Edmund spotted the carriage not far ahead. Without slowing, both he and Caldwell retrieved the pistols they were carrying—just in case. He wouldn't put anything past Redford.

Edmund and Caldwell split up, riding on either side of the coach forcing the driver to stop. "See here! What is the nature of your business?" the driver spat at them.

"We have come for the kidnapped lady," Caldwell said as he aimed his pistol at the driver. "Do not move or I'll put a bullet in you."

Edmund, his heart up near his throat, slid off his mount and staggered as he moved cautiously toward the door. Before he made it, the door flung open, and two shots were fired in his direction. He dove beneath the carriage in the nick of time. At the sound of Redford reloading, Edmund scurried from beneath the coach and flung open the now-closed door and pointed his gun at Redford. Hatred shone from Redford's eyes as he realized he was caught.

"Put the guns down. Slide them on the floor and kick them out of the carriage." Without taking his eyes, or his pistol, off Redford, Edmund kicked the pistols away from the coach. Still meeting Redford's glare, Edmund asked, "Lilly, are you hurt?" He could not risk looking at her. Redford was desperate, and a desperate man would do almost anything to get what he wanted.

"No." Hearing her voice confirm she wasn't hurt nearly took him to the ground with relief.

"Caldwell," Edmund yelled.

He came up beside Edmund. "Yes."

"Is the driver secured?"

"Yes. My best sailor's knot. He won't be going anywhere until some poor blackguard frees him."

"Do the same for Redford." Caldwell climbed into the carriage, clearly happy to oblige. "Lilly, you may get out."

She flew out the door so quickly that Edmund barely had

time to react and catch her. His damaged leg buckled and they tumbled to the hard ground with a loud thud. "Did you get hurt?" he asked as he breathed through the pain of rocks and sticks stabbing into his back.

"No. You cushioned my fall."

She rose off him, and helped him stand when she saw him struggling to get up. "Your leg. Is it bothering you?" Her concern was a balm to his pain.

"Yes. But I'll be fine." He walked her over to the side of the road, then wrapped her up in his arms and held her as her body shook and she broke down and cried big, gulping sobs into his chest. She was trying to talk, but he couldn't make out a single word. He kept holding her as his heart broke in two for her. For a young lady of nineteen, she'd gone through so much in her short life. Now that he'd found her safe and unharmed, he swore he would spend the rest of his life devoted to making her happy.

It wasn't long before Caldwell stood beside them. "They are both tied up. Can you help me get the driver inside the carriage? I'll drive them back to the inn and send for the constable. Lilly can ride my horse."

Edmund helped Lilly up on Caldwell's mount.

"Have you ridden astride before?"

"Yes. Several times."

He swallowed down his groan of pain when he mounted his horse. There would be time later to rest his leg. They rode side by side in front of the carriage. When they arrived back at the inn, the innkeeper sent word immediately to the local constable. Edmund, Lilly, and Caldwell sat in a private room enjoying refreshments while a stablehand guarded the carriage and its occupants.

"Let me look at your leg?" Lilly asked, her face pale and her eyes worried. Edmund didn't need her worrying about his leg. He was concerned about her.

"If I remove my boot, I'll never get it back on. There will be time for that later." He paused and lowered his voice. "Tell me what happened?"

She pushed her hair from her eyes, her coiffure long since destroyed, and the anguish he saw in them rattled his heart. "Not now. Not here," she whispered.

As much as he wanted to know, he could see she was in no condition to explain her terrible ordeal now. The constable arrived not long after. They explained what had happened, and he assured them he would see the two prisoners to London.

Edmund wanted to rent a coach, but Lilly refused. "I can't be inside a carriage right now. I need to be outside and free."

Once again, he respected her wishes.

They rode the twenty miles back to London in silence. Edmund's eyes were heavy with exhaustion but he managed to watch over Lilly just in case she nodded off. He would not allow her to be hurt on his watch. She'd been through enough.

Edmund watched from atop his horse as Blackstone, Emmeline, and Vivian hurried out the front door when they arrived at Emmeline's townhome. Blackstone immediately stepped forward and helped Lilly down, and then, with his arm around her waist, he escorted her inside the townhome. It was the right and gentlemanly thing to do, but still, a stab of jealousy pierced Edmund's insides that someone else had the privilege of putting an arm around her. But what right did he have to be jealous? He'd managed to ruin whatever relationship he and Lilly had again and again. He pushed the thought from his mind—that didn't matter now. The only thing that mattered was that Lilly was safe and away from Redford.

"Are you getting down?" Caldwell asked with worry.

"I don't know if I can. My leg has gone numb again."

Caldwell signaled to a footman standing outside the front door. "Lord Langford needs help getting down from his mount." Between the footman and Caldwell, they were able to help him dismount and lend a hand in getting him into the house. The stairs were a bugger; Edmund kept thinking he was going to fall backward and break his neck. When he finally reached a comfortable chair and his leg placed on a footstool, he breathed a sigh of relief.

THE SIX OF them sat in the drawing room as a servant brought in tea. Aunt Vivian served Lilly, who sat beside her on the settee with Emmeline on the other side. "My dear, drink this. It will warm up your bones and help settle your stomach and nerves."

"What did you put in it?" She may be numb and fighting sleep, but she was sure she'd witnessed Aunt Vivian pour something from a decanter into her tea.

"It is brandy. Just a little. It will help you relax and sleep." Aunt Vivian patted her knee. "You have had a terribly shocking ordeal, and you need rest."

Lilly needed much more than rest. She needed to forget what happened. She needed to never see Redford's evil face again. She quivered. Unfortunately, she believed his face would plague her during sleep for many nights to come. The room was uncomfortably silent as all eyes watched her. Why? Were they waiting for her to scream? Start blabbering to herself? She may do those things, but she would wait until she was in the privacy of her chambers. Then she could fall apart. "I imagine you want to know what happened?"

Emmeline took one of her hands in hers. "We do. But only if you are ready to talk about it."

She truly didn't know if she'd ever be ready. "What I want to know is will Redford ever be free again?"

"Not if I have anything to say about it," Langford said as his rubbed his upper thigh. Lilly didn't think he was aware he was doing it.

"How?" she asked.

"The magistrate will know by now what happened, and will no doubt send word soon asking you for an audience. When you are ready, he will arrive and take your statement." He paused. "You don't have to meet him alone. I will be with you if you'd like."

"Thank you. I will think on it. Meanwhile," she took the last sip of the brandy-laced tea and winced, "if you will excuse me, I'm going to rest. I'm not ready to talk about it."

⟫⟫⟫⟫⟫⟫⟫⟪⟪⟪⟪⟪⟪⟪

As soon as she was gone, Emmeline said, "Tell us what happened. I was so afraid for Lilly. I drove mother and Blackstone mad as I paced the floor."

Edmund told them what he knew. As he said the words, he was thrown right back to the moment they'd caught up with the coach. His heart had pounded inside his chest and he found it hard to hear anything. All he had wanted to do was get Lilly and never let her out of his sight again. He would profess his love and beg for her forgiveness for being an utter arse.

However, when he finally saw the horror on her face and in her eyes, he'd almost vomited. When he held her trembling body in his arms while she sobbed, his heart had broken for her. He knew at that moment he would do anything for her. He should have shot Redford on the spot. Or, at the very least, beaten him to within an inch of his life. It would have been no more than he deserved.

The vacant stare in Lilly's eyes just now as she exited the room tortured him anew. He would do everything in his power never to see that look in her eyes again.

CHAPTER TWENTY-SIX

DAISY WAS WAITING for Lilly when she dragged her feet inside her chambers.

"My lady," Daisy said as she hurried to her side. "You must be exhausted from staying out all night. Would you care for a bath?"

Lilly would love a bath but didn't trust herself not to fall asleep in the tub. "Perhaps later. Right now, I'd like to change into my night rail and sleep the whole day away." After Daisy helped her with her clothing and tucked her in bed, Lilly lay on her back with her eyes open. Tired as she was, she was afraid to close them, afraid of what she would see.

Sleep called to her, though, and she succumbed to it. At first, she slept peacefully, her body and mind recovering from the night's ordeal. Then, out of nowhere, her peace became turbulent.

The carriage she rode in bounced her around, causing her entire body to become bruised and battered. The darkness inside the carriage was oppressive and didn't leave space for even a breath of air. Across from her sat a man dressed all in black. The hood of his cape covered his features. When he abducted her she never got a glimpse of his face. Who was he? And why had he taken her? Afraid to voice her questions, she stared at him, hoping he would speak and ease her fears.

Unfortunately, when he spoke, her fears were anything but eased. He spoke with a deep, guttural, almost animalistic voice. She couldn't see him doing it, but she could hear him repeatedly smacking and licking his lips. The sound made her stomach clench with sickness. He reached up to his hood with gloved hands that looked deformed, and she gasped and then held her breath.

When the hood fell back, a scream tore from her throat. He had the face of a gargoyle. Was it a mask? After all, she had been attending a masquerade ball when he abducted her. Of course, it was a mask. Gargoyles were not real. With wide eyes, she continued staring at the man, and when he removed his mask, another scream escaped her lips.

The face staring back at her was Langford.

No. No. No. Her mind silently screamed out. Not Langford. He would never hurt her. He began laughing. Deep, deranged laughter shook the carriage, bouncing off the walls and entering her ears. She covered them with her hands and shook her head from side to side, praying the noise would stop.

When it was finally quiet, she cracked open her eyes and fainted dead away as the insane face of Redford flashed before her eyes instead.

"Lilly, wake up."

She bolted up, almost crashing into Emmeline, who was right beside her, her hand covering her pounding heart. "Why are you here?" Lilly's head swirled with fog, similar to when she overindulged on sherry with Henry when he still lived.

Emmeline's worried expression softened. "You were having a nightmare. I could hear you down the hall."

"Oh. What time is it?"

"It's half past one. Langford is downstairs worried sick about you. He left briefly to clean up and change his clothes after that long ride, and now that he's returned, I don't think he'll leave until he sees you. Are you up for a visit?"

"No, but there is much to discuss. Please send Daisy up, and then Langford at two."

One of Emmeline's brows shot up. "Do you think it is wise to meet with him in your room alone?"

Emmeline did not have to come right out and mention what had happened the other times he'd visited her chambers, but it was implied. Indeed, it was not wise, but Lilly didn't have the energy to go downstairs, and she'd promised him at the masquerade they would talk. And honestly, the sooner they did, the sooner she could look to her future, whatever it held.

"No. But I am nonetheless."

Emmeline hugged her close. "I hope you know what you're doing. And I'm here for you when you are ready to talk. Please don't think you have to deal with this by yourself. You have family and friends worried about you."

"I know. I just need time."

DAISY HELPED HER dress quickly and finished doing her hair just as a knock sounded on her chamber door. Lilly's hands shook as she pinched her pale cheeks to give her a healthier glow. "Please let Lord Langford in on your way out, Daisy."

Her maid eyed her warily, no doubt conflicted about letting the earl in her room. But Lilly knew she would do as she was asked. "Yes, my lady."

Panic hit Lilly as she wondered where she should sit when she greeted Langford, and she decided to hurry to the chaise longue, facing the hearth. Sitting perched on the end, her posture straight and tall, her hands folded in her lap, she tried to exhibit ease and grace even though her insides rattled the rafters. Perceiving his presence behind her, she said, "Come sit beside me, Langford."

He inhaled and exhaled audibly. "I think it is time you used my given name."

Very well. "Come sit beside me, Edmund."

"Thank you, Lilly. Don't mind if I do." He leaned heavily on his cane as he made his way toward her. The paleness of his complexion and the pain she saw flashing in his eyes at each step gave away how discomforted he was.

The cushion dipped as he sat close to her. Close enough that his thigh brushed against hers. "You wished to speak to me."

His hands shot through his hair. "Yes. There is much to discuss. I will start with what happened with Redford. How are you faring? Are you feeling comfortable to speak of it?"

"I am fortunate not to be in Gretna Green and married to him. Indeed, I am lucky to be alive because I believe that his ultimate goal was only to attain my funds."

"No doubt." He turned sideways and took her hands in his large warm ones. Comforting heat spread throughout her body. "I know I asked you when we rescued you, but did he hurt you? Did he take advantage of you?"

The anguish radiating from his dark-brown eyes and his concern for her made her answer quickly. "No. He did not hurt me besides pulling on my arm as he dragged me away from the ball and into the carriage. He didn't touch me otherwise."

Edmund exhaled loudly, and his face and eyes softened with relief. "Thank God." He intertwined her fingers with his. "I've never been more frightened in all my life. This is all my fault. If I hadn't put his name on that blasted list—"

"We've been over this before. It's not your fault. Redford told me he targeted me because I was a young widow anxious to find love and had no parents looking out for me. He took advantage of my situation. He knew exactly what to say and do." She tightened her grip with Edmund's fingers. "I would like to pretend I never met the man." She paused and took a breath. "Redford came up behind me at the masquerade ball. He dragged me out the servants' entrance." Lilly, with a knot in her chest, explained all that happened until he and Caldwell rescued her. It didn't ease her mind as she'd hoped it would, but it did feel good to confide in someone.

Reaching out with his hand, he placed it under her chin, tilting her head up to meet his compassionate eyes. "If I could wave a magic wand and make those memories disappear, I would." He leaned forward, placing his tender lips on hers. "I would do anything for you."

She rested her head upon his shoulder. "Will you talk to me?"

He brushed his cheek against the top of her head. "What do you want to know?"

"I want to know what you were thinking when you asked me to marry you."

Her hand rested against his chest, rose and fell as he inhaled and exhaled. "I felt so connected to you when we made love—both the first and second time. The first time I ignored it. Especially after I found the papers. And I will readily admit I acted badly. Uncle Henry was wise for what he did, preparing for your future without him, and I acted like an arse.

"The second time I messed things up by proposing as I did. It was hasty and poorly considered. I've had time to think and I never should have asked after spending the night in your bed. Please know it had nothing to do with feeling a sense of honor or duty or because I had bedded you." He placed his hand on top of hers, which rested on his chest, and squeezed gently. "I asked you to marry me because I love you. And since that day I have fallen deeper in love." Another squeeze. "You are strong and brave. And I am so proud of you."

"Thank you," Lilly whispered.

"I have a question," he said, his voice more relaxed in tone than when he first started speaking.

"Yes?"

"What were you thinking when I blurted out that awful proposal?"

"Before you asked, I was feeling relaxed and happy. I finally felt as though we understood each other. We had talked about my life with Henry, and his death. But when you asked me to marry you, it sounded careless and insincere. My heart shriveled up and died. My mind screamed at me to run away and hide."

He kissed the top of her head and his fingertips caressed her hand. "I am so sorry. I never meant to hurt you. I have much to learn about you and how to treat you as you deserve. I hope you will allow me the chance to do so."

"I would like that," she said as her heart melted and she realized they could be each other's future.

"I would also like to apologize for my rude and bad behavior since the moment we met. I have no excuse to give you. Just know that nothing resembling it will ever happen again."

"You are forgiven."

"I would like to invite you to my home for a private dinner tomorrow night," he said, his voice still not back to its confident tone.

The answer came easily to her. "Yes."

"I will send my carriage for you at six." He untangled his body from hers, and she missed the connection instantly. "I will leave you to rest." He bent over her and kissed her cheek. "Until tomorrow."

"Edmund," she said right before he exited, "I love you, too." Sighing with contentment, Lilly laid down on the chaise and drifted off with a smile on her face.

EDMUND, WITH THE help of his cane, moved around the dining room, adjusting the vases overflowing with flowers on the table. His nervous energy had driven his housekeeper, Mrs. Lewis, mad all afternoon. But everything must be perfect for tonight. The rest of his life rested on this evening going perfectly. If he didn't calm down, though, he was liable to vomit the moment Lilly entered the front door.

"Sit, my lord," Mrs. Lewis said. "Everything will be perfect. The cook has outdone herself with the menu, and if you don't relax, you won't be able to eat anything. Do you have the ring?"

Inside his jacket pocket, Edmund's fingers curled around a black box holding a ring of emeralds and diamonds he had commissioned for Lilly. After he blurted out the first proposal, he had visited a jeweler. Though up until yesterday, he wasn't convinced Lilly would ever wear it. And he couldn't give her the Langford family ring Henry had given her. Their marriage deserved something new, something that symbolized their new and blossoming love. A future full of happiness, contentment, and hopefully babies—many babies. Lilly would make a wonderful mother. Love, caring, and devotion were ingrained into her, as were patience and understanding.

"Lady Langford is here," the butler announced. "She is waiting in the drawing room, my lord."

Straightening his cravat, Edmund made his way with feet that barely touched the ground. While pausing in the doorway of the drawing room, a smile tugged on his lips, and his heart accelerated when he took in the vision before him. Standing at the chessboard, with her fingers caressing the pieces and a faraway look on her face, was the woman of his dreams. She was dressed in a deep green that made him think of her lovely eyes and the ring securely tucked inside his jacket pocket.

"Thank you for coming, Lilly."

Without taking her hand off the chess piece, she looked his way, smiled shyly, and everything in his world righted. This widow of his uncle, who had tossed his world upside down the moment he met her, was also responsible for making it right again.

"It seems strange to be here again. I only spent time here twice, but it is a handsome home and one I've missed. It has a masculine air about it, and since we never spent a great amount of time here, I never made changes."

"I'm sorry if it makes you uncomfortable being here." Bloody hell, he hadn't thought about causing her any pain or sorrow.

"No. Not at all." As she moved around the room, she touched several decorative pieces. "It feels good to be here. Soothing and comfortable."

They were interrupted when a servant entered to announce dinner was ready.

Edmund held out his arm. Gracefully, Lilly placed her gloved hand on his forearm. That light touch had heat coursing through his entire body. He hoped she felt it as well. Instead of a footman seating Lilly, Edmund did the honors. He had asked that only two footmen be present, and they had been instructed to place the food on the sideboard as he wanted to serve Lilly himself. This dinner was for her. And hopefully, after dinner would be for them.

Making his way to the server, Edmund spooned fish stew from a tureen and placed a bowl at each of their places. He sat, unfolded his napkin on his lap and said, "I hope you enjoy tonight's menu. Mrs. Howard slaved all day making your favorite foods when I told her you were coming for dinner."

Sitting to his right, Lilly spooned the thick soup into her mouth and moaned. "Delicious. Just as I remember. I'm surprised she remembered my favorite foods."

"You are quite unforgettable." He poured wine into two stemmed glasses.

Pink tinted her cheeks as she continued eating. "Have you decided to make any changes to the townhome? Or Langford Manor?"

"Uncle Henry had impeccable taste. I find nothing needs to be done, although I am thinking of redecorating the main bedchambers at both places. Nothing major. Mostly furniture, wallcoverings, and accent colors. Do you have any suggestions?" Pushing back his chair, he removed both empty bowls from the table to the server and filled two plates with roasted potatoes, buttery green beans, and rare roasted venison with a dark gravy.

"Whatever color and style you choose will be perfect, I'm sure," Lilly said. "This looks delicious."

"It does." Before he partook, he refilled both their wine glasses.

Once the main course was finished, the footman placed nuts, assorted fruits, and confections on the table before them and removed their plates. Edmund filled a dessert plate with an assortment for both of them to share. As the time to propose properly crept upon him, he topped off his glass of wine and ignored the sweat soaking the back of his shirt.

"Our cook . . . I mean, your cook makes the lightest buttery shortcrust of anyone."

He wanted to say she'd had it right the first time but ignored the urge to utter the words. "It's a lovely night. Would you care to stroll in the gardens?"

"Yes. That would be nice," she answered as Edmund pulled out her chair.

Instead of holding out his arm, he curled his large hand around hers. They stopped in the front hall to retrieve her wrap from the butler, then exited the front door, making their way around back to the private gardens. All the while, he kept her hand in his. They were skin-to-skin since they'd both removed their gloves for eating and left them on the dining room table. The heat from his warm hand heated her insides even though there was a slight chill to the air.

Lit lanterns scattered throughout the garden made for an intimate glow. "This was always my favorite place to be in town, whether night or day," Lilly said as she breathed in the night air. "Jasmine. I have three favorite scents: roses, lavender, and jasmine. All of which grow in this garden."

Walking hand in hand, they meandered through the granite stone path's twists and turns until they reached a garden bench. To Lilly's surprise, a tray with a champagne bottle and two flutes rested on a garden table. "What is this?" she asked with a smile and a flurry in her heart.

Edmund picked a jasmine blossom off a nearby plant and tucked it behind Lilly's ear. "Be patient, my dear. All will be revealed in due time." Picking up the champagne bottle, Edmund removed the cork to a loud pop, and liquid immediately fizzed over the side. He filled each flute half full. He handed her one while turning out a graceful bow. "For the lovely lady. Please have a seat."

Since her knees threatened to buckle, she wisely sat before she collapsed onto the ground. Edmund joined her on the bench.

Edmund took a black box out of his jacket pocket. Lilly followed his every move with bated breath. "Lilly, my dear, I have loved you from the moment I met you when you turned around from the window at Langford Manor, and your beautiful face lit up with a smile. So flabbergasted was I, I lashed out. I've asked for your forgiveness for the cruel words and know that I never meant any of them." He brought her hands up to his lips and kissed each of her fingers.

The warmth from his lips traveled up her arm and wrapped around her heart.

"Lilliana, will you make me the happiest gentleman alive, and marry me and become my countess?"

Tears trickled down her cheeks, and her entire body pulsed with joy. "Yes, I'll marry you."

Edmund slipped the emerald-and-diamond ring onto the third finger of her left hand. It fit perfectly. "I love you. And will love you until my dying breath."

Her eyes fell to her trembling hand and the gorgeous ring adorning it. The design and stones were everything she would have chosen. She looked up into the amber-tinged, brown eyes of her now fiancé and said, her voice wavering, "I love you. And will love you until the end of time."

Champagne flutes were forgotten. Edmund stood, pulled Lilly into his arms, and kissed her with all the passion and love they shared.

EPILOGUE

Nine months later

"**H**OW ARE YOU feeling, my love?" Edmund asked as he brushed his lips against hers and their son's forehead who suckled on Lilly's breast. "He is perfect. Thank you for giving me a son." He joined her on the bed, pulling both his wife and their son, George Henry Weston, the future Seventh Earl of Langford, close to his overflowing heart. "I've never been so frightened in all my life. If anything . . ." His voice faltered as tears clogged his throat and trickled down his cheeks. Filled to the brim both with fear for the life of his beloved Lilly and their son and the joy that they were both well and here with him, his emotions could no longer be contained.

He suspected his sailing days were behind him, though he would continue with the company he shared with his two best friends. But traveling was out of the question unless Lilly and George accompanied him. He didn't think he would survive a day without them in his heart and in his life.

SHE SQUEEZED HIS hand. "I'm fine. The babe is fine. I won't lie and say it was easy, but look at our little miracle. He has your features. He will break ladies' hearts throughout England."

While she'd labored for two days with George, she honestly hadn't known if she would live through the pain, which felt as though it would tear her body in two. She had been present during several healthy births, but Annabelle was the one that kept flashing into her mind. The midwife kept reassuring her the baby was in the correct position, however, and that he would come on his own time, which he did to sobs of relief and joy from her. Sitting with her husband, whom she loved beyond reason, and their newborn baby boy, who already owned her heart, she looked up and closed her eyes, silently wishing that her parents and Henry could see their beautiful family.

THE END

About the Author

Christine Donovan is an International Bestselling Author who writes romance that touches the heart, soothes the soul and feeds the mind. In addition to writing historical romance set in the Regency era, she also writes contemporary romance.

When she landed her first job at sixteen as a cashier at a supermarket, the first thing she did each week on payday was stop at the local bookstore and buy the latest historical romance. It was a dream of hers back then to become a romance author.

She lives on the Southeast Coast of Massachusetts with her husband. She has four grown sons, two granddaughters, two cats, and a black lab named Luna. In her spare time, she can be found at the beach, reading, painting, or gardening. She loves to tackle DIY projects.

Website: authorchristinedonovan.com
Newletter: www.authorchristinedonovan.com/newsletter
Amazon: amazon.com/Christine-Donovan/e/B00APR743Y
Facebook: authorchristinedonovan
Instagram: christinedonovan6